Daddy Boy

A Novel by Carey Cameron

DADDY BOY

Algonquin Books

of Chapel Hill

1989

Published by

Algonquin Books of Chapel Hill

Post Office Box 2225

Chapel Hill, North Carolina 27515-2225

a division of

Workman Publishing Company, Inc.

708 Broadway

New York, New York 10003

Design by Molly Renda.

Library of Congress Cataloging-in-Publication Data

Cameron, Carey

  Daddy boy: a novel / by Carey Cameron.

     p.   cm.

  ISBN 0-912697-84-9

  I. Title.

PS3553.A4318D33   1989

813'.54—dc19   88-28549

First Edition

Per Giovanni,
con cui ho viaggiato lontano

Daddy Boy

Part One

CHAPTER 1

Busy said that after Jennifer was born, she was taken in to see Daddy every morning. Then after Sonny was born, they went in to see Daddy together. Alice—who had been our nurse at Daddy's house, along with Busy, but who went over to Mother's house with Mother after Mother threw a candelabra at Daddy because she said she was tired of being lectured about how to wear her hair—Alice and Busy would set them down at the start of the hall. Daddy would stand at the other end of the hall with his hands on his knees, laughing. Sonny and Jennifer would crawl to him. Then, Busy said, after Butch was born, *he* was taken in to see Daddy. Sonny and Jennifer didn't have to go in anymore. Then I was born, and *I* was taken in to see Daddy. Butch didn't have to go anymore. Then I kept on, having to go in to see Daddy, because there was no one after me.

Jennifer whispered to me that Mother threw a candelabra at Daddy because she said she was tired of being lectured about how to wear her hair and that Daddy said that every woman he'd ever married had a steel plate in her brain, and that he then took Mother by the ankles and dragged her along the rug.

Once I asked Busy if Sonny, Butch, or Jennifer couldn't

go, just once. Busy put her hands together and whispered harshly that Sonny, Butch, and Jennifer had their tennis, swimming, horseback riding, and golf lessons, and Jennifer had her hula lessons, and besides, Daddy loved me. "Oh my *Gatt*, how he loves you," Busy whispered, her regular voice coming through on the 'Gatt,' so that I jumped, "more zan *anyvon* in zee *werld!*"

Jennifer whispered that Busy whispered like that, whispered so that her regular voice broke through, because she was Jewish and had had to hide from Germans during the war. She'd had to whisper the whole time, she was so close to them, but sometimes, peeking out of the place she was hiding in, the things she saw were so awful that her regular voice just broke through.

Jennifer whispered that you couldn't ask Busy about it, though, couldn't ask her about Germans or what Jewish was or the war, because her regular voice, coming through, would get shriller and shriller, until it broke your eardrums, like Caruso's voice. Jennifer whispered that you couldn't ask most people about most things.

. . . .

Midge always prepared Daddy's breakfast tray the night before. She would put coffee in a thermos and cover each dish with Saran Wrap so that she didn't have to be up before it was time to take in Daddy's tray. Midge was the cook but she slept late so that our breakfasts and sometimes even our lunches, if Daddy was not up before them, were made by Busy.

Carmen or Judy could have made our meals but Busy always said, leaning into the refrigerator, her chipped red nails playing over the dish covers inside it, "Dat's all rrrrrrright, I'll be yoost fine!"

"Any-*ting* you say, Busy Girl!" Judy would say, imitating Busy's accent. Judy and Carmen would laugh, Carmen's gold tooth flashing under the buzzing fluorescent light of the pantry, on twenty-four hours a day. Judy had an accent, too, but a different one from Busy's, and looked kind of Chinese, because she was from Guam.

One of them, Carmen or Judy, would rush back to Midge's room after Daddy had called them on the intercom to say he was up. Midge would come out ten minutes later, her face shiny with moisture cream, the way Daddy said he liked women's faces in the morning. Midge would stow her hairbrush in a kitchen drawer, pour the coffee out of the thermos and into a silver pot, take the Saran Wrap off the toast, and, smiling to Judy and Carmen, lift Daddy's tray.

"Patetic," Busy would whisper as Midge walked by.

. . . .

On my way down the long, dark corridor that leads to Daddy's room, I pass Midge coming the other way. I flatten against the wall as she walks by.

Sounds are coming through the open door at the end of the corridor. Daddy is on the telephone.

"How many barrels? One hundred thousand? That's thirty-five thousand a day, that's . . . Tommy Boy, that's . . ."

I walk in.

" . . . O.K. I got to go now. Here's my precious. Call me later. O.K., Tommy Boy. Bye. Yeah. Bye. Bye. O.K. Bye."

Daddy hangs up the phone and skips over to me on bare feet, in the Hawaiian trunks and matching sport shirt he wears every morning. He picks me up and starts to swing me, first hugging my chest against his chest, so that it is just my legs flying out, then faster and faster, until he is holding me only by the wrists and I am flying out, all of me, like a flag. "Thirty-five thousand a day. That's one thousand four hundred fifty-eight dollars and thirty-three cents an hour, that's twenty-four dollars and thirty-one cents a minute. Twenty-four dollars and thirty-one cents a minute, twenty-four hours a day, for Daddy's precious! Ha ha, ha ha, ha ha!" Daddy stops swinging me, throws me upwards and catches me in both arms. "We can kiss dry holes good-bye forever, Robin Girl, cause we really made it this time! Twenty-four dollars a minute, twenty-four hours a day! Whee!" Daddy throws me across the room onto his unmade bed. I land on my back.

"Daddy!" I shout, laughing and screaming.

Daddy walks over to one of the windows, opens it, and yells "Whoo!" through it. He goes to another window, throws it open, and yells "Whoo!" through it again.

Startled birds fly from the banana trees.

Daddy spies Alejandro weeding a flower bed. Daddy cups his hands around his mouth. "Another strike, Alejandro Boy!" he calls through the window.

Alejandro crosses himself. "Miracoloso, Senor D!"

"That's another fifty cents an hour for you, Alejandro Boy!"

"Gracias, senor!"

"Another fifty cents an hour for all the gardeners!"

"Gracias, thank you, Senor D!"

Daddy has prune juice, black coffee, a packet of gelatin, grapefruit, and toast cut in strips. Daddy pours the packet of gelatin into the prune juice and stirs it with his finger, which is long and thin, with three coarse black hairs on the middle joint. He stirs the prune juice until it is thick.

Midge said gelatin thickened the blood. Daddy called Midge "Darlin'" and said it didn't and Midge shut her eyes and said, "It thick-kens the ba-lud."

Daddy dips the strips of toast into the juice and flips them rapidly into his mouth, going "Mmh, mmh, mmh," in the back of his throat.

Daddy also went "Mmh, mmh, mmh," as he put Tabasco sauce on his soup at Ship's or after sips of hot coffee or when he walked uphill, rolling one foot over the other because he was pigeon-toed, but then rolling his arms over, too. He went "M-m, m-m, m-m," like a horse galloping, when he talked to Tommy Boy in Texas and went "Wah!" when I opened the shower door on him and said, "Surprise! Surprise!"

Daddy breathed heavily through his nose when he signed checks, sitting in the projection room off the bar (put in by the movie director who had owned the house before) that Daddy had had turned into an office. He burped silently, blowing out his cheeks, after meals, he sniffed in one nostril and blew out the other on the driving range, he slept with no pyjama bottoms, and after swimming, he pounded one side of his head and then the other to get water out.

Men, really grown-up men like Daddy, were explosive and hairy and full of little holes. Daddy had holes on his nose, little craters, with hairs growing out of them. When they were long enough, Daddy called Midge, gave her some tweezers, and asked her to pluck them. Daddy's hairs had little wads of white on them after they were pulled out. A tear came out of the far corner of Daddy's eye and he said, "Midge's making Daddy cry, uh-hu, uh-hu, uh-hu! Isn't that funny, Robin Girl? Midge's making Daddy cry!"

"Niggers," Daddy says, rustling the newspaper.

At first I think it is just another noise Daddy is making but then he says it again: "Niggers." Daddy turns the newspaper towards me and rustles a corner of it near a picture of colored people walking in the street. He crumples the newspaper shut and slams it onto the table beside his tray. He bounces forward on the sofa and starts dipping the few remaining strips of toast into prune juice and flipping them into his mouth.

"They come from the jungle," he says, "and now they want rights."

I looked at Daddy.

People said Daddy was handsome and I thought so, too, Friday afternoons, arriving at Daddy's house for the weekend, running to him under the porte cochere, after having seen other people's fathers for a week. By Saturday, though, I couldn't tell what he looked like anymore, because he had become just Daddy. When he said "niggers," though, he became ugly all of a sudden. It wouldn't be that he would change exactly, it would be that I thought I could see things under his skin, bumping and moving, things that made the hairs and holes you saw when you looked up close, things that, in another minute, would change him into a snake or a toad, one of the purple and green spotted toads that appeared in *Playboy* cartoons (the scary ones, not the dirty ones, the only ones Butch would let me look at long enough to let me see what they were. The other cartoons and the pictures and the fold-out Butch would flash at me for a second. "See?" he would say, then, "That's enough!" slamming it shut an inch away from my nose). The green swirls of his

Hawaiian trunks and shirt looked like toad's skin.

Mother said that we were never supposed to say "nigger" about colored people, nor "kike" about Jewish people, nor "beaner" about Mexicans, nor "chink" about Chinese people, nor "jap" nor "nip" about Japanese people, nor "dago" nor "wop" about Italians, nor "kraut" about Germans, nor "frog" about French people, nor "greaseball" about anyone who was short or dark or spoke with an accent.

But why would we want to use that word about colored people? We never even saw any! And what were Jewish people exactly?

Mother shut her eyes and said she was just telling us for when we went to school.

Daddy starts to make other noises: "Bee-bee, hm, mh, bee-bee," softly and gently in the back of his throat. He pats my stomach. My stomach fits comfortably into the hollow of his hand. I can feel the warmth of his hand, reaching all the way into the very middle of me. I can smell his Royal Briar wafting over me. "Bee-bee, mh-hm, mmm, rrrlh, rrlhhhhh. . . ."

I closed my eyes. *It was O.K. for Daddy to say "niggers,"* I guessed. *I didn't know why but it somehow was O.K.*

"Stand up now," Daddy says, taking his hand away. I stand on the other side of the coffee table, facing him. "Turn around," Daddy says. I turn around. "Now lift one leg up." I lift one leg up. "Now lift the other." I lift the other. "Now touch your toes."

"Daddy . . ." I say, turning my head to look at him.

"Now touch your toes," Daddy repeats. I touch my toes. "Now back up here a second." I back around the coffee table until I am in front of him. I feel one hand on the middle of my back and one hand on my lower back, pressing. "You've got to go like this," he says, pushing in against my lower back. "See?" He takes his hands away. "Now turn around," he says. I turn around. He puts a hand on either cheek and looks at my mouth. "Now let me see your teeth." I pull my lips back from my teeth like a dog growling. Daddy pulls his lips back, too. Daddy turns my head from one side to the other.

Daddy's eyes then drift up from my teeth to my eyes and start going back and forth, from one eye to the other. He tilts his head back and looks at my eyes through lowered lids. I can feel his breath brushing me, like doctor's breath. His hands, on either side of my head, hold it still. Daddy's eyes then go from looking back and forth to looking only at my left eye. The thumb of the hand nearest that eye touches my eyelid gently. Daddy wants to know if I am doing O.K. on my bike: he saw me flip over the day before, trying to go straight up a grass bank out of the formal garden. Alejandro, who was clipping bushes nearby, said my head landed two inches from the stone gutter. "Two inches from the stone gutter! Two inches from the stone gutter!" I went from gardener to gardener and from maid to maid, telling them.

Daddy wants to know if it is because of my eye that I flipped over. Could I really *see* where I was going?

I looked at Daddy's eyes.

Somewhere on their way between my teeth and my eye, Daddy's eyes changed. They became like the eyes of people we knew from Daddy's house, and then saw being actors on TV, eyes that made you feel as if, if you were to climb into the TV and jump up and down in front of them and say,

"Hi, Olive!" or "Hi, Florence!" or "Hi, the Lewis kids' mom!" or "Hi, Mr. Kahn!" or "Hi, Mr. Whatever-your-name-was, who was at Daddy's house last weekend and taught us how to do the yo-yo trick!", they would not say hi.

They were the eyes Daddy had had, I guessed, *when he had pulled Mother along the rug. Mother had said, "Cornelius, it's me, it's* Elizabeth," *but Daddy had just kept pulling.*

I had told Jennifer, the first time she told me about Daddy pulling Mother, that I didn't think that Mother knew *Daddy, and Jennifer, whispering the way Busy did, so that her regular voice broke through, said that I had to be the* stu*pidest person in the whole* world.

Mother had known Daddy, she had thrown a candelabra at him and then had gone away, leaving footprints in the rug, like Daniel Boone. Indians didn't leave footprints because they tied twigs to the backs of their moccasins. Twigs didn't work on rugs so Daddy had had to use Mother's whole body.

I say that maybe I *wasn't* able to see where I was going.

Daddy makes me shut the other eye and keep my head level. He puts a hand in front of my eye and starts to raise it, telling me to tell him when I can't see it anymore.

When Daddy's hand is about halfway up I say I can't see it anymore.

Daddy shakes his hand in front of my eye. "Here, *here* you can't see it anymore?"

"*Un*-uh."

"How many fingers am I holding up?" Daddy holds up two.

"Four?"

Daddy puts his arms around me and starts rocking me back and forth. Daddy tells me not to worry, just do my exercises and keep going to Mrs. Kiebler and by God, if she doesn't help me, he will get the finest eye exercise woman in the country to live at the house all the time and help me. Anything can be done with exercise. Franklin Roosevelt was actually walking, for an hour every day, right before he died.

Daddy's eyes stopped staring and started going back and forth and went from foggy to shining when he said "Franklin Roosevelt," shining not in the way they shined when we arrived at Daddy's house for the weekend and Daddy saw us running towards him under the porte cochere—that was only on the surface—but shining deep down inside them. It was a shine I saw even before I knew how I was able to see it; then I realized that I had been somehow *taken down into* Daddy's eyes: that was how I was able to see it, because a part of me had Daddy's eyes all around me, shining, and I felt in that part of me, things being twanged.

I thought it was a good idea to tie twigs to the back of my moccasins, but at the same time, I wanted the Indians to find me.

· · · ·

I was born with no muscle in my left eyelid, so that it only opened up a quarter of the way: that was why grown-ups in supermarkets, thinking I was winking, winked at me, then winked again, then looked embarrassed and walked away. It was called a "ptosis." It was spelled with a *pt*, but pronounced just *t*, like Ptolemy, who was one of the Pharoahs. One in a million people had it with one eyelid or two. Grandaddy Drayton had it and one day, when I was a grandmother, maybe one of my grandchildren would have it, too.

Mrs. Kiebler was German. Mrs. Kiebler would make me sit in a dentist's chair in her living room and make me roll my eye up as far as it would go, then, with my eyeball still rolled up, she would make me shut my eye, so that it ached and pulled all around. When I had done it five times, she would let me have a pfeffernuss and when I had done it ten times, she would let me have a piece of strudel.

I had sweated, and there was a lump in my throat, the first few times I had gone to Mrs. Kiebler's, because I couldn't understand why Daddy would let me go to her, why *Busy* would. I couldn't ask Busy about it though, because, answering me, her regular voice, coming through, would get shriller and shriller, until it broke your eardrums, like Caruso's voice, the parchmenty pieces flapping in the breeze, so that I not only could not see out of one of my eyes, I could not hear, either: it was part of a plan.

· · · ·

The telephone rings.

"That must be Tommy Boy calling me again," Daddy says. "Excuse me now, Robin Girl." Daddy crosses the room, picks up the phone and sits down in an armchair by it. Daddy leans back and puts a foot up on a knee.

"Hi, Tommy Boy. Now what do you think is the possibility of there being other strikes in that area?"

I went into Daddy's dressing room.

The dressing room was lined with mirrors. It had a mirrored ceiling and mirrored doors. Every day, when I was at Daddy's house, I went around Daddy's dressing room in the same way. I opened one door and walked into a walk-in closet. There were stacks of white shirts with alligators on them, and red and blue golf sweaters, made of squiggly wool. I counted the shirts and sweaters. I opened another door and saw lines of shoes on slanted shelves. Sometimes I even said "hi guys" to them. I opened another door and looked into a shallow tie closet, full of pink and blue and silver ties. The ties were on clips that flipped one way, then the other, in perfect sequence, like a chorus line.

"Well, the fact that Central Western's got a lease on that shouldn't stop us."

There was a mirrored dressing table as well, built into the wall. There was a bowl full of pennies on it. I stirred them with my fingers and took a few every day. There was also an army of little wooden hairy people with signs on them, presents from Daddy's girlfriends. All you had to say was "Be Mine" or "Love Me and Leave Me" and grown-ups would think you were very funny.

Jennifer whispered that she knew what Daddy did with his girlfriends.

"What?" I said, which meant, not that I wanted to know what Daddy did with his girlfriends, but that I did not think Daddy *had any girlfriends. Jennifer had girlfriends: she had Vicki Kay. PePe LePew the skunk had a girlfriend but she was a cat and boys in cars with girls squished up right next to them, when they had all that seat to sit on, had girlfriends, but I did not think* Daddy *had girlfriends. I thought you had to be thinner to have girlfriends. I thought you had to get dressed up and go out.*

"Is Dolores his girlfriend?" I finally asked.

"Was."

"Is Tamara his girlfriend?"

"Was."

"Pepita?"

"Was."

"Ingrid?"

"Was."

"Shanti?"

"Was."

"Is . . . was . . . every woman who's ever been at Daddy's house his girlfriend?"

"If they're not now, they were at one time."

"Gosh. . . ."

"I can't believe how stupid you are. . . ."

"Are Midge, Judy, and Carmen girlfriends?" I asked after a while.

"Gol! I just can't believe how stupid you are!"

Jennifer said they were after Daddy for his money.

Sonny said they were nice.

Butch said they were foreign and had hairy pits.

We didn't know if Daddy's girlfriends were always foreign, but they always had accents, and when we would ask them where they were from, they would always say things like, "My father was an Ecuadorian plantation owner and my mother was a Burmese princess but I was raised in South Africa and I've lived in Oslo most of my life," and when we would tell Mother, coming home from Daddy's house on Sunday nights, about all the amazing places they were from, Mother would say that that probably meant they were from Ohio.

Daddy said they were showgirls.

We didn't know if they really were or had been showgirls, for Daddy called almost all women showgirls—Daddy hardly ever said "woman," only said "showgirl"—but when we asked them, they always said, "Yes, well, I've done a little kicking."

"They want *what*?"

There was also a gold watch on a chain suspended in a glass dome. The thick gold was dented and scratched, the numbers on the face were fine and tapering and there was a sprig of flowers (Daddy said they were lilies of the valley) painted faintly in the center. Daddy said the watch had belonged to his daddy. There was a portrait of Grandaddy in the house that Daddy had had painted by Mr. Fraley. In it, Grandaddy's eye wasn't closed at all. The portrait hung in the hall, next to the one Daddy had had Mr. Fraley paint of me, in which my eye wasn't closed at all either, but was perfectly open and green like the other, and seemed, together with the other eye and Grandaddy's two open eyes, to follow me when I walked by in the hall, so that I always tried to run by. Grandaddy's hands were spread out over something that looked like a Graham cracker box but that Daddy said was the edge of a pulpit.

I could have lifted the dome on the watch but I never did. I was afraid the lilies of the watch, on meeting the air, would wilt, the watch would disintegrate and fall down on the wooden base of the dome in a perfect cone of ash, like the blond hair of Guenevere, King Arthur's wife, when archaeologists opened her casket. Right in front of their eyes it disappeared, like cotton candy in your mouth, the only way to prove that she was she.

Mother drove all the way downtown. It was hot. My thighs stuck to the seat and came away with the sound of cloth tearing. A nurse took me into a room that smelled of shots and burned hair. She turned a plastic E *around and made me say which way was up, then put electric clothespins in my hair which crackled and glowed in the dark when they pulled a big lever, like in* Frankenstein.

I screamed and cried and when Mother came back in, I tried to run to her, but the nurse stood in front of me and held me back until she had removed all the clips. I ran to Mother and jumped up and wrapped my arms and legs all the way around her. Mother bounced me up and down and said, "There, there, there, there."

On the way home, bumps sprouted out behind my ears, little painless bumps full of white grains which I scraped off with my fingernails but which grew back in a couple of hours. Mother kept looking in the rearview mirror and when I turned around to see what she was looking at, Mother started to tell me about how nice *Daddy had been, how very* nice. *How he had put braces on her when she was twenty-seven. "We've got to do something about that overbite," he said. How, when he would call her up at the Barbizon and ask her out and she would say she had a date, he would say, "Well, bring him along!" How he would take her and three or four soldiers out to the Plaza for dancing and did not mind if he did not dance with her all evening.*

Then after a little while, still looking constantly in the rearview mirror, Mother started to sing "Some Enchanted Evening." She sang it over and over again, her voice swelling louder every time, shutting her eyes on "stran-ger!", the high note, so that the car wheels went up over the curb.

"Of all the goddamned. . . ."

Also on the dresser, scattered among the little wooden hairy people, were rocks Daddy called 'core samples' that Daddy had hit when he was drilling at two hundred, five hundred, sometimes even a thousand feet and that had come up, glowing hot. I couldn't touch them, either.

Those rocks, Daddy said, had been parts of walls, floors, ceilings, and pillars surrounding pools of oil underground. I imagined Roman baths until Daddy said the pools underground were full to the brim and bursting and could be all different kinds of shapes: kidney, barbell, teapot, stringbean. The earth was more like Swiss cheese, then—the rocks the cheese, the pools the holes. The pools were made from the bodies of little greasy lizards lying right on top of one another and dying and being compressed until they were nothing but their grease, or oil. After five million years, you could get enough oil to squeeze out of a washrag, after a hundred million years you could get enough oil to fill a nice-sized swimming pool; after a billion years, you could get enough oil to fill a football stadium and after fifty billion years, you could get enough oil to fill a dish the size of the state of Rhode Island and a mile deep. The walls, floors, ceilings, and pillars from which the pieces of rock were taken were made from harder, drier animals, or the harder, drier parts of animals: hard-shelled beetles, sea shells, tusks, teeth, calluses and bones. They were compacted, had acid dripped on them, were struck by lightning, rained on, frozen, thawed and baked, baked and thawed, for billions of years, until they were rock-hard. Then Daddy had come along, and with his drill, as big as a mosquito's snout, in relation to the whole world, and in a few months, which the Bible or someone had said were but the flickering of an eyelid, in relation to all time, punctured the rock that had taken billions of years to make, and the oil that had taken billions of years and more lizards than there were people in the world to make came burbling up, for Daddy, for us.

"Don't give 'em an inch, Tommy Boy."

Daddy hadn't always been rich, though, and hadn't always lived at the ends of long, thick-walled corridors and had not always had lots of showgirls to go out with, one after the other. Daddy had lived in flimsy houses, where screen doors had kept banging in a constant wind. He had been cold and hungry. He had shared bathrooms. He had put newspaper in his shoes and across his chest when the wind blew hard, and sometimes, he had so little money and no work and it was so cold that all he could do was lie in bed in some cheap room in the dark with all his clothes on and the covers pulled up to his chin, not even able to read. ("But you could've turned the heat on!" we said. "But you could have bought candles!" But then we remembered: so little money, so *little money*.) He had been married to three showgirls before Mother, none of them as beautiful as she. He had not even started to go out with beautiful showgirls until he had made his first money and gone to Arthur Murray's in Hollywood and Colette, who was a gossip columnist, had seen him, learning the box step, through an open door.

He had worked on drilling rigs in Texas and Oklahoma. Worked in the sun all day, with rattlesnakes crawling up his pants. Fished them out and swung the guts out of them. Learned to drink beer and wrestled half-breeds, who pounded his neck against a stone until the only thought in his head was a quiet, wondering "Hey, I'm gonna die!" Caught the drill bit as it came down from the monkeyman and, legs spread wide, guided it into the hole. *Caught* the drill bit and. . . . The muscles in Daddy's neck stood out. He held an imaginary pipe in his hands. *Caught* it again. Jumped off the floor yelling, "She's gonna blow!" when he heard a rumbling under his feet. Ran smack dab into the monkeyman scrambling down off the derrick and he and the monekeyman rolled over and over each other, trying to get away in time. They were not more than fifty yards away when with a rumbling and then a blowing and a whistling, like the sound of Niagara Falls stuffed into a hole one foot across, the green-black oil gushed out, up through the derrick and out over the top, carrying tools, pipe, hats and jackets with it. Seemed as light as water, the way it gushed, but it fell on Daddy and the monkeyman and the roughnecks and the monkeymen around the trailer with a thud, thud, thud, weighting them down as they reached for each other to throw each other around. And it was so thick, that oil, that they had to be constantly poking at their nostrils to keep them open, and wiping their mouths so they could speak.

"We'll go to court if we have to, but I think we'll be able to work it out our way . . . you know . . . now how's Margaret?"

Daddy was still friends with the men he had worked with in Texas, even though they worked for Daddy now. I imagined Tommy Boy and the men from Texas to be a little like Li'l Abner, with enormous shoulders and tight jeans, but when they came to Daddy's house, they were bald and hunched over and wore brownish suits that turned brownish-violet in the sun.

"May I help you?" Judy would ask.

"Ah, we all er ah frinds frum. . . ."

"Tex-ahss?" Judy would be putting on her English 'ahss.'

"That's right."

When the wives of the men from Texas came along, Daddy would take one look at them and tell them to go charge up something to him at Saks. He would say they needed something the color of champagne, to go with their hair. He would laugh when he saw the bill. "You little showgirls just *love* to walk all over old Daddy Boy, yes you do!"

Sitting in the bushes looking up at Daddy's house, Jennifer whispered to me that Grandaddy Drayton might very well have had a shut eye, but the real reason I had one was because Mother married Daddy for his money. That was God's way of punishing Mother. That was why each of us had something wrong. That was why Jennifer had a deviated septum and why Sonny had a trick knee and why Butch had an outie navel and pigeon toes. Everyone breathed a sigh of relief after Butch was born because all he had wrong with him was an outie navel and pigeon toes. They said, "Maybe even the next one will even be perfect!" Then I was born and everyone went "Eek!" and ran screaming from the maternity ward, while God's voice above them boomed: "Yea, even unto the last one, ye shall not be perfect!" That was God's way of punishing, too: making something go sort of right for a while, then, blam! it went even worse than before.

"You be sure to arrange that meeting for me. There'll be no problem with the leases. I'll make sure. Bye now, Tommy Boy."

Daddy hangs up the phone and comes into the dressing room. He kneels down next to me. He draws a kidney-shape on the rug. "This is the way that oil field was," Daddy says.

He rounds the kidney shape out with a dotted line. "This is the way it's going to be. This is the way Daddy Boy's going to make it."

. . . .

Don and Minnie lived in an apartment above the garage. Minnie had moved in there with Don after they were married. At first Minnie had just lived above the garage as Don's wife, but then Daddy saw her and said, "Why don't you come on and work for us? There's always room for one more!" Minnie came to the house every day but she never stayed in the same room with Carmen, Midge, or Judy because she said it made her mad, seeing them tripping over one another, just to get Daddy to notice them. Minnie was always off in some corner, dusting.

I made a lot of noise walking up the creaking wooden stairs that ran up along the outside of the garage to Don and Minnie's apartment. Minnie either yelled, "Come in, Robin!" or she stayed silent. If she stayed silent, I turned, little more than halfway up the stairs, and walked back down again, because Jennifer had whispered that Don and Minnie hadn't been married very long. "Don and Minnie haven't been *married* very long," she would whisper, or "You know Don and Minnie? *They* haven't been *married* very long!"

At the bottom of the stairs, I always broke into a run.

I liked Don and Minnie's apartment. It was very small, and everything in the house was worn or soft or rounded. The tables were chipped and scratched, the wooden chairs at the kitchen table were worn away in the seat so that the light wood showed, the sofa in the living room sagged in the middle, so that when I lay down on it, it became the most comfortable sofa in the whole world. The armchair in the living room was worn away on either arm so that the cotton stuffing came out, like wads of Kleenex.

Minnie was usually sitting in the armchair when I came in, her feet up on a battered footstool in front. "Hi hon," she said when she saw me. "Hon, could you hand me an ashtray?"

I went into the bedroom to get an ashtray and brought it to her.

"Thanks. And some matches. They're in the kitchen."

I got them, too.

"Thanks." She lit a cigarette, shook out the match and flicked it into the ashtray. It landed with a tiny *clink!* She blew the smoke out, batting her blond hair back from her face at the same time.

"And Busy, she doesn't know what she wants, but she's there, tripping over herself, and over Judy, Midge, and Carmen just to get Mr. D. to notice her, too." Minnie hunched her shoulders and rolled one, then the other, imitating Busy when she ran, and stared at me with dark brown eyes that she could make look very worried, like Busy's.

I laughed.

I liked it at first when Minnie talked about everyone up at the big house. It was like being on another side. All you had to do was get on it and you saw everything, *everything*, in a new light. After a while, though, of Minnie talking, I started to feel as if I didn't know where to look.

My eye caught on something. It was dark red, like heavy curtains. It was the inside of my eyelid. I was looking up into it completely. I kept my head turned so that Minnie wouldn't be scared, seeing just the white. It was the inside of my eyelid that I had to look up into at Mrs. Kiebler's and that I looked up into on my own whenever grownups talked, their voices going on and on, like organ music. I would look up into my eyelid and dark-red-out half of everything I saw, to make the time go, and play, on the dark-redded-out half, like in the movies, scenes of the great battle that was going to happen one day, between all the boys in the world and all the girls. The boys would be lined up on one side of Daddy's driveway and the girls would be lined up on the other side, behind thick bushes. The boys would shoot arrows and bullets and throw rocks at us, the girls, but we would hide quietly in the tunnels we'd made in the thick bushes. We would be so quiet that the boys would think, after a while, that we were all dead. They would come over to look and we would reach out of the bushes and grab them. It would be an am-bush. The boys would take swings at us but they would not be able to reach us, our arms would be so long.

I rolled my eye further, further than I ever had at Mrs. Kiebler's, trying to see how they *looked* as they swung at us, trying to see how we looked. It was like trying to throw a rope over something very high.

Jennifer whispered that after they had dinner, Daddy brought his girlfriend back to our house. If they came back to our house on the weekends when we were there, they had to be very, very quiet so as not to wake us up. They tiptoed back to Daddy's bedroom and lay down on Daddy's bed, side by side, facing each other, with all their clothes on, even their shoes. They kissed and hugged for a while, then they got up and took their clothes off and lay back down again. They kissed and hugged some more, then Daddy rolled over on top of her.

"Come on. . . ."

"That's what they do!"

"How do you know?"

"I just do."

A pause. "They don't really do that."

"Yes they do!"

"But . . . WHY?"

"But your dad, he's a saint. . . ."

My eye rolled back. I turned my head to be able to look at her again.

"He's got to be the sweetest man in the whole world. Did I show you what he gave us?"

"No."

Minnie ground out her cigarette and pushed herself up off the armchair. She walked into the bedroom on stockinged, swollen feet. I followed her.

"Look," she said.

In the corner, a brand new wheeled cart supported the television.

"Isn't that great? I was up at the house the other day and Mr. D. asked me, 'Minnie Girl,' he said, 'do you have a TV?' Mr. D. is always asking questions like that, out of the blue. 'Yes, I do,' I said. 'Where do you keep it?' he asked. 'Well, Mr. D., we keep it in the bedroom, but if we want to watch it in the living room, we take it out there.' 'Do you *carry* it?' 'Don does. It's kind of heavy,' I said, without thinking about it, and the next day *this* arrives. He's so thoughtful, your dad. He really picks up on the little things. It drives me *crazy* how some of the people up there take advantage of him. I mean, he does these things out of the goodness of *his heart.*"

Jennifer whispered that, no matter how early we got up, we would never be able to see Daddy's girlfriends leaving. Daddy's girlfriends always managed to stay just out of sight, like the toys in the story, that stopped playing every morning just before the little boy woke up.

"It gives me the creeps, that story," I said.

• • • •

They begin before we are awake, rolling in round tables on their own and, on dollies, big vases full of birds of paradise and piles of white napkins and red tablecloths with thick pieces of felt to go underneath them, and crates of knives, forks and spoons and five different kinds of glasses, including one shaped like a slipper to drink champagne out of. Men get up on tall ladders and hang decorations from the chandeliers, oil rigs with colored lights on them and stars and tinsel floating around them. Busy runs up and down stairs on high-heeled plastic shoes all day long, calling to us to keep out of the kitchen as it is full of colored people.

Jennifer and I peek through the kitchen windows and see a pot on every one of the ten burners on the stove and every burner lit. Jennifer sits back on the dirt, hugs her knees, and says, "Doesn't that make you feel *good?*"

An old, rusty truck drives up to the house half an hour before the party. It is driven by an old Mexican. Two Mexican boys cling to the sides of it. Daddy comes out with his sleeves rolled up and his collar spreading out from his neck like two wings and tells the driver to drive down to the swimming pool. Then Daddy tells everyone except for the colored people in the kitchen to go down to the swimming pool.

The truck drives up over the curb and down the slope to the pool, leaving two tracks of flattened grass behind it. We run in the flattened tracks. The two Mexican boys hang onto the truck and watch us running behind them and laugh.

I start to smell something. It smells very good. It grows stronger as the truck drives faster.

Jennifer shuts her eyes as she runs and says, "Oh, have you ever smelled anything so wonderful in your whole *life?*"

The lights are on in the swimming pool, lighting the people who stand around it up from below. The truck stops a few yards from the pool. The Mexican boys jump off. They are wearing high rubber boots. The truck turns, backs up to the edge of the pool and stops. There is a grinding, then a whirring sound. The back of the truck starts to rise and tilt. It tilts further and further, until something shifts and rolls inside. The back panel of the truck swings outward. Clumps of white start to fall into the pool, large clumps with smaller clumps falling around them, landing in the pool with a plop, plop, plop. Then the great mass that is still in the truck turns over and slides out under the panel all at once, falling into the water with a soft thud and rocking gently on the water in a white mound.

"Ooooh," everyone says as the white mass falls into the pool, then, "Ahhh!" as the perfume wafts over us.

"Oh, Daddy, neat! Oh, I love it!" Jennifer says.

"Wonderful, fabulous," everyone says.

Daddy smiles. "Gardenias," Daddy says. "Had 'em flown over from Hawaii."

The Mexican boys draw long-handled brooms out of the cab of the truck and, smiling broad smiles lit by the light of the pool, spread the gardenias evenly over the water, lifting their brooms over Jennifer, Busy, Midge, Judy, Carmen, and me as we stoop along the edge of the pool, picking up gardenias and putting them in our hair.

Gardenias they were that party, but the party before that they were yellow roses from Texas and a party before that, pink orchids from Mexico.

Guests don't start to come until after we are in our pyjamas. At first it doesn't look like there are going to be many people. A few people come and kiss each other and then there is a long wait. Then more people come, then more even sooner, women in dresses that are full at the hips and gathered at the knees, like popcorn popping, until we can't believe how many guests there are, and new arrivals coming in the door push the guests who are already in the living room along in droves. Busy says there are two hundred guests, and Don, who brings up our dinner, a selection off the hors d'oeuvre plates—toast with caviar, tiny shish kebabs, shrimp puffs, and chicken livers and water chestnuts wrapped in bacon—says there are five hundred.

We watch the party from the balcony overlooking the living room, dangling our feet, with dustmop bedroom slippers on them, through the balustrades. Some of the people look up and smile at us and wave and nudge other people who also look up and wave. Some of the people who wave then break away from the crowd and climb the stairs to see us. As they climb the stairs, I pray that they won't be famous, because famous people make my heart beat fast and make me feel as if I have to go to the bathroom and make the word *famous, famous, famous* resound in my head, until I almost say, "You're famous," right to their faces.

They sit down between us, putting their legs through the balustrades. The women have to hitch up their tight skirts all the way above their stockings to put their legs through. They shout at their friends below and throw balled-up napkins at them ("Check her pits when she raises her arms," Butch says about the women. "Check 'em now, check 'em") when they won't look up. Then they turn to us and ask us what our "impressions" are of such-and-such. They pull the corners of their mouths down, trying not to smile when they ask us that. I squirm and say, "I don't know. . . ." and Jennifer looks at the ceiling and says, "Um, I think, um, I think. . . ." and without waiting for her to finish, they say, "Your dad's amazing, you know? He really is. You must never forget that."

I searched the crowd for Daddy until I found him, in the middle of a group of women, making big circles with his right arm in the air above his head. He was showing them how to lasso a dogie, I knew, and explaining to them that a dogie was not a dog but a calf, a veal.

"Amazing," I thought, "amazing." It was amazing how I could have a father who was amazing and spend whole days not thinking about it. Then, when someone said Daddy was amazing, or when I remembered on my own that people thought so, it was as if a big bubble burst, covering Daddy and everyone around Daddy with sparkling dust, like the kind of dust that poofed out of Tinkerbell's wand as she flashed around the Fantasyland castle at the beginning of the "Walt Disney Show" at eight o'clock on Sunday nights.

I didn't know why it was exactly that people thought Daddy was amazing, but when they said he was, I always acted like I thought so, too. Daddy's being amazing, I guessed, had to do with the way the rest of the world was. Grownups knew more to compare. We saw the rest of the world sometimes, on the way from Mother's house to Daddy's house on Friday afternoons or from Daddy's house to Mother's house on Sunday nights, as we peeked down the side streets that ran off of Sun-set (seeing houses with one-car garages or no garages at all), and we really saw the rest of the world in Life *magazine, seas of people kind of bald-looking with bowls out for rice. Not everyone discovered oil. Not everyone, either, was handsome like Daddy was or had so much energy at an age people said was old and had to be, for Daddy had white hair. That was what grownups said, and what I knew I would see in time, but for the moment, the amazing part was, not so much that Daddy was amazing (for someone had to be) but that of all the souls that God sent down (from the kind of pediatrician's waiting room that was the part of heaven for unborn souls) to be in the children that Daddy made, God had to send down* us. *The really amazing part was that* I *was in* me.

It was O.K. for Daddy to say "niggers," then, I *guessed, O.K. for him to drag women along the rug and roll on top of women and get women to trip over themselves and do and say a lot of other things that, if other people did or said them, would be* mean, *because he was amazing: so many people said so.*

CHAPTER 2

Mother says we are all spoiled little Beverly Hills children and don't know how to walk in the woods. You walk sideways, like this, see? Mother faces sideways on the hill and digs in with the uphill edges of her shoes.

Mother promised to spend Saturday with us, so Saturday morning, Sonny, Butch, and Jennifer told me to hang around Mother's dressing room to see what she was putting on, just to make sure.

I held my breath as I watched Mother's hands in her closet, moving hangers along the rod inside.

"Pedal pushers," I said to Jennifer, who'd been waiting in the hall, and Jennifer said, "Oh, whew!"

Jennifer carries a thermos. Sonny carries a blanket. A man walks behind us carrying a large picnic basket. We try not to look at him. He looks like a man from Mars, with no eyelashes or eyebrows, tiny pointed ears, a nose that goes down only half as far as a regular nose, with nostrils set flat into his face just below it and lips that are in places turned in instead of out.

Mother waited until about five minutes before he was supposed to arrive and then told us that a man who had been burned in the war was coming. It seemed a shame to keep such a beautiful house to ourselves on such a beautiful Saturday when there were so many unfortunate people in the world. . . .

"Kee-reist!" Jennifer said, running to her room and slamming the door shut behind her. Then from behind the door Jennifer shouted that she wanted to have one afternoon, *just one afternoon* without some . . . weird person there.

Mother called through the door that she did not want to hear that kind of talk, that Sam needed her cheerfulness, that Sam needed all our cheerfulness.

Sonny spreads the blanket on a piece of ground overlooking the live oak that stands at the very bottom of the canyon. Jennifer sets down the thermos, then Sonny and Jennifer and Butch run off down the canyon.

"Watch where you're stepping!" Mother calls after them. "There might be snakes!"

Mother sits down on the middle of the blanket. Sam sits down beside her, then leans back on an elbow and stretches out his legs. Mother looks at him and smiles. Mother leans forward and starts rummaging in the picnic basket, pulling things out and setting them on the dirt beside the blanket.

Squinting up at me, Sam wants to know if I know that I have The Most Wonderful Mother in the Whole World. He had been walking down the street, minding his own business, but not feeling especially happy that day, not for any particular reason, but because "Well, you know . . . ," Sam shrugs, "life." He didn't think it could be seen, when suddenly, this beautiful woman came up to him and just smiled.

That was what made Mother so beautiful, really beautiful. Sure, she was beautiful on the outside, everyone could see that, but the fact that she didn't concentrate on herself and seemed to know how other people were feeling, feeling *inside* themselves, was what made her beautiful, through and through. . . .

I run off down the canyon.

"Watch where you're stepping!" Mother calls to me, too.

Jennifer and Butch were together underneath the live oak that grew at the very bottom of the canyon. They were working out the rules of a new game. Sonny was by himself in the distance, underneath a cascade of vines that grew at the end of the canyon, over a spot left hollow by a landslide. He was trying to pick a vine strong enough to support his weight for a swing over the gully, making little Tarzan yells as he jumped up.

"O.K., here she comes," Butch said.

Jennifer and Butch came walking towards me.

I felt my heart beat fast and crossed my legs to keep from going to the bathroom because I never knew when Jennifer and Butch, together, were going to pay attention to me and it was so so different from when Jennifer, alone, paid attention to me: it was more like in my waking dreams in which, twigs strapped to the backs of my moccasins, the Indians somehow found me. *That was when they turned into cannibals and didn't eat me exactly but licked me and had teeth primed on me. The electric clock in my room sounded like drums beating. It made my insides pump.*

Jennifer and Butch grabbed me on either side, held my arms and walked me, tripping, into a fort they had clipped with long-handled clippers in an oleander bush.

They squatted down, brushing oleander leaves out of their faces, until they were looking at me eye level, and stayed that way, staring at me.

Butch was like chocolate. His skin was always brown and he had full, chocolate-boy cheeks. Jennifer was like a honeybee, all yellow and brown stripes. She had blond hair on her head, dark brown eyes and eyebrows, fine blond hairs on her face, long blond hairs on her arms and the most moles.

"Cyclops," Butch said.

"Bullwinkle," Jennifer said. She was breathing hard.

"Turd face."

"Butt breath."

"Knee-walking butt head."

"You're as ugly as Godzilla."

"You're as ugly as a witch."

"You're as ugly as a frog."

"You're as ugly as a toad."

"You're as ugly as a snail."

"You're as ugly as Alice."

"You're as ugly as a piece of B.M."

"You're as ugly as a chunk of throw-up sitting on the floor."

"You're as ugly as toe-jam and boogers."

"Combined."

"You're so ugly we wish you were dead."

"You're so ugly we wish someone would put a stick of dynamite under you and blow you up."

"Yeah. And then take the pieces and wrap them in cellophane . . ."

"And throw them in the bottom of the ocean . . ."

"Where they would be eaten by sharks . . ."

"And crapped out in shark B.M.'s . . ."

"That's what you're as ugly as!"

They laughed.

I laughed, too.

Even though I knew they were being mean to me, even though Sonny and Mother said they were being mean to me and friends of Butch's and Jennifer's, hearing them, sometimes said, "Why are you being so *mean* to her?" it still seemed funny somehow. It was because of the way they panted. It was because of the way their black eyebrows became like divebombers diving towards their noses, like the eyebrows of cartoon characters, when they were planning something mean. It was because of the way Jennifer, panting so much, and seeming to be thinking about it so much, was trying to act like someone younger than she was, like someone Butch's age, or someone even my age, like when she shoved her big body into my dresses and sang baby songs.

"Look at her!"

"Look at how dumb she is!"

"And ugly."

"Yeah. So ugly."

"Too ugly to go to school."

"Yeah, some people are so ugly they break mirrors . . ."

"But you, you're so ugly you'd break blackboards!"

They laughed harder.

I laughed harder, too.

"Who am I?" Butch said in a dumb-sounding voice, looking at me with one eye shut.

"Look at me," Jennifer said, drawing one eyelid out like an awning and folding it until it somehow stayed like a letterfold, showing the red.

"Ew."

"Eeeeeewwwwwwwwggggggggghhhhhhhhhh!"

There was a crash through the oleander bush. Bodies fell against me, pushing me against the springing branches, then fell off.

Sonny and Butch fell onto the ground outside the bush. Jennifer fell on top of them. Sonny pinned Butch's head in a circle of arm and held it. Jennifer started jabbing Sonny's armpits with the points of her fingers, trying to get him to release his grip. Sonny pinned her head with his other arm. Jennifer and Butch dug one foot after the other into the ground, trying to twist out of Sonny's grip, until they were moving in a circle, with their heads in Sonny's grip in the middle of that circle, fixing their eyes, Jennifer's brown and Butch's brown on the outside, then green, then yellow around the pupil, on me every time they came around.

"Cyclops!" Butch and Jennifer panted. "Bullwinkle!"

Sonny pinned their heads tighter.

"Children! Boys! Stop that fighting!" Mother calls, sliding down the embankment.

"What's the trouble here?" Sam asks, sliding down behind her.

"Cyclops!" Butch hissed at me as he was brushing himself off.

Sonny leapt on Butch again.

. . . .

Sonny had black hair, dark brown eyes and was taller than Jennifer and Butch and twice as tall as I was. His height and his hair made him seem very grown up. Black hair was more grown up than brown hair and brown hair was more grown up than blond hair. Blond hair was sissy. It had no stuff in it. Wisdom and kindness came down from dark heads. God had black hair before he got old.

Sonny would tell me things as he was walking his bike up the hill at Daddy's house to ride back down again or in his and Butch's room, at Mother's house or Daddy's house when Butch wasn't around. He would look out the door to make sure Butch wasn't coming, then lock the door behind us. He would sit on one of the twin beds; I would sit on the other twin bed, facing him.

Sonny told me what "divorce" meant, and "custody" and "alimony" and "child support." Sonny also told me not to pick my nose, not to chew with my mouth open, and not to pick up my fork before the head of the table had picked up his or her fork. He'd read that in the encyclopedia, under "table manners." No one taught us manners, he said, neither any of the people at Mother's house nor any of the people at Daddy's house because they either didn't know themselves or weren't around us enough to care. Daddy never taught us because he never ate with us and Mother never taught us because she was so distracted by their divorce. Sonny told me Daddy had been divorced three times and Mother never. Sonny told me, too, that it *wasn't* queer to like poetry, or classical music, or your mother, even though Butch and Jennifer acted like it was, and that there were places in the world, whole islands, where people liked poetry, even the unrhyming kind, and held hands with their mothers, even when they were fourteen.

Sometimes Sonny would read me poetry then, reaching under his pillow for a thick red book. His favorite was a poem called "Out, Out." When he got to the part that went, "Don't let them cut my hand off, sister," he would stop reading and just stay, staring down at the book and breathing, which was the way older boys who didn't cry anymore cried, so that I would almost cry, too, about that boy (even though I didn't understand what really happened to him, I knew it was totally sad) and about a lot of other things, too, but then I would think of Butch and Jennifer, with their cartoon eyebrows, and so I would say instead, "That's nice."

Sonny would lie for hours on the flowered green sofa in the living room. The flowers on the sofa were quilted and stitched all around so that they stuck up and were soft. He would lie with one eye half open. He would be so quiet that I wouldn't even know he was there until I turned the corner, then he would put out an arm towards me while I just stood there and watched. His arm would seem to stretch, like Jimmy Olsen's rubber arm, and be as flexible as a tentacle. It would wrap around me, then reel me in, wrapping around me again and again, until I would be crushed up against Sonny, my arms crisscrossed against my chest like the wings of a cooked squab.

Sonny would ask me who my protector was and I would say it was Sonny. Sonny would then ask me if it was true that he always beat up anyone who was mean to me and I would say it was true. Sonny would then ask me if I knew why Sonny always beat up anyone who was mean to me and I would say I didn't and then he would say it was because I was Sonny's Robs, Sonny's little sister, Sonny's lit-tel sis-ter. Then Sonny would say "Coo-oo!" raising his voice on the last "oo" against the back of my neck.

He would wait for Alice or Mother to come by and do that to them, too, though he wasn't strong enough to roll them up all the way. He would just hold them at arm's length. Mother would laugh at first, but then she would say, "Honey, now. . . ." and Butch and Jennifer would dance all around and call Sonny Eddie-Puss.

. . . .

Mother starts to put on her pedal pushers, then hears a grinding in the driveway and stops, turns, runs to the window and looks out.

An old, dusty car with a different-colored license plate is coming around the drive. Mother stays watching until a man, fat and pale, in a rumpled light-colored suit and translucent pink-rimmed glasses and a straw hat falls out of the car, looking at Mother and yelling, "Hey-ah, 'Lizbeth, he-yah ah ay-um i-yun Hollywoo-ud!"

"Whah Beauchamp, you silly old thing," Mother yells right back, in an accent she has all of a sudden that sounds like his accent, "this isn't Hollywoo-ud, it's Bre-untwoo-ud!"

Beauchamp he was called that time, but other times he was called Dudley or Spotswood or Rush, which was short for Rushton, names you never heard in California. In California, men had names like Craig or Kyle or Carl. Mother said Beauchamp, Dudley, Spotswood, and Rush were perfectly normal Southern names: men from the South had names like that because the South was more baroque.

Once I told Mother that they sounded like the people from Texas, and Mother, in a voice that sounded almost impatient, said that they were *not* like the people from Texas, they were *much* more well-born.

"I said they just *sound* like the people from Texas!"

"They are not like, nor do they sound, like the people from Texas. They have a much more well-born accent."

"Isn't Texas south?"

"Texas is south but it is not *the* South."

Mother runs from the window to the closet, tripping over the pedal pushers which have fallen to her ankles. Mother kicks them off and throws them into the bottom of the closet, on top of a pile—that Alice said she wasn't touching and that Mother said she didn't *have* to touch—of other kicked-off pedal pushers, girdles turned inside-out with the stockings still attached, hairnets, hairpieces, and a scattering of hairpins, a sprung Slinky, an andiron, a half-eaten slice of bread, dress shields looking like funny bras, a patty of Silly Putty with a piece of the comic strip "Blondie" printed on it, a half-eaten slice of salami, warped tennis rackets, the skeleton of Butch's horned toad, some party invitations, some keys, a blouse encrusted with bubble gum, a file of papers, deodorant, a report card, a spangled scarf, tea bags.

"Lady born and lady bred," Mother says, half singing, "dresses her feet and then her head." Mother extracts a pair of at-home shoes from the pile and puts them on, then pulls a long, flowered bathrobe off the rack above and slips it over her head. She picks up the hem of it and stares at it for cat stains. "Go run down and say hello to your cousin Beauchamp," she says to me.

I went towards the front stairs, then at the last minute, turned and ran down the back stairs. I went through the kitchen to the dining room and peeked out the double doors of the dining room to the front hall.

Mother runs down the stairs giggling, hair and bathrobe floating up. "Mama!" Mother calls to Na-Na, "Mama! Beauchamp's here!"

"Beauchamp, Beauchamp!" Mother says when she gets to the bottom of the stairs, taking his hands, then stepping back and looking at him from head to toe.

"Lizbeth, Lizbeth," Beauchamp says, "and Florence! How are you, Miss Florence?" Beauchamp asks, turning to Na-Na, who has been led by Alice from her soap opera and is standing in the dining room door.

"Biscuits, hot biscuits," Na-Na says, reaching for him with trembling arms.

Na-Na was Mother's mother. She had moved in with us a couple of months before, from the Shangri-La Guest Lodge in Santa Monica. Blood didn't go to her brain all the time, which was why she only talked about food, except when she saw a tie clip or a pair of fat ankles, and then she screamed, "Common! Common!" Mother said she was like that from eating too much salt, from years of putting salt on her sliced tomatoes until they were white on top, because that was all they had to eat sometimes, just sliced tomatoes, and Na-Na had to give them taste, or salt and pepper sandwiches, or a tureen of peas, or fatback quivering on a bed of wilted lettuce, but Alice, biting dry skin off the inside of her lower lip as she polished furniture hard, said they could have *planted*, couldn't they? They could have *dug*. They could have done something besides swat flies and talk about what good blood they had at My Old Kentucky Home (Alice called it that even though she knew it was in Virginia). *Her* six brothers and sisters on their farm in Iowa, and her father with a stroke and her mother with burns on sixty percent of her body—they were poor but they *ate*. And then Mother's relatives following Mother out to Hollywood as soon as she had her success: her brother who'd been in the car accident with the minister's wife with whom he had been . . . going out and her other brother who had multiple sclerosis but who went insane first became convinced he knew of a communist plot drove to Washington with his leg out the car window to keep it from folding up he said and got all the way to J. Edgar Hoover before they realized he was insane, and who knew who else, as if Mother didn't have enough on her already.

Mother takes Beauchamp by one arm and Na-Na by the other and leads them into the den.

I got on my bike and made my rounds.

I made rounds of things in the yard every day to see how they were doing and to deliver messages to them. I delivered messages by riding my bike in different patterns. I couldn't deliver the messages by speaking because there were transistors planted and spies everywhere, Union spies, peeping over window sills on the second floor. I drove around and around the driveway and around the tennis court and around the big box containing the swimming pool heater motor. I rode out the driveway and around the man sitting in the car across the street. "Hi, Mr. Vanucci!" I called.

"Hi," Mr. Vanucci said.

Most of the time, when Mother was at home, there was a man sitting in a car across the street. Sometimes there was an ice cream man in a white truck, but I had given up asking him for ice cream because he always said, "Whoops! I've just run out!" and I had given up asking him why he didn't go get some more because he always said he was tired and was waiting for his daddy to come pick him up.

Sonny and Butch rolled cherry bombs under the ice cream man's truck. The ice cream man held onto the dashboard and squeezed his eyes shut when they exploded.

Mother said that wasn't a very nice thing to do and took the ice cream man some coffee. After that, Mother took the ice cream man, or the man sitting in the car across the street, coffee every day. In time we learned their names: Mr. Vanucci, Mr. Ludwig, and at night, Mr. Dorn. Mother invited them into the kitchen as well but they said they'd lose their jobs.

Mother and her lawyer, who was a friend, and Na-Na went next door to the Andersons' for cocktails. The ice cream man crawled into the Andersons' bushes. We saw the soles of his black shoes poking out of the bushes.

"Hi, Mr. Ice Cream Man," we said. "Mr. Ice Cream Man, what are you doing in there?"

"Leave me alone," the ice cream man said.

Coming out of the neighbors', Na-Na got stiff and wouldn't go in the car and started to laugh and say, "Oh, Elizabeth, oh, Elizabeth," over and over again, which meant she was going to wet her pants. Mother called Sonny to come help push his grandmother but still she wouldn't go and so Mother's lawyer got in the car and pulled Na-Na in on top of him. The ice cream man sat in the bushes and wrote something in a little book.

Daddy called Mother the next day. Mother laughed on the phone and said, "Oh, I'm sorry, Cornelius, I just can't talk anymore," and hung up while Daddy was still talking. Then Mother turned to us and, still laughing, said that Na-Na, our own grandmother, had been seen in a car, lying on top of a man, and worse, that our mother had been seen in the same car, *watching them!* For a good twenty minutes! Mother laughed until she cried, then wiped her eyes with a wad of Kleenex, which she always had, up her sleeve or pressed into a patty under her pillow.

Mother and Beauchamp walk through the front door arm in arm.

I threw my bike down and hid behind a statue of a boy balancing a cornucopia on one hip.

"Now there's Donald Jansen, president of the North Corporation. His wife and I go to the same beauty parlor and of course, I know them from parties. Yes, Jan-s-*e*-n, that's right. And Harrison Goode. He designed some new kind of airplane engine. A very interesting man. Director of one of those think tanks overlooking the ocean. You may have seen one of them on your drive down. And Al Mandel, he's in television. A good friend of mine. You can tell them I sent you. You can tell all of them I sent you. And Sam Goldman, an associate of Weiss in the filming of *Last Train from Cairo*. Hm . . . that's all I can think of right now. But that ought to get you started."

"Would it be all right to say that I know Cornelius?"

Mother puts a hand on his arm and looks up the driveway. "Mr. Vanucci!" Mother calls.

Mr. Vanucci looks up from his newspaper.

"Come on over here," Mother says.

Mr. Vanucci gets out of his car and walks to us with his head down and a small smile on his face. "I ain't supposed to be seen on your property. . . ." he says.

"Oh, Mr. Vanucci, come now!" Mother says. "You're my friend! We're good friends! Mr. Vanucci, this is my cousin . . . now write that down in your book. . . ." Mother pauses while Mr. Vanucci takes a black book out of his pocket and turns it to the right page. "Bee-chum, B-e-a-u-c-h-a-m-p, Kee-yah-tah, C-a-r-t-e-r. I know Cornelius is not going to believe Beauchamp is my cousin, but he really is. Beauchamp, this is Mr. Vanucci."

"Hi," Beauchamp says.

"Pleased to meet you," Mr. Vanucci says, shaking his hand.

"Mr. Vanucci is supposed to harass and distress me," Mother says.

"It's nothin' personal, Mrs. Drayton," Mr. Vanucci says, looking at the ground.

"Oh, Mr. Vanucci, I know that! You're only doing your job! We're friends, aren't we?"

"I can't say nothing about that neither, ma'am," Mr. Vanucci says, smiling his small smile.

"Well, we are. I can say it." Mother puts her hand to the side of her mouth, as if she were telling a secret: "Mr. Vanucci and I are *friends!*"

Everyone is quiet for a second, then Mother says, "Isn't Mr. Vanucci a lovely Italian?" She puts her arm through his. "Where did you say your parents were from?"

"Brooklyn, ma'am."

"But before that?"

"Calabria."

"His mother came out to California to be with them," Mother says to Beauchamp. "How old is she?"

"Seventy-five, ma'am, and still does all the cooking. Makes the best lasagna in the world!"

"Isn't that lovely?" Mother says.

Everyone is quiet again, then Mr. Vanucci says, "Well, I guess I got to be going back." He puts out his hand to Beauchamp. "Bye."

"It was a pleasure to meet you, Mr. Vanucci!" Beauchamp says, shaking Mr. Vanucci's hand again.

Mr. Vanucci turns and walks away from them.

"Bye, Mr. Vanucci!" Mother calls after him. Mother turns to Beauchamp.

"Oh, *Elizabeth* . . ." Beauchamp says in a very sad voice.

Mother presses something into Beauchamp's hand. Beauchamp's hand closes around it, moves to his pocket, and releases it inside. "Thank you, Elizabeth."

Mr. Vanucci turns towards them again as he walks around his car to the driver's side.

. . . .

Mother sits on a sofa in the den. We sit on either side of her. She is wearing pedal pushers. She has a scrapbook up on one her knees, the one Butch ripped pages out of and took to school to prove that Mother had *too* been on the cover of *Life* three times. Mother makes a valley in the middle of the sofa, into which we are constantly sliding. The more we try to pull ourselves out of the valley, the further in we slide, so that finally, Butch and I, who are farthest in, each have a leg up on one of her legs.

Mother was not going out that night, nor was anyone coming over. I was not going to have to worry for another twelve hours.

There is a poem on the front page by Daisy. Daisy is Mother's friend. Daisy made the book, pasted in all the pictures.

She lived with Mother at the Studio Club. She comes over sometimes now and talks with Mother until Mother gets tired and goes to bed. Daisy stays up the rest of the night in the living room and chain-smokes. She was always a good friend, Mother says, and talented. There is a picture of Daisy in an oval to one side of the poem. She is leaning over the railing and smiling, with a cigarette dangling from two fingers.

"'To Cornelius who dominates her hours,'" Jennifer reads out loud. "What does that mean?"

"That means he had a whip or something."

"Daddy with a whip?"

On the first page is a picture of the house Mother grew up in. It looks like a haunted house, tall and unpainted. The people on the front steps look haunted, too: three women in long black skirts and shirts with high collars. They are Mother's three old-maid great-aunts, whom Na-Na and her children went to live with after Na-Na's husband had died in Florida. Out in the woods they lived, in that house, without any heat, plumbing, electricity, or men, and sometimes not much food, sometimes all they had for lunch was sliced tomatoes or a tureen of peas or salt-and-pepper sandwiches or fatback quivering on a bed of—

"Pa-leese," Jennifer says.

Butch makes the sound of a violin.

Mother turns the page.

There is a picture of some colored people with no teeth, then a picture of a man tilting a jug up and a spotted dog next to him with writing underneath that is supposed to be something funny. You can tell from the streaky way it is written and the exclamation point after it. Then there is a picture of Mother as Apple Blossom Princess during the year of the blight. Then there is a copy of the front page of the

Baltimore *Sun* with Mother's picture on it because she had fallen off a horse while working as a secretary in Baltimore making twenty dollars a week and broken her hip and was so pretty and there wasn't much happening in Baltimore that day. Then there is a picture of Charles Fitzmartin Kilroy Blowfut, Mother's cousin who stuttered and had a bump on his head from a World War One and who kept the front page of the Baltimore *Sun* with Mother's picture on it folded in his pocket at all times. Then there is a picture of Charles Fitzmartin Kilroy Blowfut's prize-winning chickens, which Charles Fitzmartin Kilroy Blowfut had taken to the Madison Square Garden Poultry Show, and beside the cage of which, on the train, Charles Fitzmartin Kilroy Blowfut had read an article about a new profession called "modeling agent" and how a certain "modeling agent" in New York named John Robert Powers was looking for tall girls with regular features. Then there is a picture of Charles Fitzmartin Kilroy Blowfut, his chickens, and John Robert Powers, whom Charles Fitzmartin had gone to, right off the train, only to be ignored by the secretaries in John Robert Powers's office, until John Robert Powers, who was what Mother called a sentimental Irishman, passed Charles Fitzmartin on his way to lunch. Then there is a torn yellowed invitation to a 1937 dance at West Point that Mother had finagled as a way of getting to New York. Then there is a picture of Mother's older sister, whom Na-Na, even though Mother had been living on her own for six months, would not let her go to the dance without, whom Mother had persuaded, on their way back South from the dance, to stop in New York, and who had immediately felt self-conscious, right there in Grand Central Station, in her cotton country-print dress and wide-brimmed hat, while Mother had not.

Then is a picture of Mother with John Robert Powers, whom Mother made cry by letting her hair down and turning this way and that and talking about the house she lived in in Virginia with her mother and brothers and sister and old-maid aunts, registered in "Historic Houses of Virginia," that didn't have any indoor plumbing and how there *wasn't* any money except for the small pension her mother got and the pension Aunt Evie got from working at the Library of Congress. Then there is the first picture, ever, of Mother's modeling career, that John Robert Powers sent her to have taken that afternoon, after which Mother had started making twenty dollars an hour, as opposed to twenty dollars a week, and never went back to Baltimore, ever.

Then all the little flat gray pictures stop and the big splashy pictures and the magazine cut-outs begin, with so much glue on the back of them that they make the rest of the pages in the scrapbook ripple and crackle when you try to squeeze them together, like a stack of paper fans. There are pictures of Mother, with short hair, in advertisements for Colgate, Borax, Fels Naptha, Duz, Ajax, Viceroy, Chesterfield, Bayer, Hills Brothers, Knox hats, Amana ranges, Lenox china, tin collecting, paper drives, the USO. There are pictures of Mother, too, on the cover of *The Saturday Evening Post* or inside in a bib apron, with shiny pink cheeks, serving a turkey to a table full of children, grandmothers, and grandfathers and one empty chair because the father is away at war.

Then there are magazine covers, covers from *Redbook, Look, Ladies' Home Journal, Bride's Magazine, True Confessions, True Romance,* the *Life* covers, scotch-taped back in, *McCall's, Vogue, Harper's Bazaar, Argosy, Modern Yachting,* the *New York Times Sunday Supplement.* Then there is a big article, in which pictures of Mother as a little girl are blown up, and over the pictures are the words, slanted far to one side, with lots of underlining and exclamation points: *SHE WAS A BEAUTIFUL BABY AND BABY, LOOK AT HER NOW!!!!!!!* Underneath the pictures are words in smaller print: "a tomboy at ten," "demure at sixteen," "ravishing at 20."

"And not a thought in her head until she was thirty-six," Mother adds.

"Who?" we ask.

"Me." Mother turns the page.

Then there are pictures of Mother with a blond woman in the middle of a crowd of sailors who are all smiling and holding up their hands. Mother and the other woman are being voted The Two Girls the Navy Would Most Like to be Shipwrecked With. Then there is a picture of Mother shaking hands with Franklin Roosevelt in his wheelchair. Then there is a picture of Mother shaking hands with Eleanor Roosevelt. Then there is a picture of Mother taking off her shoes at a party and looking surprised.

Then there is a small yellow newspaper clipping from *The Northern Neck News* about Mother, a Cover Girl, Visiting Her Home. Above the article is a picture of Mother bending a blossoming dogwood branch down next to her face.

Then there are pictures—which we think are advertisements until Mother says with a sad voice, "Aw, look at how sweet they all were . . ."—of Mother with one man or another in uniform. The men are either standing with their arms around Mother, or they are sitting down, straddling benches, the soldiers or sailors with their legs spread wide and Mother, with her back to them, jammed between their legs, leaning her head back on their shoulders, and smiling at the camera, or they are standing in front of planes that have

Mother's name painted on them, that Mother says were shot down in the war.

"All of them?"

"All of them. The boys were never found."

"Not even *pieces* of them?"

"*Butch.*"

Mother kisses her finger and puts it on each one of the soldiers' and sailors' photographs.

Then there is a picture of Mother with a lot of other women getting on a train. Then there are movie stills of all the full-length movies Mother had been in, always in an evening dress, always standing to the side, and always trying to look mean or mad. Mother says they always made her play the other woman because she couldn't act. Then there are stills from all the screen tests she'd done for more important roles because directors kept *hoping* she could act, kept getting down on their knees in front of her and pleading "Act!" but Mother says that all that having-to-walk-to-the-mark-on-the-floor-while-looking-here-and-saying-something-there was too much like patting your head and rubbing your stomach.

Then there are stills of all the serials Mother was in after the studio had not renewed her contract. Mother says they were a comedown for her, being in movies the scenes of which they re-took only when the horse went to the bathroom. We think they are the most fun to look at, though: stills of Mother wrestling gorillas and drowning in quicksand and driving a stagecoach, tugging at the reins with an Indian climbing up the back, stills about which we asked when we were very little, "Was it *really* scary with that Indian climbing up the back?" and Mother said, squeezing us, and talking in a high, baby voice, that "the only really *scary* part was the fat producers waiting to goose" her "as soon as" she "stepped off the set!" There are stills, too, of Mother lying down in a faint with men fighting around her and dynamite fuses burning beside her and ceilings covered with spikes descending towards her and pagan temples collapsing, their giant blocks that Mother says were cardboard about to fall on top of her. There are more stills of Mother lying down in a faint than there are of Mother doing anything, so that Daisy printed at the end of them, in large fancy letters, like the heading of the *Los Angeles Times*: THE ACTRESS WHO HAS SPENT MORE TIME UNCONSCIOUS ON THE SCREEN THAN ANY OTHER ACTRESS. Mother says the directors found that it was easier to have her unconscious than to try to do anything with her.

Mother turns the page.

Then there is another yellowed newspaper article with a copy of the photograph that was at the beginning of the scrapbook, of the house that Mother had grown up in, and next to it, a movie still of Mother in her khaki outfit, leaping over a chasm, and over the pictures is the headline: FROM HISTORYLAND TO HOLLYWOOD IN ONE LEAP.

Then there is a picture of Mother dangling from an end of a long wooden lever, about to be lowered into a big pot. Daisy has cut out a piece of paper in the form of a bubble and printed something on it and pasted the point of the bubble next to Mother's mouth. "Oh, won't some millionaire come and get me out of all this?" Jennifer says, reading the words in the bubble.

Then there is a picture of Daddy standing in front of an oil well, and newspaper clippings of Daddy. Then there is a big cardboard folder with a drawing on the front of it of a woman with a bathing suit top on and a big, ruffled skirt and around her stars, with curving lines beside them and little dots around and below the curving lines to show that the stars are shooting this way and that. Inside the folder is a photograph of Mother and Daddy, sitting at a table, with soldiers and sailors fanning out on either side of them.

Some of the soldiers and sailors look familiar to us. Mother says they are her cousins and brothers, whom Daddy would take out, along with her other boyfriends, when Daddy and Mother went on a date, and whom Daddy had given jobs to after the war, Daddy was so nice, and who came to visit us now sometimes. "Look, there's Beauchamp," Mother says, putting her finger on one soldier, "and there's Rush and Spotswood. Look how lovely they were. . . ." Rush and Spotswood are Mother's brothers, our uncles, but it is hard to think of them healthy in restaurants and easy to get them mixed up because they are both in wheelchairs now.

They are all smiling, but Daddy's smile is wider than anyone else's. Daddy's smile is so wide it looks as if the corners of his mouth were being held back by little rubber bands, like the kind that fit over hooks on the braces of Jennifer's back teeth, only his are going over his ears.

"*Is* Daddy a millionaire?" I ask suddenly, looking up into the space, black now, above my left eyelid.

"*OF COURSE DADDY'S A MILLIONAIRE!*" Jennifer, Butch, and even Sonny shout, all around my head, so that I have to put my fingers in my ears and squeeze my eyes shut.

"Children!" Mother says. "I don't want to hear that kind of talk. I don't want to ever *hear* you mention about how much money your father has. It's a very ugly thing to do."

"Is it as bad as saying '*nigger*'?" Sonny asks.

"Yes."

"Is it as bad as saying '*Jew*'?" Butch asks.

"Worse."

We look at her. Mother's voice is sounding almost the way people's voices sound when they are mad, but we know Mother doesn't get mad. Her voice becomes gentler: "I don't want you ever to *mention* how much money your daddy has or talk about all the things you have at your daddy's house to anyone. Money can be a very good thing but it can also be a very destructive thing. It can take away your wanting-to-do-things. It can make people like you for the wrong reasons. I *especially* don't want you to mention it to any of your friends at school. I've tried to get you into unpretentious schools, where there are children who don't have all the things you have at your daddy's house. I didn't want you to be in schools with a lot of other rich children who would simply be reinforcing the wrong attitudes that money can give. I wanted you to get an idea of how *normal* people live. It might seem sometimes like it would be fun to talk about how rich your daddy is, and if you were to say it, it might make you feel important for a while, but in the end it will only get you into trouble."

Butch, Jennifer, and even Sonny glare at me.

I wanted to tell Sonny, Butch, and Jennifer that I *knew* what the things were that you weren't supposed to say, I really really did, it was just that sometimes—I didn't know if it had to do with having an eyelid hanging down or just being young, but I guessed that one was like the other—I heard things—things that had been said around me many times before—as if I were hearing them for the first time. It was as if I heard things but had never before *thought* about what they meant. It was as if things had been received by me *but through my eyelid* and were there now, only I was unable to see them. That was what grownups meant by things being "over your head." I wondered if it was like having no blood in your brain for a second: I wondered if I had inherited that from Na-Na, just as I had inherited my eye from Grandaddy Drayton. I wondered if it was like having a steel plate in your brain, like Mother and every other woman Daddy had ever married had, or being unconscious, more unconscious than any other actress, like Mother was, with a whole temple collapsing on you: I wondered if I had inherited all that as well.

"*Is* Daddy a millionaire?" Jennifer asks after a while.
"*Jennifer . . .*" Mother says.
"I know but I just like to hear it. . . ."
"*Jen-ni-fer. . .*"

The telephone rang.
"Tell them we're dining, Alice!" Mother called from the sofa.
We heard Alice pick up the phone. There was a pause.
"No, this is her housekeeper," Alice said.
Another pause. "Ah, I see, just a moment . . ."
Alice came into the den. "Mrs. Drayton, it's the—"
Mother wrinkled her forehead, shook her head and mouthed the word *no*. She got up out of the sofa and walked quickly into the kitchen. She whispered something on the phone, then ran back through the living room, not saying anything to us, through the front hall and out through the front door, still in her pedal pushers. She got in the car, started it, and drove out the driveway. The ice cream man started talking on a little radio.

"How long is Rush going to be in jail?" Jennifer asked Alice.

"Until your mother bails him out, I guess," Alice said.

"*Sweet potatoes!*" Na-Na said.

"How did you know it was Rush?" Sonny asked Jennifer after Alice was back in the kitchen.

"I just tried it out," Jennifer said, examining an imaginary manicure.

Butch whistled. "Pretty smart, Jennifer."

"Is he the one who was just here?" Sonny asked.

"No, that was Beauchamp," Jennifer said, "another cousin out of the woodwork."

"Is he the one with multiple cirrhosis?"

"Multiple *scle*-rosis. No. Sclerosis is what Spotswood has. Beauchamp's just a poor sap. Dudley's the one with cirrhosis. Cirrhosis of the liver."

"Dudley?"

"Another broken-down cousin. He used to visit us sometimes. God, how can anyone have so many broken-down relatives."

Rush, Jennifer whispered: you could remember what he was like from his name, Rush. Rush rushed. He rushed from women and the police. He rushed because he stole. He got women to fall in love with him and take him into their houses and then he stole from them. He had been in a car accident, with a minister's wife with whom he had been . . . going out, trying to get away from the police, then after the car accident, when he was in the wheelchair, women fell in love with him faster, and he stole and he rushed even better. Because he was more attractive somehow. Because people felt sorry for him and trusted him.

I thought love had to do with getting up out of a wheelchair but Jennifer said bending over to hug him was good enough for them.

Rush liked California because the houses were all on one level. One afternoon when the woman was out, he wheeled into her bedroom, over to the bureau with the dolls on top, the dolls planted in big skirts and the music box and the postcards from Mexico. He found the key in the music box, underneath the disc with the Spanish dancers on top. He unlocked the drawer and took out papers and money and earrings and a brooch, then quickly closed and locked the drawer and put the key back and wheeled out the front door, down the ramp set up specially for him and down the driveway. He wheeled to the gas station on the corner. He called a taxi from there and waited in the office of the gas station until it arrived. The taxi driver and the gas station attendant both lifted him into the taxi, then folded the wheelchair and put it in the trunk, all the while saying that someone must have been awful to leave a fellow like him all alone.

. . . .

Right before Mother left was the worst time, because I knew she was going to leave and that was as bad as her being gone. I had to wait through the time of knowing she was going and through the time she was actually gone. Right after she left was also bad because I was the longest from seeing her again. Being in the middle of the time was also bad because I was the longest from seeing her on both sides and yet it wasn't as bad because I had already gone halfway. I knew what waiting half the time had been like and knew that it could be gone through again.

An hour was six cartoons and five commercials and the beginning and the end of the show. An hour was eating scrambled eggs alternated with petting our dog, Spot, all over, named after Spot in *Dick and Jane.* First I ate some scrambled eggs and petted one side of her back, then I ate some more scrambled eggs and petted the other side. Then I ate some more scrambled eggs and petted the outside of her legs and combed through her toes with my fingers. Then I ate some more scrambled eggs and petted the insides of her legs. Then I ate some more scrambled eggs and petted her stomach, circling with my finger around each one of her eight nipples. An hour was going next door to see Mrs. Anderson and drinking juice, seated on a high stool by her dishwasher. The steam came out of the dishwasher and made my face go loose. "Mrs. Anderson is my friend," I thought, "my friend." An hour was rolling over Ray the gardener's ornamental rocks one by one and watching the almost clear sow bugs and the sow bugs dogfood pink wriggle in the light and counting one, two, three on each sow bug that I saw.

. . . .

Mother had black rings around her eyes the next morning. She served us poached eggs out of a fat porcelain dish.

"Rush's in jail, isn't he?" Jennifer asked.

Mother put down the serving spoon. "How did you hear that?"

"Alice told us."

Mother went into the kitchen. The swinging door went *whap!* behind her, sucking in the curtains in the dining room. She said something to Alice. Alice mumbled something. Mother's voice rose. Mother was sounding almost the way people sounded when they were mad. Alice mumbled something again. There was a series of mumblings, Alice's voice low like organ music, Mother's voice high, back and forth.

Mother came back in. She sat down and served the rest of the eggs, pushing the spatula underneath them roughly and dropping them onto plates so fast that one of them slid off the other side and landed broken on Butch's placemat.

"Mom!" Butch said, but Mother went on serving.

We looked at one another again. We had never seen Mother act that way before. We had never seen her go on for so long without smiling. We waited for her to stop acting that way, to smile, so that we could start smiling, but she didn't stop. Mother really *was* mad. We didn't think Mother *got* mad. Midge got mad, her round face, behind its moisture cream, twisted into a Laurel-and-Hardy grin in the corridor on the way from Daddy's room, Alice got mad, biting hunks of skin off the inside of her lower lip and plunking dishes into the sink with a crash, but *Mother* didn't get mad.

I felt my heart beat fast. Mother getting mad made her seem not like Mother, and Mother, not seeming like Mother, made everything else seem different, too, until finally I felt as if I were not sitting at the table anymore, but in a chair in space, with no jacket on.

That was the way Mother had looked when she had thrown the candelabra at Daddy, I thought, *that was the last and only time she had ever been mad before.*

Mother said she thought it was very silly of Alice to admit that Rush was in jail but very bad of Jennifer to instigate her telling and very irresponsible of Jennifer to do that in front of us. Mother said she was trying to do things on her own now, quietly, without Daddy. She was trying to do what she could for her relatives by herself and it was up to Jennifer to support her in her efforts and not try to undermine her by talking about it in front of children who were too young to cope. . . .

Looking down and drawing with her fork in the egg stains on her plate four neat lines at once, Jennifer said she was tired of all the broken-down relatives coming over, or if it wasn't broken-down relatives, it was someone retarded or with their arm blown off or something. Jennifer said that Mother had three hundred dollars a month child support, per child, and out of those twelve hundred dollars a month, Mother could *do* something for those people, but at a distance, so that we wouldn't have to have them *around* all the time. Jennifer said it was perfectly all right with her.

Mother rose out of her chair.

"Jennifer . . ." Sonny said.

Jennifer turned to Sonny and said she was tired of his little precious baby sister, too, tired of having to look at her *every day*.

"Don't you say that. . . ." Mother said.

"Cornbread," Na-Na said, "cornbread with butter and . . . piccalilli."

"Tired of *her*, too. God, she's only seventy but she acts like she's nine hundred and three!"

Mother stepped towards Jennifer. Jennifer turned out of her chair and ran out of the dining room with her lunch box banging against her legs. Mother walked quickly after her saying, "Don't you say that! Don't you *ever* say that again!"

• • • •

I lay awake, sweating under too many covers. I was afraid to get out of bed and go to the bathroom. I thought I would get gallstones. Gallstones were big then. Jayne Mansfield had them, and Alice told me you got them from holding it too long or too often.

The air in front of the wallpaper shimmered silver-blue sand. They were atoms, and many of them, in shimmering clusters, were called molecules. I was the only person in the world who could see them, but I couldn't tell people about it, couldn't even tell Alice because people would put me on display with a sign underneath me, THE GIRL WITH THE MICROSCOPIC VISION, and then they would kill me. It was what Alice called My Compensation. Blind people were good in music, deaf people could draw and paint well, I, with my eyelid hanging down . . . Alice said she didn't know what My Compensation was yet, but that it would probably show itself soon.

I couldn't tell people about it, couldn't even tell Alice, because people were not supposed to be compensated so well.

I lay awake, sweating. I could see other things, too, things children were supposed to *want* to see, things that thought they were being *nice* appearing to children, but that I hoped would never appear to me: There would be Jesus, in a diaper with bloodhound eyes, who appeared to children who were good or to children who were bad to make them good, so that I tried to be good, then bad, then good, then bad so fast that Jesus wouldn't appear, because he always had to know ahead of time what kind of child he was appearing to, and so that by the time he had prepared himself to act in one way towards me, I would have changed. There would be Jerry Lewis, who picked children out of crowds at muscular dystrophy telethons and sang to them. There would be Mr. Manners, only two feet tall, a stack of paper napkins under his arm, and there would be a doll, one of my dolls, coming to kill me.

I tried to keep a sweet expression on my face as I lay in bed, hoping my dolls would be moved with pity as they approached. I kept my hands on my chest, left of center, so that if they tried to stab me as I slept, the knife going through my hands would wake me and I would have a chance to defend myself, flailing with split hands.

Mother comes in. "Still awake?"

"Would you sleep with me?"

"No, I must sleep by myself in my own bed."

"Can I sleep with you in your bed?"

"No, you have to sleep here, because if I let you sleep with me, Sonny, Butch, and Jennifer will be wanting to sleep with me, too."

I think for a minute. "*Please* can I sleep with you?"

"No."

"Please, please, please!"

"No, no, no!"

"Please, Pleeee-ase!"

"No."

"Please."

"No. Are you scared of something?"

"No!"

"Something you saw on TV?"

"NO!"

"Then what are you scared of?"

"I'm not scared of anything! I just want to sleep with you!"

"But you can't. Look, I'll sing The Westminster High School song for you. Would you like to hear The Westminster High School Song?"

"O.K." I am soaked with sweat.

Mother stands by the bed and starts marching in place:

> For our Westminster High School falls in line,
> We're going to win again another time,
> For our Westminster High School dear i-l,
> For our Westminster High School dear i-l, i-l,

Mother starts to take little marching steps back and forth:

> And if you want to find some pep and vim,
> Just watch our WHS boys fall right in,
> And when the gang's all here our school will shine
> Down the line, rah, rah, rah!

Mother jumps up and down on the "rah, rah, rah," then begins the song again, trotting in little circles around the room, breasts and behind bouncing:

> For our Westminster High School falls in line,
> We're going to win again another time,
> For our Westminster High School dear i-l . . .

Mother runs out again. I hear

> For our Westminster High School dear i-l, i-l,
> And if you want . . .

sung in the hall. She runs back:

> . . . to find some pep and vim,
> Just watch our WHS boys fall right in,
> And when the gang's all here, our school will shine
> Down the line, rah, rah . . .

Mother runs out.

> . . . rah! For our Westmin . . .

Mother runs out. Seconds pass. A minute. I hear "ster"

sung from the other end of the hall. More seconds pass. Fifteen minutes. An hour.

A big noise woke me up. I thought I had been dreaming of Mother being chased by men in striped bathrobes across a tile roof. I thought I had been dreaming of one of the men slipping and falling, then running into the distance with a pat, pat, pat, but then I realized that the sounds were real.

I stayed in bed, sweating, and listening. My dolls were in the corner, unmoving. I looked quickly to one side without moving my head to see how much distance there was to the door. I waited until the thinking about me, that the dolls did in waves, had passed over me. I threw off my covers and ran to the door.

The door to Mother's room was open. Her light was on. Jennifer and Butch, in their pyjamas, were standing by Mother's bed. Sonny was in Mother's bed, far to one side, the covers jammed up under his arms. Mother was standing by the window, looking out on the red tile roof.

The telephone rang on the bedside table. Mother walked to the table and picked it up. She listened for a while, then made a face and took the telephone receiver away from her ear, letting the voice babble in the air, like Scrooge McDuck's. She put it back to her ear.

"Yes, I'm in bed with a man. He's about five feet tall. You want to speak to him?" Mother handed the phone to Sonny.

"Hi, Dad," Sonny said. Sonny listened for a second, then gave the phone back to Mother.

A pause. "Oh, I can't very well take her to Dr. Reynolds in the middle of the night now, can I?" Mother listened again. "I'm sure you can," she said after a while, "I'm sure you can do all that." Mother hung up. She was shaking.

She leaned back on the pillows and shut her eyes. "Your daddy is still trying to prove that I'm a bad mother," Mother said. "He's trying to catch me . . . with other men. And if he can't catch me with other men, he accuses me of planning to take Robin to New York to have her eye operated on without his consent. . . ."

"Why doesn't he want to have Robin's eye operated on?" Jennifer asked.

"Because that's the only thing he has left, that's the only way he can still have some kind of . . . power over me."

Mother sighed on the word *power* and kept sighing, even after she'd finished talking, until she was almost flat under the covers. We stepped to the edge of the bed and watched her, waiting. Mother sighed so flat because she had so much on her: Daddy, Rush, Spotswood, Beauchamp, Dudley, Na-Na, my eye—they were all things on her. I wondered if they lay on her the way Daddy lay on his girlfriends, then figured it had to be another way. They had to sit more than lie. We watched her, waiting: you could almost see them, sitting on her, making her sigh flatter than other mothers, the way we sat on beach rafts with the nipples undone at the end of a day at the beach before putting them back in Mother's station wagon. "Whuuu" the air went out as we sank slowly. That was why Mother didn't have to pick up her closet, when we did, and why you couldn't ask her to do things, like get your bicycle fixed, and why you couldn't ask her why she *couldn't* stay home a little more or why she *had* to have so many weird people over, at least not in that tone of voice: she had so many things on her. That was why Mother was wonderful: because she had so many things on her but still just smiled. Mother was wonderful to balance Daddy's being amazing.

"Poor Mother," Sonny said.

A tear trickled out of the far corner of her eye. She breathed in. "But it's just a few more days. Then the judge will say that I can have you for sure and your dad will have to be at least a *little* sneakier about his detectives."

Then suddenly, the way it always happened, Mother starts to talk about how *nice* Daddy had been to her, how very *nice*, and charming, in the kind of way that made you think, "Are you kidding?" She'd been up at Lone Pine on location, making those humiliating serials, getting up at five-thirty to sit for the makeup man and then getting eaten by red ants or boiled in oil, when this Texas oilman, who looked like Cary Grant but who didn't know how to dance because his father had been a preacher, whom she had met in New York but who had followed her out to Los Angeles, flying ahead to meet her at every stop of the train with flowers and once with a porter with a wheelchair because he thought she was looking pale ("'Porter! Porter!'" Mother growls on the bed, imitating him, her voice full of phlegm; Mother takes a deep breath), but who she thought was somehow *playing* at being a Texas oilman, she couldn't believe Texas oilmen were so much like . . . what she had thought, would call her. He'd say, "How much are you getting paid up there?" and she'd say, "I'm making a hundred dollars a day," and he'd say, "Well, I'll pay you that much, I'll pay you more, to spend time with me." And she'd say, "I can't have you *pay* me to spend time with you!" And he'd say, "That's what I like about you, Lizzie Girl, you're not common. I can't *stand* common women."

. . . .

Peter came when we were eating chicken noodle soup on the porch. We stopped eating for a second while Mother, standing beside him, told him our names one by one. "Hellao, hellao," Peter said, in a voice that sounded almost English. Peter talked like that because he was from the East.

"*Sausages!*" Na-Na said. "*That's what I like!*"

Peter had gray hair and blue eyes. He was thin and wore a sweater that buttoned down the front. It was different from the sweaters that buttoned down the front that Daddy wore to play golf in, their full sleeves gathered at the wrists like a mariachi's blouse and made of squiggly wool: Peter's sweater was made of straight wool, with sleeves that fit snugly over the arms. Peter's sweater was more like the sweaters of pipe-smoking fathers on the "Donna Reed Show" or "Father Knows Best," who I guessed were from the East, too (though you couldn't tell from the trees on the show, and there was never any snow outside).

Mother told Peter to go find a chair in the next room.

"Harvard man," Mother whispered to us when he was out of the room.

Mother smiled at Peter as he came back in bringing a chair. He put it next to Mother and sat down, then cleared his throat, smiled at all of us, and inched a little closer to Mother. Mother asked him questions. She asked him how long it took him to drive out from the East Coast, how often and how many times he stopped and where he stopped. She asked him how things were in the East and how his painting was going. He said he hadn't been doing much painting lately because of driving and before that getting ready for the trip and before that thinking, ever since he met Mother, of . . .

Butch slurped his soup. Jennifer giggled.

"What do you think of my babies?" Mother asked.

"Babies?" Peter said in a very quiet voice. "Oh, you mean your children here! I think they're just fine! Yes!" He smiled at us. "I think they're fine! Heh, heh." Peter laughed. "Jennifer is the oldest, isn't she?" Peter asked Mother.

"Yes," Mother said.

"How are you?" Peter asked, looking at Jennifer.

"Huh?" Jennifer raised her head.

"I said, 'How are you?' "

"Fine," Jennifer said, her voice wriggling, looking down at her plate and pressing her lips together to keep from laughing out loud.

Peter asked Jennifer how old she was and where she went to school and what grade she was in. Jennifer answered him, squirming after every answer, and hitting Butch underneath the table (you could tell from the way her shoulder moved), while Butch sat beside her, hitting back.

Peter asked Jennifer what her interests were.

"Interests?"

"What subjects interest you."

"You mean in school?"

Peter shrugged. "In school. Or out."

"I don't know. . . ."

"Do you like painting?"

"Put 'em on the griddle, fry 'em up . . . "

"Mother, *please,*" Mother said.

"Yeah . . . sort of." Jennifer's lips were pressed together even harder. Her face was red.

"What kind of pictures do you paint?"

Jennifer looked at him.

"Who is your favorite painter?"

"Um . . . Rembrandt?"

"Only name you know!" Butch shouted.

   .   .   .   .

Mother asked Peter if I could go to the beach with them. Mother and Peter waited until Sonny, Butch, and Jennifer weren't around, then Peter picked me up and carried me out of the house with them and into the car.

We drove on the road along the beach. Mother gave me her scarf to trail out the window. We drove past hot dog stands. Some were like castles, some were like Swiss chalets, some were like the adobe missions of Father Junipero Serra. Some were like log cabins. Some were big hats and some were big people. Each one of them made me wonder how it came to be there and what it was like inside.

We drove off the highway and saw the beach stretching ahead of us, wide and curving, with almost no people on it.

"Beautiful," Peter said.

Beautiful: the word sounded different. It was because I'd never heard a man say it about anything other than a woman. It was because I'd never heard it said just by itself, without anything before it or after it.

Peter parked the car. Mother and Peter got out and started to walk.

"But what are we doing?" I called after them.

"We're taking a walk," Mother said. "Come on."

Take a walk: I'd never done that before, just walk, without going anyplace. I'd heard people talk about taking walks, I'd heard people tell other people to take a walk, but I never thought people actually *took* them. I tried to think of Daddy or Busy or anyone at Daddy's house taking walks but couldn't. Peter took walks because he was from the East. Mother took walks with Peter because she had been from the East and being with Peter made her be Eastern again.

"Isn't it wonderful here?" Peter said, taking Mother's hand.

"Yes," Mother said.

People from the East talked about California being wonderful, I thought. People from the East held hands.

"I mean the colors, the smells. Just take a deep breath, Elizabeth!"

"Oh yes, yes," Mother said, breathing in, "yes," as if she were thirsty and Peter's words were something to drink. Mother breathed in again and again, moving her arms up and down with each breath. She started taking longer strides. Peter speeded up. I had to run to keep up with them. "Mm-hah! Mm-hah!" Mother said. "When I was married I couldn't go on any walks. 'What do you want to walk for?' Cornelius would say. Once I found an empty house in the Hollywood Hills. Nothing in it but wall-to-wall carpeting and a stereo. I dressed the children in leotards and we all went and interpreted the sunset. Mm-hah! Mm-hah!"

"I can't imagine how anyone could *resist* walking on a beach like this," Peter said after a while.

I looked from the distant mountains to the sand dunes to the sloping wet sand to the ocean to the sun, low over the water. I pretended the mountains and sand dunes were parts of a giant ski slope and I was skiing on it, up to the sun. Then I saw how the sun shone on the water and on each retreating wave and how the water rolled and foamed, dragging grains of sand, black or metallic but some lilac as well, and red and yellow, back with it, reshaping the grains into different patterns of big and little *v*'s and then stroking the *v*'s, once they were made, with rippling fingers.

Beautiful: I saw how you could say it, just like that.

I would find out about Rembrandt, I thought. I would wear a beret. I would sit on a sofa and have modern paintings squished on the wall behind me. I would look at things people at Daddy's house—and Mother, until she met Peter —didn't think were beautiful, didn't notice one way or the other, with eyes that had become, somehow, both of them, completely open, and think, "Beautiful, beautiful." It would be like having fresh wind on your face. I would sail to the islands where people liked poetry and classical music, and hear the voices of Butch and Jennifer fade behind me on the dock. I would listen to opera. I would eat liver, brains, tongue, oysters, frogs' legs, fish eggs, and even tomatoes.

CHAPTER 3

The people from Texas come into the living room looking at the chandeliers. They walk stiffly in their new clothes. "Hey there!" the men say to us when they see us. The women smile. They sit down on one of the sofas. After a while the men get up and start looking at things around the room, swinging their arms back, then bringing them forward and clapping them together in front of themselves. The women recross their legs.

"I wish Daddy would come," Jennifer says under her breath. "It's so embarassing."

Daddy had stopped having big parties and had started having people over for drinks, then taking them later to Trader Vic's. Daddy said he liked big parties, but for the time being, while he wasn't feeling as good as usual, he thought he would just have smaller groups of people over.

Dr. Fayman came over before anyone else came, in a tuxedo, carrying a black bag. Daddy, dressed in gray suit, white shirt, and silver necktie, met him in the hall. "Daddy Boy's got to get a little shot now," Daddy told us. Daddy put down his drink and went ahead of Dr. Fayman through the living room to the phone booth at the base of the stairs, put in by the movie director who had owned the house before because he had had parties at which the guests were always getting phone calls.

I saw the black and gray backs of their suits through a window in the door that stopped just above their waists. There was just enough room in the booth for the two of them. Daddy moved his elbows back and up and hunched over. Dr. Fayman hunched over, too. They stayed that way for about a minute, then they both straightened up and came out, Daddy smiling at me and rubbing his behind.

"I'm havin' a little problem with my blood being too thick, Robin Girl," Daddy said. "It's not going fast enough through my veins. I've told Dr. Fayman Boy about it, so Dr. Fayman Boy's giving me something to make my blood thinner, so it'll run faster. It's like what you do in the oil business with an old well: shoot salt water into it to make the oil flow faster.

"Your daddy's a tired old well, but a recovery well, too, that's gonna rise again and be the biggest, meanest, damndest well in this whole country, isn't that right, Dr. Fayman Boy?" Daddy slapped him on the back.

"Yes it is, indeed, Mr. D.!"

"Heh heh yes well. . . ." Daddy picked up his drink and went back to his room to rest until all the guests came.

Busy comes down, then Don, then Minnie, even though Minnie said it didn't seem right, her mixing with Daddy's guests, but Daddy said he wouldn't think of Don going out in the evenings without her.

Then Daddy's lawyer friends come with their wives, then Colette, the gossip columnist who had been the first person in Beverly Hills to see Daddy, through a half-opened door at Arthur Murray's, learning the box-step, and had called Rhonda Fleming right away. "You've got to see this," she had said. "You've just got to come over and see this."

Daddy had to invite Colette to his parties and had to let her toy poodles "run" (which meant leave hard, dry number twos) on the lawn every day at three o'clock or she would write bad things about him in the paper, and besides, Daddy said, he owed her, he would always owe her, for all the beautiful showgirls he knew.

Colette had blond hair swooshed up into a permanent tidal wave over one ear and had had her face lifted ten times, she said, and had got her mouth back in shape after each operation by saying "Papa, potatoes, poultry, prunes, and prisms" between talking to people and kissing. She wore beige shoes and carried a beige handbag.

Colette was like one of Daddy's girlfriends left to bleach in the sun or like one of Daddy's girlfriends left to go back to what she had been before Daddy met her.

If Daddy met a woman he wanted to be his girlfriend, and she was blond, he would make her dye her hair a dark color and go charge up some dark, shiny clothes to him at Saks. Then Don would stop taking the old girlfriend's children to the orthodontist with us and start taking the new girlfriend's. Then the old girlfriend would stop coming to Daddy's house for cocktails and the new one would start coming over. Then the old girlfriend would start calling Daddy on the phone and Daddy would start saying "pipe down" to her. Then the new girlfriend would redecorate part of the house. Dolores took out the Grandma Moseses in the bar and put in their place paintings of big pink women in see-through nightgowns and high-heeled satin bedroom slippers with pompoms on the toes. Tamara took out the grandfather clock in the living room and put in its place a table with a marble top and fancy gold legs that she called "Louie Says" and on the top of it a gold statue of big man with a beard she called "Low Coon" wrestling with a snake, with a lot of other little men caught in the snake's coils and a clock set into one of the snake's bulging eyes. Pepita took the pots of azaleas and ferns off the terrace and put in their place giant dark-brown fat-bellied tikis, made of compacted palm-tree fibers, like the kind they had at Trader Vic's. Ingrid put a purple and turquoise canopy over the bed in the guest bedroom, suspended from the fist of a flying cupid, and took out the plain mirror in the guest bedroom and put in its place a mirror shot with spidery gold lines. Daddy would not let them touch his bedroom, though. Shanti took out the low-pile carpets and the Persian rugs and put in their place a white wall-to-wall carpet, running throughout the house, with a pile three inches thick.

"Oooo . . ." Sonny, Butch, Jennifer, and I would say when we saw what they had done, "pretty!" and Daddy would put his arm around Dolores, Tamara, Pepita, Ingrid, or Shanti's head, until her head would be nothing but a little black poof of hair in the middle of Daddy's arm, and say that no one had taken care of little Daddy Boy for a long time.

Then the old girlfriend would call us on the phone, sometimes putting her son or daughter on first, so that if Daddy picked up the phone, he wouldn't know it was really her calling. She would ask us if we thought she'd always been nice to us. We would say that we thought she always had been nice. Then with a voice trembling like the organ music on "As the World Turns" she'd ask us to *tell* Daddy, then, how nice she had always been to us. We would tell Daddy what the old girlfriend had asked us to tell him. Daddy's new girl-friend would usually be there and they would both laugh and then Daddy would shake his head and say, "That poor little showgirl, that poor, mixed-up, crazy, sad little showgirl."

Then the old girlfriend would start to follow Daddy, com-ing up to Daddy on the driving range, and Daddy, seeing her coming, would duck behind a palm tree and then go to his office in Sacramento or Tulsa for a while. Sometimes Daddy would even take out a court order against one of them that Alice would see in the newspaper and come and get me out of school to show me.

Then Daddy would give the new girlfriend a Cadillac. Then Daddy would give the new girlfriend a fur coat and a ring. He would hold the ring in a box high over her head and she would say, "Oh gimme, oh gimme, gimme!" and Daddy would say, "You have to jump for it, Dolores, Tamara, Pepita, Ingrid, or Shanti Girl!" and she would start to jump for it, giving little yelps as she did.

Then Daddy would meet another woman he wanted to be his girlfriend and we wouldn't see the one who had been his girlfriend for a while. Then Daddy would start to be friendly again, but just as a friend, with the old old girlfriend, the one who had been his girlfriend before the one who had *just* been his girlfriend. He would take her to the driving range with him (picking her up from her beige-interiored house), or she would drive her beige car over to Daddy's house to let her dogs "run" on the lawn or swim the length of the pool four or five times, fitting a flowered bathing cap on over hair which she had let go back to beige or blond.

Daddy would watch her from the terrace overlooking the swimming pool, mumbling, "Look at that old biddy in her bathing suit," then cup his hands around his mouth and shout, "Go, Dolores, Tamara, Pepita, Ingrid, or Shanti Girl, go!"

Colette writes the names of the people from Texas in a little book.

Then some famous actors and actresses come, only they are not quite as famous as the ones who had gone to Daddy's big parties. They are ones you see on channels five, nine, and eleven, instead of on two, four, and seven, but still they make me feel as if I have to go to the bathroom, and still we look at the people from Texas, the way we look at any un-famous people at Daddy's house when they meet famous people, to see if they will do something when they shake hands with them. The women look more at the ground than at them and the men snap their fingers and point and say, "You're . . . you're . . ." so that their wives whisper to them later, "You shouldn't have said that . . . like that."

"I wish Daddy would come," Jennifer says again.

Then Rita comes.

Rita was Daddy's new girlfriend. She had re-done the dining room. She had taken out the antique sideboards and flowered curtains and put in their place built-in sideboards with pink lacquered doors with frosted glass pineapple slices for handles and pink satin French curtains: rows and rows of stuck-together *u*'s that were raised and lowered by a complicated system of pulleys.

Rita wasn't foreign, though, just from Philadelphia, she said, where her parents were what she called "Society People" ("Thank God," Butch said, "no hairy pits"), and didn't have any children, as there were no children going with us to the orthodontist now. ("Thank God," Butch said again,

[77]

"they're always such wimps, those kids, neurotic, shuttled around. . . .")

Rita had black hair, white skin and a nose that was long and thin, with pinched nostrils and two bumps, half-emerged, for the tip. Rita said she had been in a car accident but Mother said she'd had a nose job, one of the early ones. Mother said she could remember Rita as a tall teenager, straight from Kansas, arriving in Hollywood just six weeks after being crowned Miss Kansas State Fair, with a voice and accent copied from Loretta Young. Rita had had a kind of little turned-up Kansas rainwater-catching nose then.

Then Mother would say, "Don't repeat that," which meant Mother was forgetting that I knew now what the things were that you weren't supposed to say—I knew them all—and was hoping I *would* repeat it, or even go so far as to ask Rita the question, "Rita? Did you have a nose job?" Mother wanted to hear of Rita's humiliation at being asked such a question and of Rita crying and balling and unballing her handkerchief up near her nose and then pounding the air with weak fists and shaking the black curls and the diamond pendants in her ears. And Mother wanted to hear of Daddy saying, "There now, Rita Girl, you know you're the prettiest, the very prettiest girl in Beverly Hills!" Mother wanted Daddy to repeat to her what had happened, even though I, coming home Sunday night, would have described the scene already to her in detail. Mother wanted Daddy to ask her where I, where that child, had ever heard such things, so that Mother could act shocked and then say innocently, "Gracious, Cornelius, I don't have any *i*dea where she picked that up! Poor Cornelius, poor Rita, I'm just as shocked as you are, I can promise you!"

Finally Daddy comes out. His tanned skin shows up shockingly against his white hair, white shirt, gray suit, and silver necktie. Daddy is the reverse of other fathers, whose hair and suits and neckties are usually *darker* than their skin.

"Hey, y'all!" Daddy says to everybody.

"Hey, Cornelius!" they shout back.

"Hey, you gorgeous hunk of man, you! Hey, you beautiful cowboy!" Rita shouts, jumping up on tiptoes.

Daddy kisses Rita first, putting his hands on either side of her face, shutting his eyes, puckering his lips, and bringing them towards her puckered lips slowly. They stay kissing upright for a few seconds, then, still kissing, Daddy puts his arms around her shoulders, his knee into her back and bends her over backwards, without ever taking his lips off hers, while the other guests scream and laugh and clap and one of them shouts, "Yahoo!"

Daddy brings Rita back up, then goes around the other women and kisses them and bends them over backwards, too, one after the other, while everyone laughs and claps and screams, the noise rising in little peaks each time he bends a new woman over, while before and after, individual voices say, "Oh, that Cornelius," or, "He's really cute." Then smiling, Daddy shakes hands with all the men, holding onto their hands after he shakes them and saying in a low, growling voice, "Come here," then pulling them towards him, putting his arms around their shoulders, and hugging them with his face thrust over a shoulder. "How are you, boy?" he asks as he hugs each man.

Daddy steps back, looks around, and pulls one of the men and one of the women from Texas close to him and puts an arm around each of them and says to the other people, "Do you realize that Tommy Boy here and Margaret Girl here . . . but let's go get a drink." Daddy leads the way, pushing the kitchen door open and holding it open while they all file past him into the pantry.

There was a bar at the house, long enough for twenty people, but Daddy said he liked drinking in the pantry, with all his girls.

Midge, Judy, and Carmen are waiting on the other side. Bowing, Daddy introduces Midge, Judy, and Carmen, calling them by their full names.

"Hey, Midge Girl," "Hey, Judy Girl," "Hey, Carmen Girl," the guests call to them.

"Hey, So-and-so Boy," and "Hey, So-and-so Girl," Midge, Judy, and Carmen call back to the guests before Daddy is able to finish his introductions, the braces on Midge's teeth flashing in the overhead light.

Midge had braces on her teeth, Carmen's gold tooth was gone, and Judy looked different, too, though it was hard to tell how.

Daddy goes to one of the kitchen cupboards, opens it, and pulls out a bottle of bourbon. "Now who wants a drink? Midge Girl, make Shirley Temples for the kids. Who wants a drink?" A couple of people say they do, so Daddy pours bourbon over ice into a couple of glasses, then pours one for himself, leans against the counter, and says, "Cheers."

"Cheers," everyone says.

Before Daddy kept a bottle of bourbon in the pantry, he had kept one in what was now Midge's bathroom, in the one-storied wing off the kitchen, only it had been some other cook's bathroom then. That was when Grandaddy Drayton, Daddy's father, who was a minister and who didn't believe in drinking, smoking, or dancing, was alive and when Mother and Daddy were still married. Daddy had gone to what was now Midge's bathroom every night at six o'clock and, sleeves rolled up, had washed the tumbler the cook before Midge used when she brushed her teeth, then had poured a little bourbon in and drunk it, in one gulp. Then he had rinsed the glass and poured some of the cook's Lavoris into it, washed his mouth, spat, and rinsed the glass and sink.

After a few sips, Daddy pulls one of the actresses up next to him. He puts his arm around her waist. She smiles at Daddy, then around the room at everyone. Daddy keeps looking at her. His eyelids are lowered. We keep thinking that, any second, Daddy is going to start looking at everyone else around the room, too, but he just keeps looking at her. Everyone stops talking. The actress smiles again and shrugs. The hand that was around her waist goes up to her shoulders, then reaches around until the tips of his fingers touch her chin. He presses up on her chin lightly. Her head rises. She looks at everyone again, rolling her eyes down to be able to do so, and smiles a quick half-smile, which makes her nose bob down once quickly.

"Cute," a voice says uncertainly.

Daddy turns her until everyone in the pantry can see her from the side.

"Have you ever seen such a profile?" he finally asks.

The actress smiles a wide smile. Everyone in the room breathes out at once. "She's beautiful, Cornelius," people say, nodding.

"She's beautiful, Mr. D.," Midge, Judy, and Carmen say.

"Oh, Cornelius, you're making me so jealous!" Rita says, rushing forward and trying to spank Daddy. Daddy jumps away just in time, laughing.

"Cute, oh cute," a chorus of grownup voices (they are almost moaning it) say.

Daddy's eyes then start to travel around the room.

I pushed myself back harder against the counter I was leaning on.

"Come here, Robin Girl," Daddy says.

My hands, behind me, held onto the countertop edge.

"Come here, Robin Girl," Daddy repeats.

I let go of the counter and took a few steps towards Daddy and the actress.

"Do you know who *this* is?" Daddy asks, smiling down at me.

My stomach, which had had a couple of butterflies in it before, began to feel like that tree, somewhere in California, which all the monarch butterflies flew to, all packed in tightly together.

"Oh *Daddy*," I say.

"Oh *Daddy*," a grownup voice repeats, imitating me, then says in a regular voice, "cute."

"Oh *Daddy*," Daddy repeats, "I just want you to tell me who this is!"

The actress smiles down at me.

I felt the butterflies fly in tighter, I felt them becoming one black-and-orange ball.

Oh Daddy, I want to say again, but instead I say, "That's . . . oh, I don't know. . . ."

"You don't *know?*"

Daddy then asks one of the women from Texas to get close to him. He puts an arm around her and then, with one arm around the woman from Texas and the other arm around the actress, he asks the woman from Texas if she knows who *this* is, giving the actress's shoulders a squeeze.

"Cute," someone says.

"Yes," the woman from Texas says, and Daddy says, "Who?"

I am not sure whether Daddy means to do it or whether it is just a flinch, but Daddy's index finger on the end of the arm that is around the woman from Texas arches backwards on the word *who*, up under the nose of the woman from Texas, making the end of her nose turn up and the middle of her nose wrinkle in ridges like an accordion.

Daddy looks at her with eyes that suddenly become foggy.

The woman from Texas stays with her nose turned up like that for about a second, her eyes darting to the left and right, then she lifts her head back further than Daddy's finger can arch, until her nose falls back again and the overhead light on her glasses blocks out her eyes. "That's . . ." she says, naming the actress, and the actress smiles and goes

"Yeehoooo!" and wiggles her behind under Daddy's hand.

"Cute, oh cute," a forest of grownup voices say, breathing out.

Then Daddy asks the woman from Texas if she ever thought that she and Daddy would someday be having a drink with the actress she said it was or with Rita Girl, for that matter. The woman says no, and Daddy says, "No what?" and the woman says she didn't ever think and Daddy says, "Think what?" and the woman says that she'd be having a drink with the actress she said it was and Daddy says that that was why he thinks life is so Goddamned Wonderful.

Then a man's voice, one of the actors' voices, says, "Well, didn't we think the same thing, too, that we'd be standing here, having drinks with a famous Texas oilman?" and Daddy's eyes snap back, from being foggy to being bright and shining, and he laughs and says, "I *like* you, boy!"

Daddy goes on to talk about the flimsy house he had lived in, where the screen door had kept banging in a constant wind, of the nights he had spent there, dreaming of the time when he would make it and of all the beautiful showgirls he would have, nothing but beautiful showgirls. He talks about how cold and hungry he had been and of the bathrooms he had shared. He talks about working in the sun all day, with rattlesnakes crawling up his pants. "'If only they were showgirls,' I used to think. . . . Fished them out and swung the guts out of them." Daddy circles his hand over his head. He talks about how he had learned to drink beer and had wrestled half-breeds, who pounded his neck against a stone, until the only thought in his head was a quiet, "kind of wistful, you know? 'Hey, I'm gonna die . . . but just let me see some beautiful showgirls first!'"

Daddy talks about how he had caught the drill bit as it

came down from the monkeyman and—Daddy comes out from behind the bar and plants his legs wide apart—"guided it into the hole. *Caught* that drill bit and—," the muscles in Daddy's neck stand out, "*caught* it again. Jumped off the floor yelling, 'She's gonna blow!' when I heard a rumbling under my feet. Ran smack dab into the monkeyman scrambling down off the derrick and the monkeyman and I, we rolled over and over one another, trying to get away from that thing in time. We were not more than fifty yards away when with a rumbling and a blowing—it was like the sound of Niagara Falls, stuffed into a hole one foot across—that green black oil came rushing up, up through the derrick and out over the top, carrying tools, pipe, hats, and jackets with it. 'Look out, beautiful showgirls,' I said when I saw that. . . .'" Daddy stands out from the bar, his arms spread wide. "'Look out, beautiful showgirls, and big parties, here I come!!!!!!!'"

People shift on their feet.

"What?" I ask, taking my eyes off Daddy.

A woman, one of the lawyers' wives whom I have never met before, has said something to me that I don't catch.

"Did you get stung by a bee or something?" she repeats, in a loud whisper.

"There's nothing wrong with her little eye," Daddy calls from across the room.

Everyone looks at Daddy. Daddy is looking at the woman. "That's my baby girl. That's my baby girl and there's nothing wrong with her little eye. That's my bee bee HM!" Daddy clears his throat. Daddy lets go of the woman under his arm, pulls a handkerchief out of his pocket and puts it over his mouth. You can see something in it, bulging.

"'Course there's nothing wrong with her little eye," Rita says.

Daddy twists the handkerchief off at his mouth. "Nothing wrong that a little exercise won't fix."

"A little exercise, that's all she needs. . . ." Rita says, nodding her head. "Are you all right?" she asks Daddy.

"'S nothing, ahem, just a frog in my throat." Daddy starts taking glasses out of guests' hands and throwing the ice and left-over bourbon out into the sink.

"Guess it's time to go now," Rita says.

Some guests start to move towards the door. Other guests and Midge, Judy, and Carmen offer to help Daddy clear but Daddy says he will be all right.

We drive to Trader Vic's in six white Cadillac limousines. Daddy drives the first limousine, Don drives the second. Gardeners drive the others. We pile into the front of the first limousine with Daddy.

Daddy had six white Cadillac limousines but drove them mostly himself. It looked O.K. at night when there were so many people, but it looked strange during the day when Daddy drove them himself, Daddy up front with all that limousine in back.

Sitting beside me, Jennifer whispers that she wishes Daddy were not driving in the front but sitting in the back with a snobby-looking lady, not Rita, but a lady in riding clothes, with a neck scarf.

Daddy clicks his heels together and bows to the head-waiter standing behind the reservations desk. "Mon capitan," Daddy says. The headwaiter clicks his heels together and bows back. Then all the waiters make a line on either side of us and click their heels and bow at us as we walk to the table. Daddy bows to them one by one.

People turn around in their seats and look at us.

There was a whole outrigger canoe suspended from the ceiling, with spears and shields attached to the sides of it, and there were fishnets and blown-glass balls that the head-waiter said were floats for the nets, but it was hard to see how they wouldn't get smashed, such delicate things in the middle of the ocean with sharks and war canoes going by them. Old-fashioned diving suits with dummies in them stood between the tables and there were capstans and port-holes and balustrades between the various levels of the res-taurant with knobs on them for tying rope. The walls were made of printed palm tree bark, with stuffed fish mounted on them.

We point the fish out to the people from Texas as we walk to our table. "That's a dolphin," we say, "and that's a mahi-mahi."

"A *what?*"

"You don't know what a *mahi-mahi* is?"

There was a giant steaming vat, too, behind a glass wall, with a fire underneath it made of crossed logs. It was like the kind of vat cannibals cooked people in in cartoons. It was where they made Special Chicken. Three Chinese men worked around it, stirring the Special Chicken with long bamboo poles. Their shirts were dripping wet and stuck to their bodies.

I looked around. *Those Chinese men really worked. I didn't think that you were supposed to look at people working that hard, let alone put them on display, like in a diorama, but neither they nor the people in the restaurant seemed to mind.*

We always had the same table. It was the only one with gardenias on it. It had the best view of the garden: stone lanterns, bonsai trees, raked gravel paths, and tiny, arching stone bridges, all lit with blue lights and backed by a high wall. It was hard to believe the intersections of three four-lane highways were on the other side.

Daddy gives us ten-dollar bills to wander with until dinner is ready. We wander back out to the entrance, re-seeing the things we have just seen, then to the gift shop, where we buy rubber hula girls who hula when you turn a small crank between their legs, wooden monkeys with hooked hands and feet to add to the chain of monkeys we already have, fake vomit, plastic ice cubes with flies inside, and a bottle opener with a golf ball for a handle, then to the small display case near the entrance, that we try never to look at but always end up looking at our second time around: a tiny shrunken head, with long black hair like wire and two blue stones in place of eyes.

The headwaiter said it was from New Guinea.

"It was a person," Jennifer says. "It was a *person*."

I looked around. *I didn't think that was supposed to be there somehow either: an actual person's cut-off* head *in a restaurant with us just there looking at it. I thought it wasn't legal somehow.*

Daddy orders the same thing for us every time: cho-cho, limestone lettuce, teriyaki steak, and fruit punch in carved-out pineapples. Daddy also orders the same thing for himself every time: something with a whole hard-boiled egg in it, sitting in dark-brown gravy.

The fruit punch is The Most Delicious Drink in the Whole World. We drink one fruit punch after another without raising our heads: the waiters just keep them coming. We drink them until our straws gurgle at the end. Butch gurgles his straw loudly and says, "Daddy, Daddy, I got a dry hole!"

Daddy squeezes his eyes shut and scrunches up his mouth. "Hee hee hee!" he laughs, moving his head up and his shoulders down with each "hee." Tears roll down his face. "Oh Butch Boy, you kill me!"

"What did he say? What did he say?" one of the men from Texas asks, fumbling in his pocket with his hearing aid control.

"What did he say?" Colette asks, pursing her lips in a silent "papa, potatoes," fumbling in her purse for her little notebook.

"What did he say?" all the other people at the table ask, leaning forward.

"He said he hit a dry hole!" Daddy shouts.

The men from Texas tilt their heads back and laugh: "Wo ho ho ho ho ho ho ho! Wo ho ho ho ho ho ho ho!" All the other guests laugh, too.

"Hee hee hee hee! Hee hee hee hee!" Daddy laughs. "Oh that Butch Boy, he kills me, he's so cute."

"He *is* cute," a guest says.

We drive up Daddy's mountain after dinner. I lean forward on the seat to let Busy undo the back of my dress, I am so full. There are no lights on the mountain, Daddy explains, for Daddy owns the whole mountain and hasn't figured out what to do with it yet. Daddy has bulldozed off the top of the mountain, looking for a place to put a house, a house where he could raise his children, spend the rest of his days. He is a tired old man. "Your Daddy's a tired old man, honeys," Daddy says, looking at us in the rearview mirror. "Daddy is just a tired old man, with four little children that the good Lord saw fit to send him in his old age, looking for a place to put a house—now, what could be wrong with that?—when some people down there—," Daddy makes a downward gesture out the car window into the valley below, "started bringing a suit against him. A suit, against Daddy Boy!"

"No!"

"Said mud had washed into their living rooms! Just a lot of money-grubbing Jews."

"I don't see how *anyone* could do that to you, Mr. D."

"No, you're too good, Mr. D., too good."

"Oh, my *Gatt*, you're so good," Busy says.

The limousine winds up the mountain, sometimes passing between two halves of a giant rock that Daddy has had dynamited, sometimes passing on the soft, outer, guardrail-less rim, so that rocks trickle above us and below us and the grid of colored lights below us that is Los Angeles tilts towards us, then away, as if we are in an airplane, circling. Children scream. Grownups draw their breath in through their teeth.

"Then there was my father going into the hospital for his gall bladder operation?" Minnie whispered beside me. "Well, I'll be darned if he didn't get a fruit basket the next morning with fruit piled on it, I mean this high. . . ." Minnie raised a hand with a cigarette smoking in it as far as she could in the limousine. "Something that big *couldn't* have been from anyone else. And then, there's my sister's kid with cerebral palsy? Well, Children's Hospital calls my sister and says that this physical therapist, the best one in the country, has been assigned to giving my sister's kid physical therapy, and this has all been paid for, and they want to know what time of day could my sister bring her kid in for her daily session. And those sessions must be at least a hundred per. Now, how did he know? Do you know what *I* think? I think he's got detectives following *my* family around or something. Anyway, after that thing with my sister's kid, I went to your dad and I said, 'Mr. D., this is all very nice, but if you think you can use my sister's kid as a way to . . . get me, *Oh*-ho-ho-no. . . .'"

Daddy waits for me to get in bed and lies down on top of the covers, half on top of me and half beside me. He puts one leg and half his chest and a shoulder and an arm on me. He squishes his nose against my cheek. His chin scratches my neck. His bourbon and Mai-Tai breath waft over me. He says he is going to stay with me until I fall asleep.

Daddy is so heavy I can't move. I try to move my legs but Daddy's weight on top of the sheets has them pulled like a cinch. Daddy feels me moving and says for me just to be quiet with Daddy Boy. Daddy's bourbon and Mai-Tai breath is heavy and slow. I am breathing twice as fast as Daddy, my breaths occurring at the same time and in the middle of his breaths, so I breathe in a little bourbon Mai-Tai every time, but his breathing is so heavy and slow that it drags my breathing out into his until finally we are breathing just the same.

I wanted to tell Daddy to get off me but didn't because I knew that that would hurt his feelings. No one had told me it would, I just knew it would. That was why Mother didn't tell him to get off her and why his girlfriends didn't tell him to get off them, a man as heavy as he was. They said it silently, between all the sentences they spoke: "Don't hurt Daddy, don't hurt Daddy," their tongues beat like tom-toms. It was as if I had X-ray vision, as well as microscopic.

I looked around, up over Daddy's shoulder to the stuffed animals I had at Daddy's house, gazing at me from a shelf. *I had liked it at first,* I thought, *when Minnie said, "Oh-ho-ho-no." It sounded like the kind of thing I and all the other girls in the world would say in the great battle that was going to happen one day, between all the boys in the world and all the girls. "Oh-ho-ho-no." I felt tears spring into my eyes. Or the kind of thing cannibals chanted as they grabbed the enemy person. Or the kind of thing Daddy's friends chanted as, cuter and cuter, they danced around Daddy in a bunch of gravy while everyone in the world acted as if that were perfectly all right. After a while though, I didn't like it so much anymore.*

Daddy says Robin is Daddy's baby girl and Daddy is Robin's baby boy. He bunches the skin of my chest up in his hands and puts his cheek and eyes against it. He says that I am a little Mommy and that is where a little milk will come out. He wants to know if I won't give Daddy some.

"Oh *Daddy*," I say, feeling as if I am choking.

Daddy says he is just kidding.

"Oh-*ho-ho-no*, oh-*ho-ho-no*," *the cannibals chanted at* me.

. . . .

Sonny loomed above me. Clouds were passing by his head, like they did by the dome of the Beverly Hills Post Office. Sonny told me that he never wanted to hear me say again that I loved Mother more than Daddy. You didn't say things like that.

I felt my cheeks burn and my stomach shrink. I knew that I shouldn't have said that I loved Mother more than Daddy. I wanted to tell Sonny that I *knew* what the things were that you weren't supposed to say, I really did. I wanted to tell Sonny that I knew that, it was just that sometimes . . . it was a bad day, like one of Midge's bad days.

Midge would shuffle to the door dividing the kitchen from her wing, a cigarette dangling from her lips, her stocking rolled down below her bathrobe into little doughnuts around her ankles. Her stomach would be pooched out, below the waist.

"I can't take his tray in today," she'd say to Judy or Carmen. "It's a bad day."

. . . .

I stood by myself in the basement, way back in back of the laundry room, way back in back of where the bikes and Flexies were stored, at the mouth of the giant air duct that sent heat all through the house.

I was looking at the air duct I imagined Daddy's girlfriends used going and coming from his room. Jennifer had said that we never would be able to see Daddy's girlfriends leaving, that they always managed to stay just out of sight, because they used the air duct. A branch went from Daddy's room to a little grill at the side of the house by the porte cochere, and from there they just looked around to see if no one was looking and ran to where there was a limousine, waiting to pick them up, and whipped into the limousine so fast that it would be *as if* we hadn't seen them.

I stood at the mouth of the air duct, half wanting, half not wanting, to see them, moving my head from side to side, from my open eye to my shut eye and back again, like a very slow-moving old person saying, "No, no, no, no."

I had asked Jennifer once whether, if I held my eye up, I would ever be able to see Daddy's girlfriends leaving. Whispering the way Busy did, Jennifer said that it was not just me, nobody could see them, because they were secret. She said that all we would ever see, at most, would be curtains rustling or a piece of silk disappearing through a crack in a door, like a snake in a hole. We could try to look after it, but it would be gone.

CHAPTER 4

When Mother and Peter go into their bedroom, they shut the door behind them quickly, as if they are trying to keep some cat from getting out. Mother and Peter have a patio off their bedroom, surrounded by a high wooden fence. Mother puts her underwear to dry on the camellia bushes while Peter sunbathes and paints modern art and listens to classical music, whistling along with it every once in a while.

Peter sunbathed nude, we thought. We saw flashes of his bare shoulders and back through cracks in the fence, but the camellia bushes kept us from seeing below his waist. Eastern people, or people who listened to classical music, wouldn't strip down to bathing trunks at the beach, but when they had a chance to be in private under the sun, they took their clothes off altogether.

"Have you seen him yet? Have you seen him yet?" we asked each other, but Peter put his hands together in front of his pyjamas when he walked in the hall, and in the powder room with the gold swans on the wall he always went silently against the side of the bowl, so that you didn't know when he was in there unless you were watching the door, and then, by the time you had run around to the back of the house and raised your head to the window, holding the ledge, one foot wedged in an air vent, he had already gone.

Peter had a scar running from his chest to his navel for he had been sick on their honeymoon in Paris. He had thrown up blood, with clots in it, and the maid, the stupid French maid, had chased Mother down the hall, yelling at her for messing up the bathroom, while Mother ran ahead, yelling, "Help! Docteur! Police! Help! Docteur! Police!" Peter could only eat white food—milk, rice, bananas, yogurt, and cheese—and only a little bit at a time, and he wasn't allowed to worry or be upset because that made bad juices.

Peter had stopped saying "beautiful" and had started saying "interesting!" Mother said "interesting!" too. Peter and Mother said "interesting!" about a lot of different things. The darker a restaurant was on the beach and the dirtier it was and the more it served frogs' legs, the more "interesting!" they said it was. The heavier a man's accent was and the more he wore the same sandals, gray flannel pants, and striped socks, the more "interesting!" they said he was. Peter asked Mother if she'd noticed that the more "interesting" people in Brentwood were voting for Kennedy. Peter said he still liked Nixon, though. I looked at Mother to see if she really thought what Peter said was interesting *was* interesting but she was looking at Peter and smiling. The less you could tell what a painting was of, the more "interesting!" it was and the more I told Mother and Peter that children at school called me ugly, the more "interesting!" looking they said I was, except for once, when Peter said, "Tell him."

"Tell him what?"

"Tell him what the children at school say to her."

"But Peter, you can't just *tell* him. . . ."

"Tell him," Peter said. He turned and left the room holding his stomach.

No one said "interesting!" to me the rest of the day. Daddy called that night and asked to speak especially to me. There were extra long pauses between his words and every few sentences Daddy asked me if I was his baby and I said I was.

Mother and Peter said "interesting!" to me even before I went to school the next day, kneeling down in front of me and looking from one eye to the other. "Interesting! Interesting! Interesting!" until they sounded almost mad.

Peter left the room holding his stomach if Mother talked about Daddy or asked questions about Daddy, standing by the front door when we came home from Daddy's house on Sunday nights, or if we forgot to say "please" or "thank you" or said "real" instead of "really" or "pretty" instead of "very," "extremely," or "quite," or if we asked Peter questions like, "If Mother died, would you keep her body on ice?" (it was very hot that day), or if we complained about Mother burning the toast on the weekends Alice was away and we stayed at Mother's house instead of going to Daddy's. If Mother burned the toast, Peter said it was because we were sitting on our ba-*hinds*, saying, "Get me this," "Get me that," not helping her! Peter wanted to know why Mother didn't simply *tell* Daddy how rude we were. And if we sat on our ba-hinds, Peter said, turning to Mother, it was because she thought she had to do everything for everybody, for all those relatives of hers, and if there weren't any relatives around, for some poor wretch she met in the supermarket.

Mother stands behind Peter and mouthes "Sh!" at us and winks and smiles and pats her stomach and when we get up to help her, whispers, "No, sit down. I don't want so many people up, milling around."

Sometimes, even when we *had* said thank you, when we were sure we had, Peter would say we hadn't. Peter would say we hadn't because he was a little deaf. Peter was a little deaf from standing on a ship underneath big guns throughout the war.

"I *did* say thank you, I *did!*" I shouted at Peter over my cereal bowl, but Mother, standing slightly behind him, winked and said, "Sh!" in the softest voice possible and tugged on her ear lobe.

I felt a lump rising in my throat. The lump turned my voice into a shrill whisper, like paper when you blew straight onto the edge of it. "I did, I did," I said, until I couldn't speak anymore and then turned out of my chair and ran, through the dining room and the living room, where Spot, our dog, and Na-Na were sitting on their towel, and through the hall with the speckled brown carpet. I ran into my bedroom and flopped, stomach down, onto my bed. The flop jolted out the lump in my throat and my crying came after.

Jennifer came in after a while and said she thought Peter had a lot of nerve getting mad, since Daddy had bought the house for *us* and Peter was just *living* there.

. . . .

I found Alice with her ear to the door, her head bent. She snapped her dustcloth when she saw me and walked away.

There were crying sounds on the other side of the door, and voices, then footsteps coming towards the door.

I ran to the end of the hall and ducked into the doorway leading to Sonny and Butch's room.

The door to Mother and Peter's room opened. Peter came out. He went outside and started watering the azaleas, transferring the hose from one pot to another and picking off dead blossoms while each pot flooded.

Sonny and Butch were by the garage.

"Peter's made Mother cry," I said.

Butch kicked a handball over the roof of the neighbor's garage and told me to go get it, then hit me in the stomach when I just stood there. I started to cry and waited for Sonny to hit Butch back, but he didn't, he just got on his bike and rode up the driveway.

Clutching my stomach, I walked around the back of the house to Alice. I tried to keep my crying down as I walked by Mother's room, to be able to find out if she was still crying. There was silence, but then I thought that maybe she had heard my crying and then stopped, the way birds did singing, to be able to listen to one another.

Jennifer, when she came home, sat down and, looking at me eye-level, wanted to know where I had been when I had heard Mother, where Mother had been exactly and where I had been. She wanted to know how I had been so sure that Mother was crying. She wanted to know what kind of noise Mother had made, was it a lot of different sounds high and low or was it the same sound, over and over again? She wanted to know how much longer it was after the first crying that Peter had gone out of the room.

. . . .

Alice wore white Enna Jetticks, white cotton stockings, and a white dacron dress. Alice looked very English, Mother said. She had English skin and an English nose, one that looked as if it were always smelling, that was hooked and cut away on the sides. Alice checked my temperature several times a night, putting her nose and lips against the side of my neck, and in the morning said, "Oh, you were perspiring so much last night when I came in," or "Oh, you were so hot I thought you were running a fever," or "Oh, I thought you were going to get a chill."

Mother said Alice was the Most Organized Person in the World. She said she didn't know what we'd do without her. Alice went from bathroom to bathroom once a week, squeezing toothpaste up from the bottoms of tubes, then rolling the flattened parts up from below. She "burped" Tupperware, holding a corner of the top up and squeezing the container before finally sealing it so that the stored food was as vacuum-packed as you could get it without using some big machine. She made sieves out of runned nylon stockings and washed pots and pans as soon as she was finished with them, so that she would not have a mess at the end of the meal. She made sure to put a fresh towel under Na-Na and Spot over their place on the sofa every morning, so that they wouldn't leave any stains, and always tried to have a little ironing on hand while waiting for something to finish cooking, or a little chopping or stirring to do while she was waiting for the washing machine to finish. In her room, her clothes never touched a bed or a chair or the floor when she took them off but went right onto hangers or into drawers.

Alice tried to teach us to be organized, too. "You pretend like the floor and the bed and the chair have *poison* on them, and if your clothes touch them, they'll be poisoned, too!" I picked up my clothes, my heart beating fast, thinking of the poison burning into my skin, my bones bleached white in seconds, as if they had been picked by piranhas, but Butch, Jennifer and even Sonny only said, "Sure, Alice, sure," and

"Goody-goody" to me when Alice was out of the room.

Alice tried to teach Mother how to be neat and organized, too. "You pretend—" Alice said, but without waiting for Alice to finish, Mother closed her eyes and said, "Yes, Alice, thank you."

"It's a mental crutch—"

"Yes, Alice, but you see, I'm just not thinking about that right now."

Alice was married to Melvyn. She spent the weekends with him. Melvyn picked her up on Friday afternoons and brought her back on Sundays before dark, about the same time we came back from Daddy's house. Sometimes our car, with Don driving, passed Alice and Melvyn's car on Sunset. We honked and waved. Alice brought back food she'd made for us over the weekend, toll house cookies and chicken salad in Tupperware boxes.

Alice was seventeen years older than Melvyn. Melvyn was twenty-seven and Alice was forty-four when they were married. When Alice was out of the room, Mother never said "Melvyn" without saying, "who was twenty-seven when he married Alice who was forty-four" or "Alice" without saying, "who was forty-four when she married Melvyn who was twenty-seven," just the way Alice, when Mother was out of the room, never said "Rush" without saying, "who was in a car accident with a minister's wife with whom he had been . . . going out," or "Spotswood" without saying, "who had multiple sclerosis but who went insane first, drove to Washington with his leg out the window 'to keep it from folding up,' he said, and got all the way to J. Edgar Hoover before they realized he was insane."

Mother said "Melvyn" in that way and "Alice" in that way because she was so proud of having introduced them and of them having liked each other. She said it was one of her greatest triumphs, Alice was So Well Organized. Mother had used what she called the oldest formula: she had gone to Alice and said, "Melvyn likes you," and had gone to Melvyn and said, "Alice likes you."

They had been married at Daddy's house when Mother and Daddy were still married. Jennifer had been flower girl. Butch had carried the ring on a black velvet pillow. Mother had helped Alice pack for her honeymoon. They had gone on their honeymoon, then Alice had come back to work for Mother and Daddy, spending only weekends with Melvyn. Then when Mother left Daddy's house, Alice had gone with her.

I asked Alice once why she was happy to spend only weekends with Melvyn. I expected Alice to start answering me in a long, low, trembling voice, like the voice she used when she told me where babies didn't come from ("No, it's not swimming in the sea that does it, and you don't get them from eating sunflower seeds, though seeds are involved"), but instead, Alice pinched her lips together and started moving dirty dishes roughly along the formica countertop and plunking them into the sink, crashing glasses and plates together.

Mother stood where Alice couldn't see her and scratched her finger in the air at me for me to follow her.

"She's sensitive," Mother whispered to me after we were in the pantry.

"But what did I say?"

"She's just being sensitive."

.   .   .   .

Alice waited outside school for me sometimes, even though I could get home on my own. She said she just wanted to be with me. Children ran up until they were alongside us, stopped, looked at us, and ran on ahead. I looked down and watched the white toes of my saddle shoes go peek, peek, peek, out beyond the edge of my dress.

Alice said that she was the youngest in her family, like me, and like I had my eye, she had been abnormally small for her age, and like Sonny, Butch, and Jennifer did on me, her older brothers and sisters used to pick on her. They called her "shrimp" and put worms in her bed. Alice said that, like me, she, too, had been good (because it was *easier* to be good than to be bad, wasn't it?) and they had picked on her for that, too. Alice said she had actually *liked* being the youngest and smallest and being picked on, though, because she knew that it meant that, in the next life, *they* were the ones who were going to be picked on and she was the one who was going to be sitting on a cloud with a lovely harp. Alice said it was hard for her not to think sometimes that she was me.

Alice then looked around and, lowering her voice, said that, like me, she, too, had been more perceptive and sensitive than her brothers and sisters.

"I am?" I asked out loud, having heard that before but pretending that I hadn't, to hear her say it again, wondering, as I did every time, if being 'perceptive' and 'sensitive' was the same thing as being a genius.

"You are. Everybody says so. Your mother. Minnie."

"They do?" I asked, having heard her say that before, too.

"Yes. That's why grownups talk to you."

"They do?" I asked, wondering, as I did every time, if being a genius meant that I would not have to go to school.

"What am I doing?"

"Huh?"

"You asked me if grownups talk to you. What am I doing?"

"Oh," I said, wondering if not going to school meant that I could have a dog cart and St. Bernard to pull it, with a flask of brandy on its neck, that I could drive on Sunset, past all the children going to school and say, "Nyah, nyah," to them.

"I used to tell Jennifer things but she doesn't want to listen anymore."

Alice then told me about things that had happened or people I had met that I couldn't remember since I had been too young when the things were happening or the people were around. Alice told me about getting married to Melvyn at Daddy's house. She told me about getting ready for the wedding in the room where I was lying in my crib. She told me about bending over to kiss me good-bye. Mother's brothers, Rush and Spotswood, had been there, Na-Na, Midge, and Melvyn, Busy, Colette, even Rita.

"Was *Mother* there?"

"*Of course* your mother was there!"

It seemed incredible, the idea of Alice at Daddy's house. It seemed incredible, the idea of all those people at Daddy's house, of Daddy clinking glasses with Na-Na, of Busy talking with Alice, of Mother talking with Rita, of Rush and Spotswood, whom I'd never seen, being anywhere at all.

It seemed incredible, the idea of Sonny, Butch, and Jennifer there, with them being all together, and me there, me there anywhere near them being all together. It seemed incredible that I could not remember such a thing. I searched in my head, not rolling my eye up because Alice said it was bad for me, but which I could do now anyway, just by staring straight ahead, in the place where I knew things like that were, but could not find anything.

"You were just a baby," Alice said, as if reading my mind.

Even though I had been just a baby, it seemed incredible that I could not even remember Alice bending over to kiss me with her veil on; it seemed incredible that I could not remember that white gauze falling all around me.

I wondered if Alice had come at me from the upper left-hand corner, holding back her veil. I wondered if that was why I couldn't remember, because I hadn't been able to *see* it. I wondered if that was *why* they had had the wedding then, because I hadn't been able to see it, and that if somehow, magically, I had been able to get out of my crib and walk down into the living room and look at them with two open eyes, they would have scattered: Daddy, Midge, Busy, Colette, and Rita to their side, Alice, Mother, and Na-Na to theirs and Rush and Spotswood into thin air.

. . . .

Sometimes Alice couldn't wait until I got out of school to tell me things. She told the principal I had to go to the eye doctor and had me called out of school early. A monitor came into the classroom to get me. On the way out, the teacher said, "I hope your eye feels better, dear."

Mother was in Europe again with Peter. Peter said they hadn't been able to see it properly the last time because he had been sick. Mother stood behind him and winked and smiled and patted her stomach, then whispered to us later that she didn't really *want* to go, she wanted to stay in California with us, but Peter's health was so delicate. . . . Mother sent us postcards of The Little Mermaid from Copenhagen, of Peter Pan from London, and from Greece, postcards of grownup men in ballet dresses with pompoms on their shoes.

One time Alice put a folded-up piece of newspaper in my hands, explaining that Daddy had married Rita. Another time she told me my uncle Spotswood had died.

"But I thought he already did!"

"That was your uncle Rush."

"Which was which?"

Alice sighed. "Uncle Rush was the con man who was in the car accident with the minister's wife, with whom he had been going out and Spotswood was the one who had multiple sclerosis, but who went insane first, became convinced he knew of a communist plot, drove to Washington with his leg out the window to keep it from folding it and got all the way to J. Edgar Hoover before they realized he was insane."

"But I thought you said *Beauchamp* was a con man!"

"He was sort of a con man, but Rush was a serious con man."

"Does J. Edgar Hoover make vacuum cleaners?"

"He is the head of the F.B.I."

"F.B.I.?"

Alice said Mother had a lot of relatives who had been, or still were, in trouble, either sick or with the police. Alice said she had never seen so many in one family. That was why Mother married Daddy, because Daddy helped them out.

Alice said Mother had always been the most beautiful woman she'd ever seen, driving around the curves on Sunset. Alice had been working at Tolefson's then. (Alice always said "Tolefson's" like that, without a "the.") She had been

waiting at the bus stop when a car stopped and this . . .
beautiful woman leaned across the seat. "Which way are
you headed?" she had asked Alice. Alice had told her. "I'm
headed that way myself!" Mother had said. Alice didn't find
out until much later that Mother really hadn't been headed
in the direction but had taken Alice anyway, just to be nice.
Mother was like that. She just did things for people. Alice
and Mother started talking. Alice told Mother what she did.
Mother got very excited: "Why don't you come on over and
work for Cornelius and me?" she had asked. Just like that.
She didn't know Alice from Adam and yet she trusted her.
Mother was like that. Just *nice.*

That was why Mother married Daddy, Alice said, she just
wanted to be nice to everybody. She wanted to be nice to
her mother, who was so vague, and to her brothers, Rush
and Spotswood, and to her cousins, who had had no work
after the war. She knew Daddy would help them. And he
did help them for a while, bailing Rush out of jail, getting
him jobs that he always ended up using as a base for more
con games, getting Spotswood into a good hospital with an
around-the-clock nurse, getting a nice house for Na-Na, then
when she became too vague, putting her in the Shangri-La,
but after a while, he started to say things like, "Do you know
that I spent over a thousand dollars last month on your
brother?" when he had just spent twenty thousand dollars
on one of his Hollywood parties! That was why Mother put
up with so much in their marriage. It was obligation on
obligation. That was why it riled Daddy so much when she
just left. But she had to. If I only knew some of the things
that he had done. Alice came in when Mother was packing
and said, "Mrs. Drayton, I'm going with you."

"But Alice, don't you want to go home to Melvyn for a

while?" Mother had said, and Alice had said, "Mrs. Drayton, I'm going with you."

That was why Daddy was being the way he was now about my eye. That was why Daddy was being the way he was being when everyone *knew* it should be operated on, when even all the people at Daddy's house knew, but never said anything because Daddy was doing the same thing to them that he had done to Mother, giving them things, getting them in deeper, until in the very middle of it, they became confused.

I wondered how Alice knew about the people at Daddy's house now. I pictured Alice talking to Minnie when I was in school. I wondered if the time I was in school was like the time I couldn't remember, in that people who I didn't think got together got together during it. I pictured an eyelid like a big blanket, slung up across the road in front of school, with the people from Mother's house and the people from Daddy's house running back and forth on the other side of it (Daddy's girlfriends with their armpit hairs flying, saying, "Eyelid? What eyelid?"; Alice and Minnie saying, "Eyelid, eyelid, eyelid") as if before the start of a play, with a wing, tacked up in the air, for Rush and Spotswood, who were in heaven, to come down just for that time.

Alice came and got me out of school to show me them, running, but could not let on about them before we saw them, could only say silently between all the things she said, "Look! Look! Stop looking at your saddle shoes and lift up your head and *look!*" but as soon as we had turned onto via de los Flores they had already found out we were coming (through guards, stationed like Indians, all the way down the line) and had gone back to the houses and the times they had come from.

"I'm *so* sorry to be telling you all this," Alice said, after we had come to the end of via de los Flores and were turning up Harmony Lane, which meant that she was *so* sorry she was bringing me home for nothing.

. . . .

Squinting in the sunlight, a girl asked me who that lady in white was. It was milk break and I had just picked my milk carton off a pile of milk cartons on a table in the patio and was standing nearby, sipping. There was another girl beside her. I said Alice was like a . . . a friend, who did things for us.

The next day at milk break, the girl who had asked me who Alice was said that she had asked her mother and her mother had said that there was no such thing as a lady in white who was like a friend. She had to be a maid.

There was a crowd gathering around us. The girl asked me why my mom didn't do stuff. I said my mom did plenty of stuff. She drove the car . . . I bowed my head and tried to take a sip of milk out of the half-pint carton I was holding in my hand but the straw gurgled at the bottom and the few drops that reached my mouth were warm and mixed with bits of wax. Fresh milk cartons sweated nearby, in wire crates.

"Are you rich?" someone asked instead.

The whole crowd's eyes were on me.

"Um . . ."

"Who do you love more, your mom or the maid?" the girl standing in front of me asked, before I had time to answer the first question.

"I don't know."

The next day, the girl said she had asked her mom and her

mom had said that having one maid didn't mean you were rich, it just meant you were well off, and that you had to love your mom more, though it was O.K. to love a maid some.

. . . .

Alice let me put on my pyjamas at six o'clock, before dinner. Then I started to put them on at five o'clock and it was still O.K. with her, then at four o'clock, then at three o'clock, until finally I was changing right out of my school clothes and into my pyjamas.

I liked not having to go outside and play, go outside where Butch waited with large freckled friends to push my face into the grass and say "Eat the dirt, eat the dirt!" as soon as I did not kick the kickball right. It made me feel special, not going outside, like Dracula.

I sat in the den in my pyjamas and watched old movies on TV. The old movies were often about wavy-haired English boys who died. Right before they died, they called poor children into their rooms and gave them their fancy toys and apologized to them for having been mean to them. Or the old movies were about angels who were sent back to earth through a special elevator in an office building in New York. The elevator went beyond and came back from beyond the top floor. The angels stepped out smiling, tightening their neckties. They wore double-breasted suits. They gave people bus money. They ended up falling in love with girls who wore muffin-shaped hats pinned to the sides of their heads. Angels were not supposed to fall in love. God was angry with them and tried to call them back. God sent the angels telegrams. The angels read them out loud: "Come back. Signed, God."

When the movie was not about dying English boys or about angels coming to earth or when I was tired of watching TV, I would go into the kitchen and let Alice tell me about my eye. Early afternoons on the way home from school were for telling me about a lot of different things, but late afternoons, when we had all that time in front of us, were for telling me the long story about my eye.

I would lean with my elbows on the kitchen counter or sit on the kitchen stool and bang my legs rhythmically against its metal legs or lie on the floor on my stomach with my chin on the backs of my hands, just in time to watch and feel the setting sun splash me and the place under the kitchen cabinets where you kicked your feet with light, then watch the bottoms of the kitchen cabinets grow darker and darker as the light traveled further and further above us in one big band. Alice had told me not to roll my eye up, so I had to watch the place where you kicked your feet grow darker and darker, until it was almost like a slot that I could slide into, on one of those rolling boards that garage mechanics used. I could have sat up, but it was nice to lie there on the floor.

Alice said that when I was born and my eye didn't open, everybody thought that it was because of an allergic reaction to the silver nitrate they put in newborn babies' eyes, but after a week went by and it still didn't open, everybody started to wonder what to do. That was when Grandaddy Drayton came up from La Jolla to see his new grandchild. Alice was there when he first saw me.

"We're worried about her little eye," Mother said to Grandaddy.

"Oh, that's nothing," Daddy said quickly.

Grandaddy started. He looked at me. He smiled, first a

very little smile, then bigger and bigger. "Oh, the precious, the precious, the little darling," Grandaddy said, his voice quivering, his hands reaching for me. "Oh, the precious, the darling, the sweet little thing, Grandaddy's only one!" He chuckled. "Oh, if she only knew how special she is!" He kissed my forehead, said "the precious" again and looked at the ceiling. He sighed. A tear trickled out of the far corner of his eye.

"What's wrong, Grandaddy, what's wrong?" everyone asked, but he didn't answer them, he just kept searching with his eyes along the ceiling, then after about a minute, he took off his glasses, bowed his head, and still holding with one hand, put the hand that held his glasses over his eyes.

"What's wrong, Grandaddy?" a single voice asked again, but he just kept on being silent. Then, after another minute, he took his hand away, looked at all of them, and said that he had just been praising the wisdom, the power, and the glory of the Lord, who had once again made His will known, for he, Grandaddy, had a drooping eyelid, too.

Grandaddy spread out the wrinkles around his eye for them to see. His eyelid was smooth where a fold should have been. There was no muscle in it, he explained, no way for it to go up. His grandmother had it and the Lord visited every second generation with this emblem of his favor.

That was the first time they knew about it. Everyone thought Grandaddy's eyelid drooped just from being old and tired. No one knew what Grandaddy had been like when he was younger and of course no one could remember his grandmother.

Grandaddy said that I would be a young girl, then a girl, then a young woman, and then a woman with great spiritual qualities, having one eye shut to the evils of the world and looking in on the soul.

Mother said that she thought I had an ironic look.

"There's nothing wrong with her!" a voice said. Everyone started and looked up.

Daddy was standing way back in a corner of the room with his hands in his pockets. Alice couldn't understand how he had gotten there. He had been standing with them just a few seconds before.

"What?" Grandaddy said, his eyes small, distorted behind the glasses he had put back on.

"I said there's nothing wrong with her!" Daddy pushed himself out of the corner and walked up to Grandaddy. "Come on, give her to me." Daddy put his hands underneath me and tried to take me away from Grandaddy while Grandaddy held onto me. I started to cry. "Stop it! Let her go!" Mother said. Grandaddy released me to Mother.

"What's all the fuss about?" Mother said. "I'm sure it can be fixed."

"But there's nothing wrong with her!" Daddy said to Mother and to Grandaddy. Then he turned to Grandaddy, put a hand on his shoulder, and spoke in a low, gentle voice. "Daddy, look, you're old, you're confused. There's nothing wrong with little Robin. She's still reacting to the eyedrops they put in her eye. There's nothing wrong with your eye, either. *Everyone's* eyelid droops a little as they get older. And there *was* nothing wrong with your grandmother's eye. You're just a little mixed up. . . ."

Grandaddy jerked his shoulder out from under Daddy's hand. "Why do you insult me? I *know* what I am talking about!"

Later that evening, standing by my crib (the door to the

nursery was open and Alice couldn't help listening), Daddy said to Mother, "I'm not saying Grandaddy's grandmother had anything *wrong* with her eye, but if she had, I mean, how could she have gotten to be a mother? I mean, what man would have . . . ?"

"That means . . ." Alice said, in a low, trembling voice.

"I know . . ." I said.

" . . . that your Daddy thought that, if she hadn't been pretty, no man would have kissed her and . . . given her a baby, a baby to go on and have you . . ."

"I know," I said again, not really knowing what I meant "I know" about.

Alice then went on, in an even quieter voice, in the kind of voice that came at the very ends of breaths, so that I kept expecting her to take a breath, but she didn't, that she'd never seen a man who thought about . . . what men and women did . . . so much. She guessed it was because his father was a preacher or something. He was making up for lost time, she guessed. She said it put a kind of spell on women, that and his money, so that they wouldn't tell him they thought my eye should be operated on, even though they knew it should, even though they told Alice, every time she called them, "It breaks my *heart* to see that child's eye like that. . . ." They never said anything.

Alice then took a breath and said she was *so* sorry to be telling me all this.

Alice then took another breath and said, ". . . but we think that, you're so perceptive, you might be able to *say* something to your daddy. . . ."

"Like what?"

"Tell him to change his ways. Make him be different. You're his favorite. Out of the mouths of babes."

. . . .

"Wo, Yippies, wo, ho, Yippies, Yippies," Butch said, pacing back and forth at the foot of my bed, waiting for an opening to spring. Yippies stood for Yipicals and Yipicals stood for Typicals and Typicals stood for Typical Priss Miss. "We were waiting outside for you, Yippies, waiting to pound your face into the dirt! God, what a Priss Miss, God what a Typical Pesky-Pitted Priss Miss. . . ."

Every afternoon, when I was back in my room, doing homework after having watched television and listened to Alice, when I heard Butch fiddling at my door, I would run from my desk to my bed, lie on my back on the bed and put my feet up in the air, because I was much better at kicking than I was at hitting.

Butch crouched low. His flattened hands started circling out from his body like a wrestler's. "You think you're pretty smart, lying on the bed. You think you can cover it up, but I passed your window about five minutes ago, and saw you, doing *homework!* What do you want to do homework for? Man, I'm *never* going to do any homework! Homework's for idiots! I'm never going to do any homework because, when we grow up, we're going to have *so much money* that we're not going to have to work and since we're not going to have to work, we're not going to have to know anything, so why should we do any homework?"

"Oof."

Butch had sprung. I had forgotten to follow him with my feet on the last turn he made. He sprang, knocking half the air out of me, then, quick as a flash, he was straddling my chest, my arms out, my elbows pinned under his knees.

"What's the deodorant race car drivers use?" Butch shouted.

"Get off—!"

"What's the deodorant race car drivers use?"

"I DON'T KNOW!"

"PIT STOP!" Butch shouted, jabbing my armpits with the points of his fingers, then, "Karate-ha!"

It tickled more than hurt. Laughing, I tried to roll my hips up and hook my legs around Butch's shoulders and push him back off me but the muscles in my stomach that were tight from laughing pushed against the muscles that made my legs go up, so that I only squirmed and laughed harder because I was so weak. Then I laughed because Butch was saying "Karate-ha, karate-ha" faster and faster. Then I laughed because Butch was so good at not letting on, not letting on at all, that he knew it was silly, his saying "Karate-ha, karate-ha" like that. I laughed until my armpits, hit over and over again, were like funny bones being hit, and I was about to scream to make Alice or Mother come but the laughs tripped up the screams in my throat and so I simply laughed louder.

. . . .

Mother, when she gets home from Europe, says it is unhealthy for me to stay inside in the afternoon. She calls up the neighbor's mother or the mother of the girl up the hill and says I am coming over to play. Then she kneels down and ties up my tennis shoes, saying, "You shouldn't do . . . *everything* Alice tells you to do." Then, still kneeling, she reaches up and zips up my windbreaker.

Peter was not there. He had stayed in the East after he and Mother had come back from Europe. California was too much for his stomach, Mother said. She missed him, she said, but she wanted to be with us. She would be with us for a while, she said, then she would go east. It was hard for her right now, it was hard for us, but one day, we would all go east, she said, hugging me.

.   .   .   .

Mother parks her car in the parking lot of the Brentwood Country Mart.

"Good morning, Mrs. Teasdale!" busboys pushing carts full of groceries call.

"And a glo-rious good mor-ning to you-hoo-hoo-hoo!" Mother calls back to them, to the tune of "Oh believe me if all those endearing young charms . . ."

People loading groceries into their cars stop and watch us as we pass by.

"Hello! Good morning! Lovely day, isn't it?" Mother calls to them.

"Hello! Good morning!" they call back.

One man bows at us over a bag full of groceries. "Yes, indeed, it is a lovely day, since I saw you!"

Mother blows him a kiss.

"Hello, Mrs. Teasdale!" the man behind the meat counter shouts as we come in.

Mother skirts around the meat counter and pretends to faint. The butcher catches her in his arms, laughing, then dips her lower, still laughing, while the woman at the checkout counter and the women at the pastry counter and the girl weighing vegetables whisper, "Beautiful, adorable, she's *such* a doll."

"Good morning!" Mother calls to the man who walks behind us taking notes in a tiny spiral notebook. "Ah, I don't know what y'all's names are anymore but good morning just the same!"

Mother stops a mother and child and points at the child's chest and says, "Are you a bold and bad Bomb Bardinar of Baghdad. . . . you got that?" she said, turning to the man in back of us.

"Bold, bad . . ." he repeats, "oh . . ." He presses down hard in his notebook and makes one thick black line across it, then shuts it and puts it in his pocket, frowning.

" . . . who tried to abombalick a bluebeard but Shah of Babelmangdad and knocked down an abominable bumble-bee of Baulsaura?"

"Who's that lady?" the little girl asks, turning to her mother.

Mother runs forward to help an old lady get a can of coffee off a high shelf. "You're too . . . *adorable* to be getting that yourself!"

"Oh, well, thank you!" the woman says, laughing.

"*You* look snappy!" Mother says to a hunched-over, shuffling man in glasses that magnify his eyes.

The man beams.

"Will there be any stars in my crown?" Mother sings as she rounds the aisle.

. . . .

Alice would tell me about her own childhood at night, after Mother had sung the Westminster High School song and waited, hands on hips, for me to ask her to sing it again. "I want to see Alice now," I'd say instead, and Mother would go and get Alice, and Alice would come in and sit on the edge of the bed. "You should be nicer to your mother, you know."

"Tell me about the apples."

Alice would tell me about the night she was so hungry, she sneaked into the basement of her house and ate the apples that were stored there. Her father heard a noise in the basement and thought someone was stealing the apples. Her father came downstairs and saw her and started to laugh and caught her and carried her upstairs saying, "I've caught my apple thief! I've caught my little apple thief!"

As she talked I would imagine her basement in Iowa to be like the basement of Daddy's house in Beverly Hills, to be huge, with roaring blowers in it to feed air ducts, even though I knew their basement had to be small because they were poor. I would get more mixed up as I got sleepier. I would mix up the stories Alice told me with the stories Daddy told me and the stories Mother told me. "Tell me about the time when all you had left was five dollars in the whole world," I'd say, or, "Tell me about how all you had to eat sometimes were just sliced tomatoes," and I would mix up houses, places, and people in the stories. I would imagine it was my father who had gone down the stairs instead of hers. Daddy had grabbed her by the wrists and picked her up off her feet so that the bones in her shoulders cracked, not in a way that hurt but in a way that felt good, and carried her upstairs, still with pieces of bitter apple in her mouth, so that the saliva came out slowly, in little surges, to balance the bitterness, and with my eyes closed I would murmur that Daddy sure had loosened Alice up and Alice would say "*WHAT?*" so loudly that I would wake up all the way with a jerk, the way people woke up when they dreamed they were falling.

Alice would be staring down at me, looking mean, but then, seeing how scared I was, she would imitate, closing her eyes and smiling, how I had murmured and what I had murmured and I would be about to open my mouth to say something when she would say, "Wasn't that silly, what you said? I don't know *where* you got that!" and I would shiver and pull up the covers, thinking of the way she blew on the *wh* when she said "where," like wind on the blue tinkling ice of the North Pole.

CHAPTER 5

Daddy said he'd talked to Mrs. Kiebler and he and Mrs. Kiebler both thought that it would be a good idea if I wore an eyepatch on my good eye on the weekends I was at Daddy's house. That would help me exercise my other eye. Daddy said he thought Mrs. Kiebler's exercises were a good thing, and I would continue to go to her in the mornings, but he thought that wearing an eyepatch would make Mrs. Kiebler's exercises work a little bit faster. Rita kneeled down and tied the eyepatch on me, saying, "Now you can be a pirate!"

. . . .

I play pirate the first weekend. I hide under the dining room table while Daddy and Rita eat breakfast, and I take parsley, reaching up and groping along the edge of the table for it. "I've caught my parsley pirate! I've caught my little parsley pirate!" Rita says, her voice faltering in the middle, grabbing my hand and pretending like she is going to pull me out from underneath the table, while I pretend to scream.

Rita was so different from Mother, who would pick up her skirt and scream when I jumped at her from behind a curtain and would shout, "A mouse! A mouse! A nasty little mouse!" and pick up her feet and pretend like she was going to step on me, then would throw pillows and paperback books and hunks of Saran-Wrapped cheese at me, and keep screaming for about five minutes, until it was almost scary.

Daddy and Rita ate breakfast in the dining room now. It was bad for Daddy's digestion, Rita said, bending over to eat breakfast off that low table in his room. Rita had also gotten Daddy to stop wearing the Hawaiian shorts and matching sport shirt that he always wore in the mornings and to wear instead the gray flannel pants, alligator shirts, and cardigan sweaters made of squiggly wool that he had always worn before just to play golf in. Rita said Daddy looked so much more dignified that way.

Daddy stands up and puts his arm around Rita's head, until all you can see is a poof of black hair in the crook of Daddy's poofy-sleeved arm, and says that no one has taken care of Daddy Boy for such a long time.

．　．　．　．

I became aware of something watching me under the table, smiling and knowing. It was red and it was there then it wasn't, it was there then it wasn't. I turned my head to be able to see it more completely. It was Midge's bright red toenails. Midge was standing at the table barefoot. She turned first beside Rita and then beside Daddy.

"How are you today, Midge Girl?"

"Fine, Mr. D."

"Did you sleep well, Midge Girl?"

"Yes, Mr. D."

"That's good. I like my Midge Girl to sleep well. Don't

I like having my Midge Girl sleep well?"

"Yes, Mr. D."

I laughed at first, covering my mouth with my hands and spluttering out the sides because it was funny, Midge's toes in the carpet with Daddy and Rita above them not knowing about them. Midge's toes in the carpet with me not having known about them for who knew how long and then their suddenly saying, "Yes, hello, we're here." Then I smiled because they were not just funny, they were "fun," too, the way Rita said "fun" sometimes, as an adjective, when she talked most like Loretta Young. They were like circus balloons. Then I stopped smiling and just thought of them, talking quietly, letting me know. Midge was trying to let me know by doing something maids didn't do, serve breakfast barefoot, to let me know that she thought I was doing things I shouldn't be doing, that everyone was. She was trying to let me know that she thought I shouldn't be going to Mrs. Kiebler and shouldn't be wearing my eyepatch and shouldn't be playing under the table, like someone younger than I was, and shouldn't be thinking that I was the one, the only one, in the whole world, to tell Daddy to change his ways, like someone older than I was, and Rita shouldn't be trying to catch me in her not-really-trying-to-catch-me way.

Midge's ten red toes then became like heads in a theater, watching. Then the toes stopped being bright red and started being fierce red, as if the toes had eyebrows, scowling. Then the toes were not in a theater anymore but in a circle, scowling at something in the middle of it, at a witch doctor in a straw mask.

"Midge," Rita said.

"My feet hurt," Midge said. She disappeared through the swinging kitchen door.

. . . .

I am a witch the next weekend. Busy makes a pointed hat for me. Midge gives me an old broom. I run through the house with the broom between my legs, cackling.

I am Dead Eye Dick the weekend after that. I point my finger and say, "P-que! P-que!" then tip my finger up and blow on it.

The weekend after that, I am a German general with a bald head. I wear a bathing cap and whisper, "Ve haff vays of making you talk!"

I am the Hathaway shirt man the weekend after that. I just stand.

. . . .

Midge stood beside the dining room table in her slip.

Rita screamed.

"Why Rita Girl," Daddy said, then, seeing Midge, "*WHY MIDGE GIRL!*"

Midge threw the serving dish down onto the table, breaking dishes and glasses and making the whole table shake. Poached eggs slid off the dish onto the floor, their yellows oozing onto the deep-pile rug. "If you call me Midge Girl one more time, if you call me Midge Girl one more time . . ." Midge moved towards Daddy with her hands up, her fingers arched. Daddy caught her wrists and held them together. "Oooh," Midge said, trying to twist out of Daddy's hand, "oooooooooh!"

"Pipe down," Daddy said.

Rita sat in her chair and cried.

"Run into Rita's room," Daddy said to us over the noise, "and find something to wrap around Midge."

"Right."

"O.K."

"Yeah."

We ran into Rita's room and opened her closet. In the front was a mink coat. Butch put his hands on it.

"Not her mink," Sonny said.

"Why not?" Butch said.

By the time we got back, Midge had stopped struggling and was laughing instead. "Watcha doin' tonight, lover?" she said between laughs. "How about a date? Ha ha ha ha ha ha ha ha!"

"Pipe down."

Daddy took the mink coat from Butch.

"Not my mink!" Rita said.

"Pipe down," Daddy said to Rita, throwing it around Midge's shoulders.

"Why, Cornelius!" Midge said. "How sweet of you! How did you know that mink is my favorite, simply one of my *favorite* things! Mmm . . ." She picked up the collar and rubbed her cheek along it, then looked up at Daddy and smiled.

"Sonny?" Daddy said, without taking his eyes off Midge, "go call Don on the intercom and ask him to come up here."

"O.K." Sonny ran into the pantry.

"Everything's going to be all right," Daddy said to Midge.

"*Of course* everything's going to be all right! Everything *is* all right! Everything's *divine*, isn't it, Cornelius? Ha! Ha! Ha!"

"Pipe down!" Daddy said, and then to Sonny as he came back in: "Did you get Don?"

"Yes. He's coming."

"Yes, well, everything's . . . my, my, my . . ." Midge lowered her eyelids and peeked at Daddy out from under them, her lips pressed together in a tight smile. Then, suddenly, she raised her head, opened her eyes, barked "*HA!*" at Daddy as loud as she could, making Daddy start, and dissolved in more giggles: "Ha ha ha ha ha ha ha ha ha. Yes, my, well, yes, yes, *HA! HA* ha ha ha ha ha ha . . . *HA!* Ha, ha ha . . . ha! And *HA!* And *HA!* And *HA!*" Midge went on, like a dog barking or a person vomiting.

"Pipe down," Daddy said. "*PIPE DOWN!*"

"That's O.K., Mr. D.," Don said, coming into the room. He put his arm around Midge's waist and pulled her, gently, back from Daddy. She stopped making noises, lowered her head, and started to cry.

"That's O.K., Midge," Don said. He turned with her and started to guide her out of the room.

"*Awfully* nice of you to give me the mink," Midge called to Daddy over her shoulder. "But you see, I've *got* a date tonight! Ha! Ha! Ha!"

"Pipe . . ."

"*HA!*"

"That poor, demented showgirl," Daddy said, shaking his head slowly after Midge and Don were out of the room, "that poor, demented, confused, mixed up, crazy, sad little showgirl. Now, why would she want to go do a thing like that? That poor little showgirl. . . . Butch Boy?" Daddy said suddenly. I saw something in Daddy's eyes snap and roll back. "Go call Judy Girl and ask her to come clean up this mess."

. . . . .

Jennifer, when she came home on vacation from boarding school, said she thought Daddy's house was the tackiest thing she'd ever seen. She had never noticed it before but it really was *tacky*. She walked through the bar with its paintings of women in see-through nightgowns and high-heeled satin slippers, the living room with its Louie Says table and the clock of Low Coon, struggling with his snake, the dining room with its built-in sideboards with frosted-glass pineapple sections set into their middles and curtains with hula dancers on them, saying, "Tacky, tacky," under her breath. "And you, you tacky little thing," Jennifer said to me, "how could you have those ... purple and turquoise throw pillows on your bed? Who ever heard of a child with *throw* pillows on her bed?"

Jennifer told everyone in the house she thought the house was tacky, except Daddy and Rita, until finally she couldn't stand it anymore and told Daddy, too, and Daddy hugged her head in a circle of arm and said, "Ha! Ha! Baby Girl! Ha! Ha! Ha!" Jennifer twisted her head out of the crook of Daddy's arm, then pushed her hair back and said, "No, I mean it, Daddy, TACK-*Y!*"

．　．　．　．

Jennifer had cable-knit sweaters and A-line skirts in every color of the rainbow, from yellow to purple. She laid them out on the bed for me to see. She wore a different skirt and sweater every day, with a circle pin or a bar or a pearl, black flats and, to go out, a plaid-lined Misty Harbor raincoat, even when the sun was shining.

Jennifer loved the East and hated California. She hated clipped lawns. "Look at them!" she said. "They look like they've been rolled up and swept underneath. It's so unnatural!" She loved long, green grass and rolling hills and horses and boys in navy blue pullover crew-neck sweaters, khaki pants, and madras jackets. Jennifer said she thought madras jackets were *so cute*.

· · · ·

Daddy stands behind the bar and makes drinks.

Daddy and Rita had drinks in the bar now. Rita said nobody was a big drinker, but that she just believed in using rooms as they were meant to be used. Nothing was sadder than a long, empty bar. It should have people at it, life, conversation.

"All I had was five dollars! Five dollars left in the whole wide world!"
"Has Dr. Grass been over?" Jennifer whispers to me.

Dr. Fayman had stopped coming over to give Daddy shots and Dr. Grass had started coming over. Daddy said he couldn't get that Dr. Fayman to see how stopped-up he really was. Now it was in his bladder. There were times when he would stand and stand there, fifteen minutes, twenty minutes, he'd turn the faucet on, hear that water rushing, think of the biggest gusher he'd ever had . . . nothing. That Dr. Fayman was suggesting he go to the hospital for a series of tests, but he knew what that Dr. Grass Boy had to do. . . .
"Daddy—" Jennifer said.
"Don't you know what to do, Dr. Grass Boy?" Daddy said, squeezing Dr. Grass's arm.
"Yes, I do, sir."

"You may ask why I didn't spend the five dollars. Five dollars could have bought a lot in those days. I could have paid off some of the rent at the boarding house where I was living. Landlady had started giving me trouble. . . ."

A woman shoves an empty glass across the bar towards Daddy, mouthing some words at him at the same time.

"What are you saying? A bloody mary? Now how do you make that again? Oh yeah, I remember." Daddy tosses the melted ice out, rattles ice in the bucket below him.

"Oh, I hate California," Jennifer whispers. "I hate California and all the tacky, Hollywoody, *vulgar* people!"

Some of the guests Daddy had over for drinks were new and unlike any of the other people who had ever been there before. Jennifer said it was because they were even tackier, "if that could be imagined." They were still actors and actresses, but they were more like ones you'd see on Channel 13—instead of on 5, 9, or 11—between fender-slapping used-car ads and midget wrestling. The men wore green and turquoise tuxedos with ruffled shirts and black piping on the lapels. The women chewed gum and talked through their noses. Colette had had another facelift, and other guests, who I thought were new and whom I was amazed to hear call me "Robin Girl" as soon as they walked in the house, turned out to be the same people Daddy had had over for drinks before he'd married Rita, only they looked different now: some people's noses turned a different way or they had noses that were thinner or fatter; other people had no wrinkles; other people had no double chins or no bulges under their eyes. Even the people from Texas looked different. None of them wore glasses anymore, and the women's faces looked as if someone had suddenly said "Ten-hup!" to them: everything was somehow up and smooth. The men from Texas had more hair. Jennifer said it was because they'd had nose jobs and facelifts and hair transplants: it wasn't just Colette and Rita getting them anymore. They'd had nose jobs and facelifts and hair transplants because they were tacky. In the East people didn't need such things: in the East people got old gracefully.

"So you see, I was keeping those five dollars intact because I was just waiting to make an investment." Daddy takes a swig of his drink. "But before I made an investment, I had to consider all the factors. Now there are four important things, factors, to consider when you are thinking of drilling a well. One is topsoil, its content. One is moisture . . ."

"And speaking of moisture," one of the women says, pushing her glass across the bar to Daddy.

"What's that?" Daddy asks, smelling it.

"A vodka gimlet."

"A vodka . . . of all the damn fool . . . Can't you wait 'til we get to Trader Vic's?"

"It's vodka and Rose's lime juice, Cornelius."

"Oh *God*," Jennifer whispers.

"Let's see, where was I?" Daddy measures the vodka and lime juice into the drink. "Oh yes, factors. One is topsoil. One is moisture. Another is salinity. Another is proximity of the prospective well to the nearest strike and the pattern of strikes in the nearest producing area." Daddy takes another swig. "Well, I'd hear about this and I'd hear about that, but nothing seemed just right. So I kept on, just lying low at my landlady's, not going out because I was afraid that if I went out, my landlady would pack my bag and put it on the front step. She was a scared kind of woman, my landlady. She was always dropping things and jumping at the noise. She'd say, 'Mr. Drayton, your rent is five weeks overdue and really I . . .' Finally I had to put my hands, just put my hands . . ." Daddy sways, takes another drink.

"Where did you put them, Cornelius?" one of the women asks.

Daddy puts down his drink and walks around to the other side of the bar. His eyes are shining. He puts his hands on either side of her head. She shuts her eyes. Daddy's face goes towards her face. His lips pucker. Then, at about the last minute, Daddy's face stops going forward. His eyes go from looking at her lips to looking at her nose.

"Dr. Grass *has* been over," Jennifer whispers.

Daddy shuts his eyes and kisses her on the mouth. Then with his eyes still shut, Daddy goes to the next woman, tilts her head back, and kisses her on the mouth, too.

"Stop kissing, Cornelius, and tell us how much money you made," one of the men says gruffly. Daddy opens his eyes. The man has said it gruffly, but you know he is just kidding. He is one of Daddy's best friends since Daddy married Rita and can talk to Daddy in that way.

"And so I said to him, 'Ted Boy, if this well doesn't come in . . .'"

"Oh, Cornelius," one of the women says, "you scare me!"

Daddy smiles and starts to move towards her, his lips puckered.

"But how much money did you make?" the man persists.

Daddy turns to him. "About a thousand."

"A thousand dollars from five dollars?"

"Mm-hm."

The man whistles. "That must have been some well."

Daddy sips his drink loudly.

"Oh, you're so good, Cornelius," someone whispers.

"Cornelius . . ." the man says.

Daddy goes on: "So I had this thousand. Enough to buy a

lease, rent a rig, and start drilling on my own. But first I rented a car and drove around the countryside. There was a little farm I was interested in. The farmer wasn't letting any oil prospectors on his place. I drove there at night with my headlights off. Climbed through the fence. Big dog came barking up at me. 'Oh Jesus,' I said, but then he licked my hand. Walked to where there was a little rise. Took some soil. You know those fancy oil prospectors with degrees in geology from the University of Texas, sending off soil samples to Houston to be analyzed? I just put that soil right in my mouth! And man, it was full of salt. That little old gingerbread house—you know, the kind with the screen door banging and the dust blowing across the front porch—was sitting on top of one of the biggest salt domes in West Texas!"

Daddy's voice rose on the last words, the way people's voices rose sometimes on TV when they talked about how America was the best country in the world.

Daddy stops talking and stares straight with glistening eyes.

Guests shift on their stools and look down at their drinks, stirring ice cubes with the tips of their fingers.

Daddy goes on: "The farmer had a daughter. She was crippled. I called on them on Sunday afternoons. She loved it when I came. She'd try to rise from the tray of beads she'd been stringing for the children's hospital in Tulsa, but couldn't no—"

"Why couldn't—" a woman, the same woman who asked where Daddy had put his hands, starts to say, but people wrinkle their eyebrows at her. She hangs her head and lets a Brillo pad of hair that has come loose from her beehive float forward to her face. Daddy stops talking and waits for a few seconds, breathing hard. People shift again.

"I tried to tell her: Franklin Roosevelt actually walked for an hour every day. . . ." Daddy's voice rises again.

"Come on now, Cornelius," Rita says. "It's time to go."

"Oh, you're so good, Cornelius," a voice whispers.

Daddy throws his ice out into the sink, then turns on the faucet and starts rinsing glasses. People reach to help him but Daddy is staring somewhere out beyond the sink as he rinses.

"Oh, you're so good, Cornelius."

Rita winks. Guests nod.

"I told you Daddy was tacky," Jennifer whispers to me.

"It's so goddamned *boring* here!" Butch says.

"You guys . . ." Sonny says.

CHAPTER 6

Alice was waiting outside school for me. She was not wearing a uniform. She was wearing what Melvyn picked her up in every weekend, a shirtwaist with a wide brown belt and a lace hanky tucked into it, a purse and patent leather pumps. But it was not the weekend. She had a thin white line around her mouth, as if she had forgotten to rinse her mouth after brushing her teeth.

Alice said she was going home to The Valley for a while. Alice said Mother thought she should spend more time with Melvyn. Alice said she had not meant to be mean with Na-Na, it was just that sometimes, with all she had to do . . . Alice said that maybe, if I told Mother she had not meant to, Mother might change her mind about making her spend more time with Melvyn. Alice said she had not meant it, either, about counting the number of beer cans in the trash, nor about picking up the phone when someone else was talking, it was just that she was so worried about us all, that sometimes, when she was at Melvyn's, she couldn't sleep from worrying about us, what with our father having gotten in the swimming pool with all those girls with no clothes on, just to get Rita to divorce him. Alice didn't know what was going to happen to us. Just so that

Rita would bring a suit against him so that he could turn around and clobber her. All those girls floating in the pool and Daddy paddling into the middle of them, then calling Rita to come look. Alice didn't know how we were going to grow up with a father like that. If we only knew the things that went on there on the weekdays when we were not there. Orgies and she didn't know what else. And the drinking, the drinking, so that she couldn't stand the idea of us children coming back to Mother's and having the same thing happening there, though it really didn't happen, she just counted the bottles and cans anyway, just to make sure. Alice said that if I were to tell Mother that it was just because of that, just because of the way our daddy was, that she was the way she was, then maybe Mother would let her come back from The Valley after a while. Alice said she thought that all that drinking and all those women, so much more drinking and so many more women, even than before, were making him be even more peculiar about my eye than he was already, so that he now was not only sending me to Mrs. Kiebler, he was also having detectives follow me to and from school, just to make sure that Mother wouldn't take me to New York to have my eye operated on.

It was hard for her to explain to Mother herself, hard for her to talk freely in front of her. Surely Mother would see why Alice acted the way she did if I explained it to her. She really didn't want to have to go spend more time with Melvyn. She loved Melvyn, but there were different *ways* of being married and she felt that her place was at Mother's house.

I said I would try.

. . . .

The room was filled with the rotten egg smell of Estee Lauder night cream that Mother wore, along with her curler cap, when Peter was not there. The shades were drawn. An ice pack lay on the pillow beside her. Balls of Kleenex, like so many rabbit tails, dotted the pile of sheets, blankets, and afghans. A vaporizer hissed in one corner.

"Hello, baby," Mother's voice called from the center of the bed. I walked closer. The back of one of Mother's hands was resting on her forehead. A tear trickled out of the far corner of her right eye. Books and magazines were scattered all over the bed, among the balls of Kleenex. I read the easier words in some of the titles: *Something Today, The Something of Dreams, Man Against Himself.*

"Why do they always blame the mother?" Mother asked, looking at me from underneath the hand that was resting on her forehead.

I held my breath, the way you did when someone was passing you in a dark, narrow hall and you didn't want them to notice you: I was afraid Mother was going to start talking to me the way she did to Jennifer when Jennifer came home for vacations, keeping her in the kitchen for hours. I held my breath and let my mouth hang open, a little bit wet, the way I looked in pictures of Jennifer, Sonny, Butch, and me that Mother had put at the ends of her scrapbooks and said "Weren't you the sweetest things, weren't you all just the sweetest things" about when she looked at them now.

Mother said she had not been able to fire Alice so she had asked Alice to please quit. She said Alice had started taking over too much of our lives, she had been getting too intimate. Mother said she had tried to do it once before, get Alice to leave, by getting her to marry Melvyn, but she had come back after a few weeks, leaving Melvyn out in The Valley by himself. She just couldn't keep away. Mother said she had been trying and trying, this time, to think of a way to get Alice to leave, but finally just had to ask her. She said all this . . . trying to be nice to everybody had given her a headache. The doctor was coming over in a little while to give her a shot and let her sleep.

Mother said it was up to me to do everything for the night, to pour one thimbleful of bourbon in a glass for Na-Na and put in some ice and water, then make sure she put on her nightgown with a robe over that and slippers, then set the table, heat up the left-over chicken, and cook the frozen broccoli for dinner. . . .

I wanted to ask Mother whether, if you went in a pool with no clothes on, it did things to the water.

"I don't know how," I said out loud.

Mother said she was sure I could do it; I'd seen Alice do it a hundred times. All I had to do was take an ice tray out of the ice box, loosen the ice cubes by pulling that little lever . . . put a couple of cubes in a glass . . . then go to the cabinet where the bottle of bourbon was kept and get the measuring thing beside it that was like a little hammer . . . help Na-Na change into her nightgown . . . pre-heat the oven to three-fifty for the chicken . . . follow the directions on the back of the package of broccoli. . . .

Mother turned on her side. "Mother has to try to sleep now. Let the doctor in when he comes." She pulled the sheet up over her ear.

I walked through the silent rooms to the kitchen, silent not just with the silence of nobody being there, silent with the silence of someone not coming back, so that they almost hummed.

"*Mom*'s going to take care of us!" I thought as I walked towards the kitchen cabinet where the bottle of bourbon was kept. I opened the cabinet and saw the bottles inside. "*Mom*'s going to take care of us!"

I took the bottle and poured a little bourbon into a glass, then put the bottle down on the kitchen counter. I stared out through the kitchen window. "*Mom*'s going to take care of us," I thought again. I put the top back on the bottle, put the bottle back in the cabinet, went to the refrigerator and opened the freezer door.

It opened with a crunch. Frost swirled inside.

I wondered how long a girl could live in there.

"*Mom*'s going to take care of us," I thought again, staring at the ice trays. The ice trays were coated with ice, a thin hard coat and a thick furry coat that you could see the hard coat through.

I put my fingers on an ice tray. My fingers stuck to the ice, burning. "Ow!" I said, taking my fingers away.

"*Mom*'s going to take care of us," I thought one more time.

· · · ·

Mother hired other maids. She hoped they would not be as "intense" as Alice. They arrived in taxis. They wore thick elastic stockings the color of Band-Aids. They each had one special thing, an icon or a brazier or a rug, that they set up in their room, after moving all the other furniture around, and called me in to see the third or fourth day they were there.

I would be in my room doing homework.

"Come, come," they would say, standing in the doorway.

"Hm?"

"Come, come!" they would say again, beckoning me.

"That's very nice," I would say after I had seen their special thing.

"*My country!*" they would shout.

"Yes," I would say, nodding.

They would open their mouths again, very wide. A few sounds would come out, but never anything that I could understand. Then they would go "Ah-ahhhhh!" pushing at the air with their hands, then grab me and hug me, pushing my nose into folds of skin that smelled like yogurt.

I wouldn't tell Mother what I thought of them; I would wait until Mother asked me, then, when Mother asked me, I would say, "I don't know," and shrug until Mother would say, "Be frank."

"I think she's kind of icky," I would finally say.

"I think she's kind of icky, too," Mother would say.

We would look at each other.

"But *kind*," Mother would say, "we must remember, she's very kind."

"Kind, yes."

Mother would wait until they had done at least two things wrong before she would ask them to please quit.

When Mother would ask them to please quit, they would pack their bags and put their special thing in a cardboard box stuffed with newspaper or wood chips and be gone by the time we woke up.

Mother would say she had not meant for them to leave *before dawn*, but after the third one left like that, Mother said she realized they probably *liked* leaving before dawn.

. . . .

In between maids, Mother tries to cook on her own. She chops up half a carrot (unpeeled), then she looks in the oven, then she moves Na-Na to another part of the kitchen, then she tears open the wrong end of a box of mashed potato flakes, then she puts a saucepan on the stove without anything in it, not even any water, and turns the flame on, so that the bottom melts, leaving smoking, melted aluminum all over the top of the stove, which Mother chips off with a spatula, saying, "Not. One. Word. Not. One. Word."

. . . .

Mother has people she meets in the supermarket over for dinner. Some are missing arms or legs. Others are black. She follows them down aisles while Butch and I beside her whisper, "Don't please don't please don't please don't."

She speeds up her cart when the amputees are at the refrigerated section, reaching over to grab a pound of bacon or a can of frozen orange juice. She reaches over for them and puts it into their cart. "That's a good brand," she says, smiling. They smile back. She meets the blacks at the check-out counter, pushing her cart as fast as she can without running, to be behind them in line. She says "nice day" to them. They smile back. She follows them to their car with her cart, even when our car is on the other side of the parking lot. She says, "I am Mrs. Peter Teasdale and it's so nice to have you in the neighborhood!" when they get to their car.

Sometimes they come home with us right then. Mother makes iced tea and they sit on the porch. Other times Mother invites them over for dinner, then calls up other blacks or amputees she has met at other times in the supermarket and invites them over for dinner, too. Sometimes she forgets whether the person she has invited is black or has had something amputated, so that a black often finds himself shaking a stump instead of a hand or an amputee often finds himself stumping into a party of beaming blacks.

. . . .

"Finally, when I threw that candelabra, your father suggested I go to the psychiatrist. 'Suggested' is hardly the word. . . ."

"Christ, Mom!" Jennifer says, holding up a lock of hair and examining it, with crossed eyes, for split ends, "all I do is mention one thing and you go off into a *whole* thing!"

"No, but listen . . ."

Mother and Jennifer sit talking in the kitchen for hours after breakfast, until bacon grease goes white on the breakfast plates, Jennifer in an A-line skirt and cable-knit sweater, Mother in a quilted bathrobe with coffee stains down the front and frayed gray cuffs. Mother will say one thing and Jennifer will bounce up and down in her chair and say, "I know, that's tacky, too!" and Mother will sigh and say, "But I've been trying to tell you about that for years!" and Jennifer will sigh and say, "I know, but you just have to have *been* East to know."

I became aware of my eyelid, hanging down, numb-feeling, like a blanket. I wondered what it was about the East, about having been there, that could cause Mother and Jennifer to arrive at such a complete understanding of who and what was tacky, so that after a while, you couldn't tell who was saying "tacky" anymore. I wondered if it was because the East was old, because it had Pocahontas and John Smith and Washington and Jefferson and the Civil War, whereas all California had was Father Junipero Serra walking up the Camino Real from mission to mission in sandals like a beatnik. Then I wondered if it was because the East was simply *away* and that California was tacky compared to any place. It was tackier than Oregon. It was tackier than *Baja* California. Then I wondered if seeing what was tacky didn't have to do with growing up as well (Jennifer jiggled when she walked in her bathrobe now, like Mother, and put bras and girdles all over herself to make her stop, so that Daddy said, "Look at that Jennifer Girl, look at that Jennifer Girl!" when he walked in on her in the bathroom) and that being East or being away was like growing up, in that they were all ways that made you *see*, either who and what was tacky, or whatever it was you had to see.

Mother said that I was growing, too, and that I'd wear all those things Jennifer wore if I wanted to, trussed up better than a turkey, but I knew you had to go East for that extra little push.

After about an hour of Mother and Jennifer talking about things they think are tacky, Mother starts to talk about Daddy. You don't hear any kind of shift; just all of a sudden, Mother says, "That's what I mean about your father!" or "And so I said to him, 'Cornelius . . .'" and you know they are talking about Daddy.

"Mark," Jennifer says under her breath, "Mark definitely has to be the most un-tacky person I know."

Mother sets down her coffee cup. "I didn't even have to lie down on a sofa. I sat in a chair in a comfortable skirt and blouse. 'What's this I hear about you throwing a—,' the doctor looked down at a folder lying open on his desk, 'candelabra . . . at your husband?' I nodded. Dr. Krile asked me why I'd done that. I told him it was because I was tired of being lectured about how to wear my hair. Dr. Krile asked me how long I'd been married. 'Nine years,' I said. 'Why did you wait so long?' *Why did I wait so long:* when he said that, I felt as if a great weight had been taken off me. I went home and found your father in the projection room signing checks with his secretary, with whom he was . . . you know . . ."

"But Mom, all I did was mention *one thing!*" Jennifer shouts.

"Where was I? Oh yes: I went into the little office your father had set up in the projection room, and there was your father, signing checks with the secretary, with whom he was having an af—oops, *les enfants* . . ."

"Come on, Mom, we know you mean to say 'affair,'" Butch says.

"Mark . . ." Jennifer sighs.

"What's an affair?" I ask.

"That's when you put your hairy banana—" Butch says.

"Sh!" Mother says.

"Mark, Mark, where *are you?*" Jennifer says through clenched teeth.

Sonny gets up from the table, puts his hands behind his head, and yawning and scratching himself, walks out of the room.

"Your father could see I was in a good mood. 'Lizzie Girl!' he said, 'I'm so glad you're feeling better. I knew that doctor would make you come round.' I couldn't tell him right then. I waited for a couple of days, until he was in the right mood, then I told him Dr. Krile wanted to see him. See him, *too*, I said. '*I* see Dr. Krile?' Daddy said. He was absolutely incredulous! 'I'm glad Dr. Krile is helping *you*, but what could he possibly want with *me?*' 'Just go, Cornelius. Do me a favor. Dr. Krile wants to get the whole picture.' 'But *you're* the one who has the steel plate in her brain!' 'Just go, Cornelius.'

"Your father sat in a chair in Dr. Krile's waiting room. I sat beside him. He was still very handsome then. Like a riverboat gambler. But he would do things handsome men wouldn't do, like he would fix me with a gaze until finally I had to say, 'Cornelius, please, that's not sexy!'"

"Ma-ark," Jennifer says.

"Your precious Mw-war-ark!" Butch moos like a cow.

"Shut up!" Jennifer says.

Mother closes her eyes. "Jennifer, will you *please* stop talking about Mark for one minute?"

Jennifer rolls her eyes.

"We weren't in that waiting room for more than a minute when your father got up. 'I'm going,' he said. 'But Cornelius, you can't go!' 'Lizzie Girl!' he said. 'This is ridiculous! We have nothing to talk about!' And he walked out of the waiting room!

"Finally I persuaded your father to really go. 'Ah, Dr. Krile!' he said, rising and offering Dr. Krile his hand. 'I just stopped by to thank you for all you have done for Elizabeth. I'm really very impressed—' 'Won't you come in?' Dr. Krile asked, holding open the door to his office.

"A few minutes later, I heard noise coming from Dr. Krile's office. Shouting and the sound of chairs being scraped along the floor. The door burst open. 'Come on,' your father said. I followed him outside. 'You. Are. Not. Going. Back. To. Him. Ever,' your father said, pointing his finger at me on each word.

"That night, as I lay in bed, I heard a pounding on the floor in front of the bed. Your father was doing exercises. He always did exercises before getting into bed when he was mad at me—push-ups, jumping jacks, running in place,

swinging at an imaginary golf ball over and over again—so
that he would fall asleep right away—"

"Mark," Jennifer says, "Mark is so amusing—"

"*Amusing* now, is it? Eastern priss miss . . ." Butch says.

"All Dr. Krile said to your father, after your father said
that every woman he'd ever married had a steel plate in her
brain, was '*Four* steel plates? In a *row?*'"

. . . .

Mark was Jennifer's boyfriend. She had come home on
vacation from boarding school with a whole trunkful of letters, photographs, cartoons that Mark had drawn of stick
figures with bubbles coming out of their mouths, like com-
ics, with words written in the bubbles that I could understand, each word in itself, but couldn't understand all put
together—which I guessed meant they were very sophisticated—and toys, corks, and bottle caps and rocks with
words written on them and hearts and his and Jennifer's
initials and little drawings and two manila envelopes stuffed
with dried leaves and grass.

"Look at what he can think up, look how amusing he is,"
Jennifer said breathlessly, spreading them out on the bed
in her room.

Jennifer said "amusing" now instead of "funny."

"Uh-huh," I said, becoming breathless, too. Mark was very
tall and handsome and sophisticated, I thought, just as
Jennifer was very tall and beautiful and sophisticated and
when he and Jennifer were together, they spoke very clev-
erly and quickly and with slight English accents, like in a
Cary Grant movie, and they wore evening clothes all the
time, and when they danced, there was always a swirl of
silk whirling around them, like in a Fred Astaire movie.

"He is just perfection. And his *family* is so nice. They live in this big house in Litchfield, Connecticut. The whole family sits down together for every meal. Mark's father—he's so amusing—comes into the breakfast room in the morning and without saying 'good morning' to anyone, yells in a really gruff voice, 'Has that goddamned hound been chewing up my paper again?'" Jennifer giggles. "And the mother, who looks so sweet and mild, with her hair pulled over at the side of her head in a little clip, says, 'That goddamned hound is the one *you* decided to buy last year and it's my paper too what is this you're the only one around here who thinks he can *read?*' just right back, and then the father winks at us and you know then that they are just *kidding* and after a while, the mother kisses the father, and I don't know, it's just really amusing, you know what I mean?"

Jennifer put her feet up on the bed and hugged her knees, putting her cheek down on them. "I just miss Mark so *much*," she said.

. . . .

"Hey, Yips, in here," Sonny whispered.

I slipped into his room and sat down on one of the twin beds.

Sonny looked both ways out the door, waved smoke back inside the room and shut the door softly. He walked towards me with a can of beer and a cigarette smoking in one hand and sat down on the other twin bed, facing me.

Sonny was in boarding school now, too. He'd been sent a year after Jennifer because Jennifer was going and Mother didn't think the two should be treated differently.

Sonny came back taller and handsomer every time he stepped off the plane, so that it seemed as if an explosion had happened, or as if he had molted, you didn't see how he could have gotten so much taller and handsomer, so fast, any other way, with the kind of dark, regular looks that made you want to snap your fingers and say, "That's, that's—," that you thought only movie stars had, but there Sonny was, just *having* them. And it wasn't just we who thought so, people in the airport turned around, too, but it might not have been for that as much as for Daddy, in the Hawaiian trunks and matching sport shirt he had gone back to wearing all the time since Rita had left, with his hands on his bare knees, laughing and saying, "Look at that Sonny Boy, look at that Sonny Boy," or for Sonny saying "*Da*-ad," each time in a more embarrassed voice, or for Butch and me circling around Sonny with our heads back and our mouths open, as if around a giant redwood.

Sonny held up the hand with the beer can and the cigarette in it and raised an eyebrow.

"I won't tell. . . ."

"Want some?"

"No, thanks," I said, trying to sound casual.

"That's O.K.," he said charitably. He drained the can in one gulp, crushed it flat, pulled a box out from underneath the bed, took off the top of the box, threw the empty can in, pulled an unopened can out, put the top back on, and pushed the box back under his bed.

"Hey . . ." he said, looking at me with eyes that were shining and with a slight smile on his lips, as if he were letting me in on a secret.

I pushed forward on the bed, hoping that the way Sonny was being with me now meant that the recent times, when he had been, if not exactly mean, just not as nice as he usually was, had been what Mother called "a passing phase."

"Can you believe how much she goes on about *the old man?* Jesus-*SSSS!*" The sound of "Jesus" mingled with the sound of the pop top being pulled off. He pulled the box out from under the bed again, cracked the lid, threw the pop top in and shoved the box back. "Every time we're together, it's 'Dad, Dad, Dad.' I mean, there're other things in life, right? I mean, she could talk about sailing or brontosauruses or something." He took a swig. "Hey . . ." He looked around, then looked back at me with eyes that were shining even brighter. He pushed closer to me. "Come here," he said.

I pushed closer, until my ear was just a few inches from his mouth.

"Do you think she still digs him?"

"I don't know."

"Hey."

"What."

"Do you know what 'to dig' someone means?"

"Uh-huh," I said, knowing that it meant "to like," but thinking that it had to mean more than that this time.

"I mean to *really* dig them?"

"Uh-huh," I said again, feeling my face glow hot.

"At *your* age?"

"So?" I said, trying to sound nonchalant.

He smiled broadly. "Hey, Yips, you're all right."

I smiled and squirmed.

He drained the beer can in one gulp, crushed it, pulled the box out from underneath the bed, threw the empty can in, pulled another can out and shut the lid. He popped the top, said, "Damn, always forget—," pulled the box out again, cracked the lid and threw the pop top back in. "Hey."

"Yeah?"

"Can you believe what a *wimp* that Peter is?"

I shrugged.

" 'But he's so sensitive!' " Sonny said in a high voice, imitating Mother, then laughing. "God."

I laughed, too.

"Hey," he said again, after a while.

"What."

"You remember how I used to like poetry?"

"Uh-huh."

"Don't tell anyone I used to like it."

"O.K."

" 'Cause I don't now."

"O.K."

"I really don't."

"O.K."

"You know why?"

"No."

" 'Cause it doesn't help. It doesn't help a goddamned thing." He looked down at the floor and shook his head.

There was some silence, then suddenly, he looked up again and raised his beer can. "This, on the other hand—"

I laughed.

"What's so funny?" He looked at me with eyes that had stopped shining and had become just surprised. "Drinking has been given a lot of bad press, but let me tell you, I think it's one of the greatest things that was ever invented! That is, if you know how to do it. Some guys say they do and then puke. I never puke. I just get groovier and groovier. We got tons of liquor at school. Gin, vodka, bourbon, whiskey, rum, vermouth, soda, tonic, even maraschino cherries. We got it all hidden in a hollow tree trunk out in the woods. We get this old coon to buy it for us. Every night, one of us goes out there with a big overcoat on to bring a coupla bottles back.

The master of our house, Mr. Sterling, he's so old he doesn't even check to see if we're in our rooms at lights out. We booze all night. We play cards, listen to music. Sometimes we even get townie girls up there. We got this fat townie girl up there and she kept saying, 'Don't you do that now, don't you do that now.' It was really funny.

"I'm handsome, right? People say I am anyway. Old ladies come up to me in the street in Eastham and say, 'You look just like James Garner!' I may *look* like James Garner, but I don't *feel* like James Garner, you know what I mean? Except when I drink. When I drink I feel like Maverick, riding into town, doing such groovy things for people, and everybody *loves* me, you know what I mean? We have these dances at school and me and some preppie girl who's had her eye on me all night, we go out to the ole hollow tree trunk and when we come back, we get out on that dance floor . . ." Sonny stood up, bent over, and spread his arms wide with a beer can sloshing in one hand. Keeping his feet in one place, he started bending one knee, then the other, so that his hips swayed. "They're playing James Brown. And we start gettin' down. And we're gettin' down and gettin' down. . . ." Sonny started moving his legs and his hips faster. "Yeah! And people swear to God that we have a kind of *glow*, you know what I mean?"

. . . .

"This is what I am going to do to you," Butch said, pacing back and forth at the foot of my bed, waiting for an opening to spring, "when you get armpit hairs. You're so queer, you're probably not even going to shave them. You're going to let them grow long and greasy and sweaty. Then one day I'm going to take you and make you lie down on your back in the desert under the hot sun. And then I'm going to take your arms and tie them to stakes driven into the desert floor, so that your armpits, your long, smelly, greasy, sweating pits, will be exposed to the grueling sun! Then I'm going to put on a gas mask and rubber gloves dipped in disinfectant and I'm going to try not to puke as I braid your greasy pit hairs. Even braided, your pit hairs will be longer than your whole body, 'cause you're so gross. And I'm gonna tie the braids at the ends with wire made of specially tempered metal, 'cause the acid content of the sweat in your pit hairs will be so high it will eat through anything else. Then I'm gonna untie your arms and you're gonna think, for a moment, that your troubles are over, but they will have just begun! 'Cause then I'm gonna take you and tie you up by your armpit hairs to a scaffold that I'll have built in the desert. And you'll hang there, under the grueling sun! And every day, I'm going to put on gloves and a gas mask and I'm going to get up on a ladder with a bucket and a brush and I'm gonna coat your pits with tanning oil, the kind of oil they use to tan leather. And the tanning oil is going to mix with the sweat and acid and grease and dirt and compacted flies of your pit hairs until your pits'll be like rawhide. Then I'm gonna take a pair of scissors and every day, I'm gonna clip a few hairs, just where they come out of your pits, so that every day, the pain will be more and more excruciating as you hang by fewer and fewer hairs. Finally, the last few hairs will not be able to hold your body up and they'll rip out and you'll go crashing to the ground, leaving bloody trailings behind on the roots of the last few hairs and bloody holes in your pits from where they were pulled out. And you'll be crouching on the ground there, begging for mercy and I'll take down your braided pit hairs and whip you . . . until you die!"

Butch sprang. I had forgotten to follow him with my upraised feet on the last turn he'd made. He landed on me with a thud, covering me with his entire body. Then, quick as a flash, he was up on his knees, straddling my chest, his knees on my arms.

"What's the deodorant racing car drivers use?" he shouted.

"You two! Stop that!" Mother's voice said. Mother stood in the doorway.

"But we were just playing, Mom!" Butch called over his shoulder. Butch stopped jabbing my armpits and started tickling me in the ribs and looking at me as if he were letting me in on a secret, too. "See? Tickle, tickle, tickle!"

I pinched my lips together, then realized that I was not going to laugh this time. It was not that what Butch was doing was any less funny, it was just that, for some time, I had been thinking that, the next time, I was not going to laugh, just to see what would happen. Then, when the time came, I always did laugh. This time, though, my lips stayed tight together.

"Tickle, tickle, tickle!" Butch said again.

I stared at Butch's mouth instead of his eyes. I was not going to give my laugh the eyes it needed to begin. I felt my lips press tighter together.

"Come on, Robs, TICKLE!"

I thought of things to keep from laughing. I thought of death. I thought of the fact that people died, of the fact that people I knew or knew of had died: Grandaddy Drayton, Sandra Bellows's, one grade below me's, grandmother just a few days before (she had cried on the playground), Montgomery Clift, Humphrey Bogart, Marilyn Monroe. I thought of the fact that Daddy would die some day, that Mother would. That Butch sitting on me would die, and that I would die, too, and that would be it, for my view of the world at least, like pulling a paper backdrop off a great big stage and finding nothing behind it and then realizing: *that was the world—*.

"Come on, Robs!"

Of the fact that this was our only chance to be alive, our only chance, out of billions of years, and in this, our only chance, brothers weren't supposed to sit on top of sisters and talk about how they were going to *kill* them.

"Come on . . ."

I felt my ribs go numb and my lips relax and my breathing get back to normal. I opened my mouth cautiously, to see if a laugh would come out again, but it didn't. I knew then that I could keep my mouth open and talk and hum and sing, all the while Butch was tickling me, because things were serious. Life was very serious.

"She's choking!"

"Oh Mom, she is *not*. She loves it. Don't you, Robin? Come on . . ."

"I do not," I said, raising my head off the bed, which made me shout in a strangely hoarse voice, "*I DO NOT!*"

"No, she doesn't love it, she doesn't love it at all." Mother's voice rose with each word. "You keep telling me she loves it but I know she doesn't." Mother took a step forward. "Stand up now."

"You little—" Butch said, jabbing me again in the armpits, hard.

"Stand up now!" Mother took another step forward and

raised her fists. You could see white balls of Kleenex stuffed in her cuffs, like rabbits' tails. "You stand up when I tell you to stand up!" Mother ran at him, bringing one fist down, then opening it at the last minute and pulling back on one of his shoulders.

"O.K., O.K.!" Butch said. He put one foot on the floor, then the other, then stood up and faced her, slouching.

"And don't slouch!"

Butch kept on slouching.

"Don't slouch, I said!" She ran at him again.

"Aw, you old biddy," Butch said, pushing her down onto the bed. He turned and walked out of the room.

Mother got up and ran after him. "And take out the trash when I ask you to. And dry the dishes. Don't wait to be asked—"

"Aw, you old bitch! Daddy's so rich that we're *never* going to have to do anything!"

"And do your homework! And . . . I'm getting tickets to the ballet and you're going to come!"

"What?"

"You heard me! It's about time you had a cultural experience!"

"Aw, go to hell!" He slammed the door to his room shut behind him.

Mother turned to me. "Poobitry," Mother said. "That's what he's going through."

• • • •

I locked my door, then took a bathrobe belt and tied one end of it to the doorknob and the other end to the leg of a heavy bureau near the door, then tried crawling under my bed, but my head wouldn't go, even when I turned it sideways, so I crawled out and crouched in the corner of the room. It was quiet in the hall. I got up and crouched for a while in another corner, then got up, my heart beating, but telling myself I'd hear something first, and dragged a night table and bookshelf in front of the corner, closing it off.

There was a small sonic boom. Curtains that had been blowing outside flew into the room. I shut my eyes as the night table and bookshelf fell over. "This is what you get for not laughing," a voice said.

I saw a white thing, like a cauliflower, with specks of purple tissue paper on it, or seaweed, the kind that came in thin sheets that were melted on rocks when the tide went out. Then I was in the ocean, swimming and swimming, up through a tunnel of water set on end. I couldn't breathe. Then breath came back, through a tiny clogged straw at first, then more and more and I felt my stomach, aching with every breath, feeling as if it were stretched and purple and wrinkled and taking up half my body, like the eyelids of a newly hatched bird.

.   .   .   .

We were reading a story, out loud, a paragraph to each student.

" . . . then Abdul called one of his servants."

"Miss Crick?" Someone raised a hand.

"Yes?"

"What's a servant?"

"I've got servants!"

Some children turned around and looked at me.

Miss Crick said that that wasn't answering the question, but as long as I was talking and as long as I had servants, I might as well tell the class what they were.

I said servants were people who cooked for you and cleaned up after you and stuff like that.

"Like maids?"

"Yeah, like maids."

"Are you rich?"

"Yes."

All the children in the class turned around and looked at me.

I waited for the trouble you were supposed to get into when you told people you were rich, that I knew wouldn't happen immediately, but that I thought I would at least see signs of, to come, but it didn't: the air seemed somehow clearer, in fact. Everything seemed somehow easier.

Miss Crick said quickly that that was enough.

From the back of the class, someone said they bet I wasn't richer than Josephine Trueblood.

Miss Crick said that that was enough again.

    . . . .

Standing up to say the Pledge of Allegiance, my grade and Josephine Trueblood's grade called back and forth. Josephine Trueblood's house had six acres; so did Daddy's. We both had tennis courts and swimming pools, with poolside bars and poolside extension telephones. Her house had columns along the front like My Old Kentucky Home; Daddy's house had doors and balconies in it imported from a castle in Spain. We both had swing sets and jungle gyms. I had a racetrack for Flexies; Josephine had a trampoline, the professional kind, set over a pit in the ground. I had a go-cart; Josephine had a horse. I had a maid who would serve me Coke with ice in a glass by the pool ("Coke with ice by the pool!" Carmen actually had said. "You're a spoiled brat and

I'm going to tell your father!"); so did Josephine. I had a governess, cook, laundress and butler; so did Josephine. My father belonged to six country clubs; so did Josephine's. My father belonged to the *Eldorado* Country Club; so did Josephine's. I had a red velvet cape; Josephine had a mink headband. My sister had a Dior dress. "What's Dior?" Josephine asked. Josephine's sister had a Patek Philippe watch. "What's Patek?" I asked. I was pale and thin like the daughters of rich people were. I would die young, like rich people's daughters did. Josephine was pale and thin, too, with long, brown hair parted down the middle, which made her face look even longer, and she had large, brown, lusterless eye, like pieces of felt or velvet cut out. I had two big brothers; Josephine had a rich person's last name and a little brother named Giles. Giles Trueblood, what could sound richer than that? Josephine had a chauffeur; he drove her to and from school. Everybody saw him every day, sitting in a Lincoln Continental, waiting to pick up Josephine and Giles. I had a chauffeur, too. "Well, where is he?" I said I had him on the weekends when I was at Daddy's house. They said having a chauffeur only on the weekends didn't really count. And having only a rich daddy didn't count. You had to have a rich mother, too. I said it did count. They said it didn't. I said it did. I said I was *so* rich, I had *detectives* following me to and from school. They asked me where they were.

"I'll show you," I said.

We walked to the edge of the playing field overlooking the circle at the end of Cabrillo Avenue.

There was a green car in the circle with a man in a Hawaiian shirt in it reading the newspaper.

"That's not a detective!"

"It is, too!"

"But . . . he's not wearing a raincoat!"

"Detectives don't have to wear raincoats!"

There was a silence. Then someone from the back of the group said, "Is that why you have a funny eye?"

Is that why you have a funny eye? Suddenly I felt as if they were very small and I were very big, smiling down at them, like God. They still said things that had nothing to do with anything, the way I had done, but had not done now for years.

"Cyclops! Bullwinkle! One-Eye!" they started shouting.

Shouting louder, I said that besides, Daddy bought a new white Cadillac every year, while Josephine Trueblood kept riding in the same old (and it was three or four years old) Lincoln Continental.

CHAPTER 7

Busy had all the shades pulled down because it was so hot. In the middle of her room was a fan as big as a kettledrum, tilted just enough on its base to shoot air up my shorts and shirtsleeves. Every fifteen minutes or so I stood over the fan. My shirt and shorts filled like balloons. Clumps of my hair were blown upwards and twirled lazily. I watched myself in the mirror and started to laugh but then stopped: I was not supposed to let anyone at Daddy's house think I was having a good time, not even for one second.

Sonny, Butch, and Jennifer were in Maine with Mother at Peter's summer house. Na-Na had been sent for the summer to Virginia. Mother, Sonny, Butch, and Jennifer had gone on the Super Chief by way of Chicago because Jennifer was afraid to fly. They went sailing every day. They wrote letters to me with sentences like, "I've got to go polish winches now. Boy, do I hate polishing winches." Maine was next door to Canada and Canada was in the Arctic Circle. Maine was cold, even in the summer. Daddy had Busy go buy out the underwear section of a ski shop for Sonny, Butch, and Jennifer before they left. Daddy couldn't understand why Sonny, Butch, and Jennifer were so excited about spending a summer in the East. The East was like Europe: it was cold and run down.

Busy said I had to stay in California that summer because Daddy loved me so much, so much more than Sonny, Butch, and Jennifer, that he couldn't stand it when I was away, he worried, but Alice had told me, telephoning the principal's office and saying it was an emergency and having me called to the principal's office to speak to her, that I had to stay in California because Daddy was afraid that if I left California, Mother would take me to New York to have my eye operated on.

Alice didn't work for us anymore but she still told me things, telephoning me once or twice a week from her house in The Valley. Mother would give me the phone winking. Alice would say that she was worried about me being at Mother's house with just Mother to take care of me, or at Daddy's house with just all those people at Daddy's house to take care of me. At Daddy's house that summer, Alice would call me (sometimes putting a neighbor's child on to ask for me, so that Daddy would not know it was her) and tell me that she thought it had been wrong of her to suggest that I say something to Daddy, it had been wrong of her to put that pressure on me. It was his business if he wanted to destroy himself, but if I ever needed a place to go, all I had to do was call and she and Melvyn would come running.

I had to wear an eyepatch all the time.

Mrs. Kiebler had moved out of her dark house in the canyon to an apartment in Santa Monica overlooking the ocean. I wore a dress to Mrs. Kiebler's, instead of the T-shirt and blue jeans I had always worn before, because putting on a slip and dress in the morning and then making sure the dress was not wrinkled gave me something to do. I wore a see-through plastic raincoat over the dress when I went outside, even when it was sunny, because it seemed like there should be something between my arms and the outside air.

Mrs. Kiebler helped me off with my raincoat, all the while talking about how I had finally become the princess Daddy had meant me to be. Mrs. Kiebler and Busy talked about how amazing it was the girls eventually *became* girls, that nature never failed.

. . . .

Mother calls from Maine and asks me if I am having a good time. I say I am. Not paying any attention to what I have just said, Mother says that I should call one of the neighbors' children up and ask if they would like to play. "But I'm having a good time!" I say again, louder. Mother then says she would have loved to take me to Maine, but this summer she thinks it is . . . *mur* . . . not to. Mother has started saying French words when she talks about Daddy. She says I should go out a lot, go out as much as I can with Busy, to Will Wright's ice cream parlor, to the movies, to the Mormon Tabernacle . . .

"But I'm having a good time!" I say, as loud as I can without shouting.

. . . .

New maids came. They came in the afternoons and sat around the kitchen table, drinking coffee with Judy and Carmen.

Daddy said we needed new maids because he didn't want any of his girls working too hard.

Judy prepared fourteen of Daddy's trays at once now, so that she only had to do anything once every two weeks. She

said her way was so much better than Midge's. She poured
fourteen glasses of prune juice and covered each one with
Saran Wrap and lined them up in the giant, built-in refrigerator, as big as a restaurant refrigerator, empty now other-
wise and smelling of shoes. She toasted twenty-eight pieces
of toast and wrapped them in Saran-Wrapped packages of
two, saying that that kind of toast never went bad, and covered fourteen trays with paper doilies and stacked them in
the pantry among the stacks of brown-felt-covered trays and
gold dinner plates left over from Daddy's parties, so that
every afternoon, after Daddy woke up, all Judy had to do
was put it all together, pour the fresh coffee she'd made for
herself and the new maids, and carry the tray into Daddy's
room, sighing and sagging under the weight of it, so that
the new maids laughed.

. . . .

Daddy goes into the kitchen every afternoon, after he has
finished his tray. He stands in the doorway in his Hawaiian
shorts and matching sport shirt with his hands on his knees,
watching them and smiling.

"Hhhhhi, Mr. D.," Judy and the new maids say, when they
finally see him, smiling in the doorway.

Daddy straightens up and, smiling a little less, steps up
to the maid nearest him. He takes her head in one hand.
"Bite," Daddy says, "bite." Daddy uses the thumb and
forefinger of his other hand to push the corners of her mouth
back, until he can see the little rubber bands hooked on her
back molars stretching and stretching.

After she has bitten about ten times, Daddy takes his
thumb and finger away, wipes them on a paper towel handed
to him by Judy, puts his hands on the back of the head of the

maid whose mouth he has just been examining, so that she automatically bows her head, and, closing his eyes, kisses her on the forehead. He then moves on to the next one.

Busy comes up behind me. She whispers that she'll make tuna sandwiches for us and starts walking back into the pantry but I tell her not to be silly: she is a governess—"*My* governess," I say, putting my arm around her (I am taller than she is now)—and she should not be doing things cooks are supposed to do. If you give them an inch, they will take a mile, I say. She is to come to lunch with me at the Hilton.

Don drives us in a limousine to the Hilton. Don looks in the rearview mirror at us and says that Minnie would be happy to make us a little something. I tell Don that that was very nice but that we will be just fine.

. . . .

Dust started to appear. It settled on the naked women in the paintings in the bar and on bowls of stale Chee-tos, mingling with their cheese powder. It settled on the Louis the Sixteenth table and on the highest undulations of the snake in the Laocoön clock. It settled on the frosted glass pineapple sections in the dining room sideboards. It poofed out of the hula-girl curtains when you swatted them and out of their thick, shredded backs and puffed out of the deep-pile carpet when you stepped and stepped on it, like a French person making wine. It settled on mirrors and windows and on soaps and sinks in unused powder rooms, and when a Santa Ana blew, it seeped through closets and settled on the shoulders of Daddy's tuxedos and cutaways and on yellowing formal shirts and patent-leather pumps that I said looked like pansy shoes but that Busy said were proper. It settled in a deep trough in back of the movie screen in the projection room, which I could see through a rip, made first by rats, then made a little bigger by me so that I could get my head through, and in piles deeper still on the movie projectors in their little room in the back, their empty reels sticking up like lacework Mickey Mouse ears.

Minnie said she tried to keep up with it for a while, but it was like trying to move a beach with a pair of tweezers, and besides, it burned her, trying, what with all those other girls just sitting around. She polished silver instead in the mornings before people came, taking it out of brown felt bags in the pantry and putting it back in. That way she did something that would at least stay for a while.

There was powdery dust, greasy dust, sticky dust, and sweet vanilla-smelling dust. I collected samples, smearing the greasy or sticky dust directly on cardboard and collecting the dry dust in tiny Glad bags, which I stapled alongside the smears, then wrote underneath the samples the date I found them and the location. I put glasses I had emptied on empty shelves and watched dust collect in them and around them, first forming a film over the sticky dried dregs at the bottom, then coating the glasses inside and out, then piling up in drifts around the bases of the glasses, leaving perfectly clean circles when I moved them. I set the glasses out and checked them every day, like a fisherman checking his nets, hiding behind a sofa if ever a new maid came by on stiletto heels, swinging a sweater, as I was checking them.

. . . .

Rita's poodle barks in a crack in the door. Rita is in her bathrobe. "Dartagnan! Dartagnan!" Rita says to the dog. "You stop that!" She turns to me. "Tell Don Cornelio I'll be right out, Robin Girl! I would ask you in but the place is too messy."

"That's O.K.," I say.

"There!" Rita says, standing in the doorway, pulling a long mohair sweater on over hair that she has let go back to strawberry blond.

"Hi there, Rita Girl!" Daddy says.

Rita stretches over me across the front seat and kisses Daddy on the cheek. "Oh, you gorgeous hunk of man, you!" Rita says, patting him on both cheeks. Rita hugs me around the shoulders. Daddy starts the car. Daddy drives slowly in the middle of the road.

Cars coming towards us honk, then pull over and wait by the side of the road until we pass by. Some drivers lean out of the cars and try to fix us with their disbelieving gaze, but Daddy doesn't look at them, he just raises his hand seignorially, half wave and half salute. Daddy's golf clubs rattle on the vast floor in back.

When we get to Wilshire, Daddy slows down to a crawl and starts pointing out the apartment buildings he owns: the Charleston Wilshire, the Savannah Wilshire, the George-town Wilshire, the Madame du Pompadour, the Del Ray and the Sans Souci.

"I bought that one from that Jew boy," Daddy says, pointing out the Sans Souci.

We drive into the Ships parking lot. Daddy noses the limousine in between two other big cars. Rita sings, "You're just as hard to land as the Ile de France." Daddy laughs.

The waitresses know Daddy and greet him as we come in. They wear turquoise uniforms with ruffled turquoise caps perched on blond hair piled on top of their heads, or if it is short, sprayed to look like it is piled. Daddy waves at one of the waitresses. "How's your boy doing?" he calls.

"Oh, just fine, Mr. D.!"

The few customers who are there having a late lunch or an early supper turn in their booths and stare at the large diamond ring on Rita's finger, which Daddy gave Rita as a divorce present. They stare and nudge each other and point their fingers underneath the table.

Rita walks by one table where people are staring at her particularly hard, turning their heads to be able to look at her as she walks by. Rita looks back at them and says, "Hi, there!" After we are seated, Daddy pats Rita on the cheek and says that she handled herself just like a princess.

We drive to Daddy's spot on the driving range. The pro is waiting for us with four wire baskets full of balls. The pro wears a shirt with wide, vertical stripes. He shakes all the time, except when he has a golf club in his hand. He shakes all the time, I think, from the years of his having to hear the wap, wap, wap of balls being hit all day long.

The driving range in front of us is a huge field of packed dirt, the biggest single piece of land in Westwood. Daddy says it will be worth a million dollars one day. There are signs sticking up all over it to mark the yards. It is covered with balls. You can't see the balls when they are in the air, you just see them after they have made their first bounce, so that they look as if they have popped out of the ground. On both sides of us are men swinging golf clubs, striking at random intervals down the line, like church bells.

A tractor goes back and forth in the field, harvesting the balls. The cab of the tractor is surrounded with wire to protect the driver. I think it would be fun to be the driver. It would be fun to have all the balls flying at me and then not hitting me.

Daddy swings. He goes "Mwraghhh!" every time he swings. He hits every golf ball longer and higher than anyone else on the entire driving range can hit them, beyond the two-twenty-five, beyond the two-fifty, beyond the two-seventy-five, over the fence at the back of the range and into the mustard field beyond.

"Wow! Look at that!" Rita says.

"You're still the king, Mr. Drayton," the pro says.

"Si, el rey, el rey Cornelio! Viva el rey!" Rita shrieks.

Daddy puts a finger against one side of his nose and blows a string of snot out onto the fake grass pad. He wipes it deeper into the plastic grass with his shoe.

"Nose drops," Daddy says.

Rita hands them to him out of her purse.

Daddy unscrews the cap, tilts his head back.

"Yessir," the pro says, standing on one leg, then the other.

"Ain't I driving like some big buck nigger today?" Daddy asks, sniffing after he brings his head back down.

"Yes, you are, you gorgeous hunk of man, you!" Rita says.

Daddy squeezes Rita's cheeks until her lips pucker and when they do, he kisses them.

After the fifteenth ball, Daddy says, "Corny Boy's tired now." There is a triangle of sweat on the back of his shirt. He eases himself down onto the bench, sniffing and sighing. "Damn," he says, "those nose drops that that Dr. Villalobo Boy gave me aren't doing the trick anymore. I'm going to have to get that doctor boy to prescribe something stronger."

Rita hits a dozen balls neatly. They fly long and low out to the one-fifty.

"Pretty! Very pretty!" Daddy says.

Then it is my turn. The pro shows me how to choke up on my grip. He puts a ball on the rubber tee for me. He puts his hand, shaking slightly, on the top of my head so that I will keep my eye on the ball and not move it up before I hit. My hair is clean and slides under his hand.

I swing five times. I nick two balls. They fly off crazily to the side, nearly hitting other drivers in the ankles. "Hey, watch it!" they shout angrily. Daddy waves to them. I want to stop then. I tell Daddy I might hit someone, but Daddy tells me to go on. I hit the other three out into the range. I hit one ball right in the center of the wood. It lands between the fifty and the hundred. It makes the iron part of the club vibrate. The vibrations travel all the way up my arm to my shoulders and then to my teeth, making me feel as if I've swallowed the ball, juicy and whole.

I tell myself I will practice. I will keep my eye on the ball and learn to hit the ball like that every time.

"Daddy," I said suddenly.

"What?" Daddy said.

"It's not nice to say 'nigger,' you know."

Daddy looked at me. "What did you say?"

"I said it's not nice to say 'nigger.'"

Daddy laughed, surprised. "Robin *Girl!*" Daddy said, "I don't call *all* colored people 'nigger'!" Daddy shook his head on the word *all*. "I just call the ones who are primitive or the ones who smell 'nigger.' Or the ones who are dishonest or lazy or have duh, duh . . ." Daddy put on an accent, "big lips and who stick deh, deh . . . bee-hinds out and kinda shuffle . . ." Daddy stood up, stuck his behind out and shuffled back and forth on the plastic grass pad.

Rita and the pro laughed. "Oh, stop!" Rita said.

"You're a stitch, Mr. D.," the pro said.

I wanted to be able to hit the ball like that every time, while at the same time, I wanted to sit in the wire-covered tractor and have the balls hit by me hit me.

. . . .

Daddy stands behind the bar and makes drinks. He doesn't have to ask what is in the drinks anymore. He pushes a grenadine and ginger ale across the bar to me.

"There's old Long John Silver!" a man standing beside me says. "How are you, Long John?"

"I have to wear this eyepatch," I say.

Judy comes out with an ice bucket on a tray. Daddy puts a hand on her shoulder and introduces her to the guests one by one. Judy bows and smiles and laughs. Then Daddy takes Judy's head and turns it so that everyone can see her profile and says, "Now *here's* one I had done a long time ago. Judy Girl came to me. She was just a little thing then. Weren't you, Judy Girl?"

"Yes, Mr. D."

"And I said to her, 'Judy Girl, it's got to go,' I mean this—" Daddy draws with his finger two semicircles on either side of Judy's nose. "Judy Girl's nostrils were a little too fleshy, a little too . . . ethnic." Judy looks to the side and smiles. All the guests smile, too. You can hear lips sliding over clean, straight teeth. "'You've got to shave down those nostrils, Judy Girl,' I said, 'and bring the whole thing up a little bit, too.'" Daddy runs his finger along the piece of skin dividing the two nostrils, tracing its upward curve. "And look at Judy Girl now. . . ." Daddy puts his hands on either side of Judy's face and brings her face towards his puckered lips. He closes his eyes.

"She's beautiful," I hear one of the guests say, about Judy.

"Just beautiful," another guest says.

"What you did for her, Mr. D. . . ."

"Oh, you're so good, so good."

Daddy is kissing another woman now. All the other women are crowding around him in a circle, laughing. "Cute," one woman says. Daddy lets go of the woman he has been kissing, turns to the woman who has just said "cute" and starts kissing her. Then another woman says "cute" and Daddy turns to her. Then another woman says "cute." Daddy is turning and turning. The women are laughing. Some are jumping up and down and clapping. Then there is a rumbling sound and like a top, slowing down, Daddy starts to wobble to one side, then another as he turns. The women stop laughing. The men stand as if alert but don't move. Daddy is bent double, still turning. Suddenly, one foot jumps over the other. He falls sideways, crashing against a bar stool. Guests rush to pick him up.

. . . .

Minnie took a drag on her cigarette and let it out. Her words tangled with the smoke. "But do you know something? I think when I said, 'Mr. D., I like my nose *just fine*,'" Minnie tapped on the side of her nose, "that he was actually *relieved*?"

My eyepatch lay beside Minnie's legs on the footstool.

"But let me tell you something. I've got it figured out." Minnie took her feet off the footstool, sat up and, twisting, pulled her body forward on the chair. "Your dad has this compulsion to—all right, I'll say it now—," she waved her cigarette in the air, "make love—you know what I mean by 'make love'—to every woman he meets. Young, old, ugly, beautiful, it doesn't matter. It's like drilling holes in the ground or something. Now this nose job, face job, tooth job thing: it's not because he can't make love with ugly women. You should see some of the women he's had affairs with. Women you would never think, in a million years—they're like—I'm not saying he *had* an affair with Busy, but they're like Busy, if you know what I mean. He would think he was doing them a favor. The only trouble was, they would start assuming they were going to spend the rest of their life with him. That's where the nose job, face job, tooth job thing comes in. Now picture this: he's making the moves on some gal, when suddenly, his eyes glaze over and he says, 'Why don't you take a little tuck?' Now, what would a woman with any self-respect say then? She would tell him to get lost! But a woman with no self-respect, a woman determined to get him at any cost, she would look at him with big eyes and say, 'Oh, really?' and *let* him give her a nose job, or a behind lift, or whatever. By doing that, he is sort of getting out of being obliged, nowadays, to make love to *every* woman he meets. He only has to make love to about three-quarters of them. He only has to make love to women without any self-respect, whom he can more easily control. And when they start assuming they're going to spend the rest of their life with him, he just says, 'Why don't you take a little tuck?' again! And on and on, until they either get fed up or start looking like goddamned Incas. Plus I guess it's also a way of changing the scenery."

Minnie took another drag. "And I got another thing figured out: why your dad, in the midst of having everyone-who-doesn't-need-it-in-the-world's face fixed, is just as busy *not* having someone-who-really-needs-it's face fixed. It's to keep her under control, too. He won't do it for her because she really *needs* it. He won't do it for her because he is afraid that if she grows up and starts looking pretty and boys start running after her, she won't be his little baby girl anymore!"

Minnie took another drag. "And there's another thing. . . ." Minnie put her hands together in front of her nose. She held them still for a second, as if she were thinking or praying, then let them drop. "I just figured this out the other day. How having-everyone-who-doesn't-need-it-in-the-world's face fixed *connects* with not-having-someone-who-really-needs-it's face fixed—*really* connects. It's as if each person's face he fixes kind of *points out* the fact that he's *not* fixing—O.K., I'll say it now—*your* face. To your mother, I guess. It's as if each person's face he fixes—this is hard now—supports his denial that there's anything wrong with you. It's as if with each person's face he fixes he's saying, 'Eyelid? What eyelid?' like Alice said he did when you were born, or saying, 'You see what kind of guy I am, I'd fix her face if there was anything wrong with it but there's nothing wrong with it!'"

Minnie fell back against the back of her chair with the sound of sighing vinyl. She shook her head. "And in every case, your dad thinks he's being the nicest, sweetest, most generous—" Minnie took another drag on her cigarette and blew it out, squinting at me through the smoke. "I don't know why he is the way he is. I can't even begin to figure that one out. Your mother's the one with the theories about that. I tell you, life's not simple but it could be a lot simpler than this."

Minnie took another drag on her cigarette, then ground it out, shaking her head. "But he's not gonna get me. No sir. I said to him, 'Mr. D., you were closer with sending my sister's kid to the physical therapist, but I like my nose *just fine!*'

"He called me up later on the phone. 'Minnie Girl,' he said, 'you're great. You're the only one I can trust.' He was in tears. I tell you, there are times late at night when *he knows.*"

She sighed. "Don's pissed off. All that energy he says your dad's spending finding out about my family when the stairs here are so dangerous and the plumbing's shot and we've got bugs—things he's *supposed* to fix. Don was going to tell your father about the steps the other day but I said, 'No, let's fix the steps at night and paint them and he'll never know.' Don thinks we can't do it but I think we can, just as soon as we have the money."

She paused. Her voice grew shrill. "I mean, the goddamned bugs are eating the floor right out from under us and he fixes people's noses. I mean, his daughter's goddamned eyelid is hanging right down in front of him and he fixes people's noses!"

"Minnie—" I said.

"But it's true!"

"I know it's true but—"

"Somebody has to do something!"

"Like what?"

"Tell him to fix your goddamned eyelid, for Christ's sake!" She was practically shouting.

"But you can't just tell him, you *can't* just *tell* him!"

I felt clammy fingers inside my throat, around the ridged tubes.

I got up and walked in the direction of Minnie's kitchen. It was hard to see where I was going. I felt something cut me across my left thigh. It was the kitchen table. I had not steered far enough around it. I put my hands forward to keep myself from falling.

"That's it," Minnie said. "Just keep on bumping into things."

My foot caught a leg of one of the kitchen chairs, sending it spinning into the room.

"Just keep on wearing your eyepatch." She threw it at me as I walked out the kitchen door.

I walked down the stairs as fast as I could, holding onto the wobbly railing. My vision started to come back to me. Then, at the bottom of the stairs, I broke into a run. I ran, ducking low under the avocado trees. Then I was up the driveway to the other side of the house, then down the slope, under the prickly shedding tree and to the umbrella tree, where Sonny and Butch had had a fort. Then, quick as a flash, I was running out from under it, sliding down the iceplant-covered embankment. Then I was climbing the kennel fence. Then, in one jump, I was on the doghouse roof. Then, in one more jump, I was on the fat gray wall that surrounded Daddy's property and formed one side of the kennel. Then I was climbing up the curving steps that formed each of the wall's four corners.

A tour bus passed. I could see one side of it, tilting towards me. I saw cameras at the windows and straw hats pressed against them.

Cross-legged, on the wall's edge, I raised my arms over my head at them and screamed.

Part Two

CHAPTER 8

We were packing. Mother, Butch, and I were flying to Boston that night. We were meeting Sonny, who was coming from boarding school near Boston, and then we were all going to Maine for summer vacation. Daddy had finally agreed to let me go.

Mother went into the bathroom and waved her finger at me from the doorway.

I followed her.

Mother pulled me into the bathroom and shut the door. She turned and faced me, with her hands behind her, still holding the doorknob. She said she had something wonderful to tell me: we were *not* going to Boston that night; she and I were going to New York and I was going to have my eye operated on!

I jumped up; Mother caught me. I wrapped my legs around her waist and my arms around her shoulders. We were both amazed that I could do that even though I was so big. But Mother couldn't hold me for long. Her arms trembled. I slid back down again. As I was sliding down I started to cry.

"There! There!" Mother said. "*Of course* you're crying because you're happy and scared and it's such a surprise.

But you're going to be beautiful, you'll see. It's almost like a fairy story, isn't it?"

"It's not that," I said. "It's just that . . ."

"I know," Mother said. "It's more than that."

Mother went out of the bathroom and told Butch. Butch looked surprised for a second, but then said, "Big deal," and went back to packing. Mother pretended not to hear him. Mother said to Butch that that meant he would be flying to Boston alone now. He could tell Sonny when he got to Boston, but after that, neither he nor Sonny were to tell anyone else. Jennifer was not going to be in Maine until much later and Mother was not going to tell Jennifer until she had gotten to Maine because Jennifer couldn't keep a secret. We had to be careful so that Daddy wouldn't find out. . . .

"Wait a minute," Butch said. "You mean you're doing all this without Daddy knowing?"

"Well, you know how . . . strange your father is about Robin's eye."

"Hey, that's pretty . . . interesting."

In the plane, Mother told me that just in case, Peter and she thought it would be a good idea if I had an assumed, that was a made-up, name, for the eye operation and so they had made one up for me already and had a bed reserved for me in the hospital and the doctor was going to operate on me under that name. It was Susan Brown.

"Susan Brown?"

"Yes. From now on, you are Susan Brown. And if anyone asks you what your name is, even any men in doctors' uniforms, you are to say it's Susan Brown. They might be detectives dressed to look like doctors. But I don't think we have anything to worry about. Oh, I'm so glad it's being done! If you only knew how awful it was to see you getting bigger every day, still with your eye shut! If you only *knew* how it broke my heart to have you come home from school and hear you tell me about how mean children had been to you! If you only knew how, all last year, I wanted to tell you, 'It's going to be done this summer!' If you only knew how I hated the idea of you in that big queer house with those queer people last summer. But it all worked out because we're going to New York and you're going to be *beautiful!*"

Mother put her arms around me, pulled me over the arm-rest, and kissed me all over my face.

. . . .

There was something on my face when I awoke. I felt up with my hands. There were bandages all around my head. A ponytail cascaded from the top, skimpy because half my hair had been caught up in bandages. I could feel a lump of it at the side of my head. People, when they saw me, would think I had thin hair, and thin hair was the one thing I did not have. Even Butch had to admit that I did have nice, thick hair.

I saw a table leg out of the corner of one eye. I tried to move my eyes to see more of the table, but the other eye, the eye that was behind the bandages, wouldn't go. And then I remembered a spinning ceiling and the squeak of rubber on linoleum and the undersides of people's chins, like sharks swimming over me, some of them with blue-black whiskers on them, that I had said "You're so strong" to, surprising myself, as they lifted me in big arms.

"One, two, three," I said to my eye, "four."

Pain came, cracking up from my left foot and down from the left side of my forehead to my eye, where the two pains met and became one hot hole of pain down which sand and pebbles slid. There were stitches. My eyeball grated underneath them.

I threw up into an enameled kidney-shaped dish. The thought "It's kidney-shaped" made me feel even sicker. "Nurse," I groaned, the way I'd heard other children groaning "nurse" the night before.

"What do you want?" the nurse said, coming into my cubicle.

"I threw up," I said weakly.

"So?"

"I . . . I threw up."

The nurse came over to the bed, picked up the kidney-shaped dish, and emptied the vomit into a plastic bucket on the floor. "If you throw up anymore," she said, "just empty it into the bucket."

"But . . . I can't move!"

"Try," she said. She turned and left the cubicle.

I lay back down on my side and stayed there without moving. The light in the room grew and faded with passing cars. I felt a lump in my throat sending a shrill whisper into my brain. In California, Alice had always been in my room at the first retch and had held my hair back from my face and made sympathetic noises as I leaned over a pink plastic wastebasket, which had been filled partially with water and placed beside my bed the night before, as soon as I said I was feeling funny. Mother and Busy did the same thing, too, though they couldn't get back all the hair around my face so that I sometimes had to shout, between retches, "My hair! My hair!"

I did not think getting my eye fixed would be like this. I knew that it would hurt but . . . I did not think that I would have to throw up alone, alone in a room that was so close to the road that car lights beamed and faded on the ceiling, like in rooms in movies in which people hid from the police. I wondered if it was because I was in the East, if in the East people said, "So?" when you said you were feeling bad and if in the East people threw up alone. I remembered billboards on the way from the airport advertising "Hotel Bar" butter instead of Edgemar and "Yoo-Hoo" chocolate drink instead of Bosco. It was so different, the East, so different. I remembered the hotel room I had stayed in with Mother the night before going to the hospital, with no bathroom, but a sink right in the room with gray pits in it that I thought was dirt at first but that Mother said was just from being old. I remembered Mother looking around the room and saying, "It's such a hideout! Exciting, isn't it? It's just like . . ." and then saying a lot of words that she explained were the titles of different plays.

I wanted to call the nurse back in and say, "But I'm . . . !"

My eye moved, sending a purple streak across the inside of my bandage, turning my whole body limp around it.

"I'm Susan Brown," I said after a while.

I was the oldest child in the ward, but Mother wouldn't let me be in a grownup ward or have a private or a semiprivate room because she said it was too expensive and being in the ward would be a good experience for me.

Some children were cross-eyed. Some children had eyes that jiggled or eyes that blinked all the time. Some children had white milky eyes that were going to be removed in a day or two; some children's already had been, the lids over the empty sockets like wilted petals, the empty eye sockets themselves as they struggled still to lift their eyelids looking the way it did under anyone's lower eyelid when you pulled it down, only going all the way back.

I went into the bathroom and threw up breakfast, lunch, and dinner on my knees in front of lowered toilets in doorless cubicles.

I looked out the window, waiting to see Mother coming down the street. The mothers who could see (for many of the mothers were blind as well) looked out for her, too, and when Mother finally appeared, announced, "La senora iss coming!"

Mother walked down the center aisle and called, "How are you today? How are you today?" The mothers smiled, showing gold teeth, and said, "Feing, feing!"

Mother sat with blind mothers who had been told their babies would not be born blind, too. She listened to long stories about brothers-in-law, fires, welfare, and said, "Ah, I'm sorry, ah, I'm so so sorry."

Mother gave me blind babies to hold. She said she was almost embarrassed that what I had was so minor. She said I should try to think about what life was like for them on the other side of their sockets. It was black. It wasn't like night, it wasn't like shutting your eyes, it was black like... black paper. Mother wanted to know if I could imagine that.

My eye scratched under the stitches in my eyelid. "*Uh-huh*," I said, surprising myself. I never knew how what I said was going to turn out. I would start to say something and my eye would hurt, making me say the rest of the words louder or higher or making me turn the words into sounds only.

Mother told me not to be so sullen. I said I wasn't being sullen, it was just that I COULD IMAGINE IT!

Mother gave the baby she had been holding back to its mother. Smiling, the mother took the baby, her watery white eyes still staring straight ahead. Mother grabbed me by the wrist. "Excuse me a minute," Mother said. The woman nodded. Mother led me out through the curtains surrounding the cubicle, into my own cubicle, and shut the curtain behind us.

"I've had enough of your attitude! Can't you realize these women and children are agonized, are *in pain?* Have you any idea what it would be like to *lose your eye?* Have you?"

"*Uh*-huh." I had not meant to say what she said was "sullen" again. It just came out.

"Answer me! Have you any idea what it would be like to lose your eye?"

"I do. I do have." My voice was normal, I thought. But still she looked mad.

"Well then, what's wrong with you?"

"There's nothing wrong with me. It's just that my eye hurts."

"I'm *sorry* your eye hurts, but it's been several days now, and your operation was such a little thing and they have such *terrible* things wrong with them. If you thought a little more about them, then maybe you'd forget about your own pain and stop acting this way."

"Acting what way?"

"There you go again. . . ."

"No . . . ah," I said, gasping at a new pain that had just shot through my eye. "How do you want me to be?"

"BE WITH THEM. BE CHEERFUL."

. . . .

I wore sunglasses out of the hospital and pyjama bottoms rolled up under my dress because Mother had forgotten to pack any underwear. My sockless feet sweated in patent-leather pumps. The innersoles stuck to my feet and came up with them every time I took a step.

Standing over me as the last bandage was removed and light pierced my eye, so that I squirmed in my seat, Mother and the doctor told me that my eyelid had to be *over*-corrected, had to be actually opened *wider* than the other, to allow for the stub of muscle to which my eyelid was attached (yes, the doctor had found a stub, wasn't that great?) to stretch, so that, until it stretched, my eye would appear to be *staring*.

"But you said—"

"It's just for a little while."

I told myself that I knew I wasn't going to be beautiful. I told myself that Mother, in saying "beautiful," had never said "right away." I told myself I knew to never more than half-believe things Mother said, and never, ever, to embroider on them, but still I had thought about it a little bit: Bandages removed to reveal me with a tiara. Bandages removed to reveal me in solid Courrèges. Bandages removed to reveal me looking like Jean Shrimpton. Bandages removed to have everyone going "Oooooo . . ." It was like in those stories of people who thought, for a while, that they had gotten their wishes but then didn't because they had forgotten to mention one thing when they made them, like eternal youth instead of eternal life, and so they just got older and older.

Mother led me down a subway entrance and asked at a token booth. We exited and walked down another way.

"Chicklets?" a voice asked.

We looked around. A black man was holding Chicklets out to us on a bright pink palm. Mother took one and nudged me to take one, too. She smiled a half-smile and nudged me to smile at him, too. "We don't want to antagonize . . ." she mumbled. "Thank you very much!" she said loudly. He put the box of Chicklets back in his pocket and asked Mother if she would have a drink with him. Mother squeezed my wrist, looked down at the ground, and started moving away from him. He followed, saying he would call her up sometime.

The train came. We stepped into a car. The black man stepped in after us. Mother looked around and, still holding me by the wrist, walked over to where a priest in a wide black hat was sitting. She sat down next to him. "Oh, Father," she said, "please engage me in conversation because that colored fellow over there has been pursuing us and I'm a little nervous."

"Sorry," the priest said, with a heavy accent. "So little English."

"Oh," Mother said. She went on to indicate with veiled looks and gestures "man" . . ."followed" . . ."scared."

"Ah, I see!" the priest said, nodding his head.

The black man got off at the next stop. Mother sighed. "Thank you so much, Father. You really saved us."

"Yes, yes!" the priest said.

Mother asked the priest where he was from. He named the country. It was very small, he said, in the Middle East. Mother asked him how long he was going to be in the United States and where he planned to go. Mother had to ask him several times, in different ways, to get him to understand the questions. "Don't miss the South," she said.

"The South?"

"Virginia. People nicer. More gracious."

"Sorry. So little English."

"South. People smile." Mother smiled. "People give."

Mother held out her hand. "North. People mmh!" Mother frowned.

"Ah, yes!" the priest said, nodding.

"And California. California nice, too."

"California, yes."

"It has attractive parts."

"Sorry."

"Attractive places."

"Mother, he doesn't know what 'attractive' means."

"No always freeways. Orange trees."

"Yes, yes!" the priest said.

At one subway stop, the priest and Mother and I rose to get off. "Ah, I see we're getting off at the same stop," Mother said. "How nice. Would you care to join me and Robin for lunch at the Museum of Modern Art?"

Mother always said "Robin" just like that, to strangers, who had no idea who or what that was. "Have you seen Robin?" Mother asked puzzled shopgirls when she lost me for a moment in stores.

"Sorry, so little English."

"I invite you to lunch!" Mother said, pressing her fingers together and touching the tips of them to her lips.

"Ah, I see! Thank you!"

As we were walking down the street, a short, dark woman stopped in front of us and let her shopping bags drop to the ground. The priest stopped. We stopped beside him. The woman started crossing herself violently. Her eyes filled with tears. The priest started crossing himself. He gave a low moan. They ran into each other's arms.

"Patr, patr," she cried.

"Diu," he cried.

Leaving one arm around the woman, the priest turned to us. "Miracul," he said. "Our country. War. Big, big. Bombs. Hide. Church. Under, under." He made a motion with his hands. "Ten days. All together. No food. Many dead."

"No food. Many dead." The woman crossed herself between tears.

Mother embraced the woman, sweeping her up onto her tiptoes. Mother then pushed me towards the woman. She hugged me in her big arms. Mother reached into her pocketbook, drew out a Kleenex, and blew her nose. Mother asked the woman to come to lunch with us. The priest translated, speaking rapidly in their language. The woman smiled at us and nodded.

The priest and the woman walked towards the museum with their arms around each other. We walked behind them.

"Isn't this wonderful?" Mother said.

Mother paid admission.

"No, no," the priest said.

"Yes, yes," Mother said.

People stared at us.

"Can I go look at the paintings?"

"No, you cannot. And what's wrong with you? Don't you want to take part in this wonderful . . . reunion?"

"My eye hurts."

Mother found a table and told the priest and the woman to sit at it while we got them food.

"Cannot we help to you?" the priest asked, rising.

"No, no, this is fine!"

"They had no food, no food," Mother said, standing at the counter with a tray. I held another one. Mother put on our trays three spoons, a fork ("But there are four of us!" I said), five rolls, a fistful of butter pats, one salad, two hot dogs, a Swiss steak dinner ("That priest must be hungry," she said), a relish plate, two slices of cream pie, a cup of coffee with milk, half sloshed out into the saucer, and a lemon wedge.

"You know New York is so wonderful," Mother announced to the man in front of her. We were standing in the line at the cash register. He turned and looked at her, then at me. He did not speak or move his face. He was in his late twenties, tall, with curly blond hair. He was wearing old-fashioned horn-rimmed glasses and a well-pressed gabardine suit. Mother told him the whole story of the man on the subway, the priest, the woman. Mother's face was turned up to his. She finished the story. She was still smiling. He still did not say a word.

It was the man's turn at the cash register. He put down his tray and reached into his pants pocket for money. Mother was smiling even harder.

"Do you know what time it is?" Mother asked him finally, her voice a little less cheerful.

He held up his wristwatch for her to see.

"I'm sorry!" she said, laughing apologetically. "I can't see. I don't have my glasses. Can you tell me what time it is?"

"T-t-t-t-t-t-t-t-t-t-t-tw-tw-ywe-twenty-t-t-t-to-en-t-t-en-t-two!" he said.

"For a minute there I thought he was impervious to my charms," Mother whispered to me on our way back to the table. "But that was just because of his stutter. He was shy."

"Dammit," I thought. "Goddammit." I felt my pyjamas rolled up under my skirt. I thought everyone could see them making my skirt balloon.

I felt my eye start to sting.

Mother put the food and silverware out on the table. I

counted the seconds until she noticed we needed knives, forks, hot dogs, napkins, more to drink. I wasn't going to tell her.

"Robin!" Mother said gaily. "We have forgotten a lot of things. We need knives, forks, napkins, hot dogs, spoons, and Father? Would you like something to drink, something besides milk?"

"That's *my* milk," I wanted to say, but didn't.

"No, no, yes, yes!" the priest said.

"Yes, yes," the woman said, nodding and smiling.

. . . .

Daddy was waiting at the bottom of the stairs leading from the plane. He didn't wave or call to me. He was breathing heavily. His alligator-shirted chest and stomach were moving in and out rapidly. His shoulders were moving up and down. His eyes were glazed. There were men on either side of him, in heavy woolen suits. I clutched in my pocket the compact of beige makeup Mother had given me, that I had used five minutes before in the bathroom of the airplane, so that my eye would not look so black and blue.

Daddy did not kiss me.

Daddy introduced me to the men standing on either side of him. One was from Switzerland, one was from Argentina, one was from Mexico, and one was from Germany. Daddy had had them flown over so that they could see what the doctor in New York had done to my eye. The doctor from Argentina smiled at me. He had one gold incisor.

We drove home in the limousine. I sat in the middle of the backseat. Daddy sat on one side of me, a doctor sat on the other. Two others sat on jump seats, facing me. One sat in the front seat, next to a chauffeur I had never seen before. I wondered if he had come from an agency.

We pulled up under the porte cochere. I felt a hand on my arm. It was Daddy's. It was very firm. He opened the door and climbed out, pulling me out after him. I felt another hand on my other arm. Daddy had me gripped between them.

"We're just going to go into the living room and you're going to lie down on the sofa and the doctors are going to have a look at your eye."

Daddy pushed me ahead of him through the front door. I felt a cool patch on each of my arms, across which a breeze was blowing, turning the sweat where Daddy's hands had been cold. Daddy's hands were not on my arms anymore.

My legs sprang forward. I ran. I ran before I realized Daddy's hands not being on my arms meant I could run. I ran through the bar, through the living room, dining room, and pantry. People came out to get me, but I managed to steer around them every time. Once or twice it even almost seemed as if they were falling back, just as they were about to catch me.

The sounds of their feet grew fainter behind me. I ran down the backstairs and into the basement, through big steel doors and into the back part of the basement. I climbed over bicycles and into the air duct.

. . . .

A siren started up somewhere. It grew louder. I turned and, seated, started pushing with my hands and pulling with my feet, out towards the mouth of the duct. My dress rode up. My underpants became so dusted that they slid on the dusty metal easily. Voices echoed along the metal, a low voice and a hoarse, high voice. The high voice was saying the same thing over and over again. "Oh," I finally made out, "oh, oh, o-o-o-o-h-h."

"Woa, here she comes," the deep voice said. "You gave us quite a scare, little lady! That's it, here you go. . . ." The flashlight was lowered. I could make out a Bel Air patrolman's uniform. He was standing on a box. Busy was standing on the floor next to him. She had her hands against her chest and was saying, "Oh, *o-h-h-h-h,*" over and over again. The Bel Air patrolman reached out, picked me out of the mouth of the duct, and put me on the floor.

"Oh, thank you, officer," Busy said, putting a blanket around me, the way people did after rescuing people from fires or earthquakes, even though it was already hot in the basement, "*thank you.*"

"Don't mention it, ma'am," the Bel Air patrolman said.

Busy put an arm around me and walked with me up the basement stairs. "Oh, *oh-h-h-h-h,*" she said. I could feel her trembling.

She opened the door leading to the basement stairs and stumbled with me out into the pantry. There was no one in the pantry and no one in the kitchen. She let go of me, lurched forward and leaned on her arms against the new refrigerator that stood in the middle of the pantry. "*Oh-h-h-h-h, oh-h-h, oh-h-h-h-h-h-h-h!*" She turned around after a while and leaned on her shoulders against the refrigerator. Her eyes were shut under her glasses. Tears streaked down her cheeks and glinted in the new fluorescent tube that Daddy had had put above. "Dat dat should haff been done," she said, breathing heavily, "and now you do dis, to your father, who is a *sent!*"

. . . .

Judy acted hurt, too, every weekend we were at Daddy's house that fall. She looked at me, then looked away, shaking her head. "Your dad's on the telephone. He's getting mad at your mom again," she said, or, "Your dad's on the telephone talking to his lawyer. He's gonna *sue* that doctor who did your eye!"

I walked around Daddy's house ready to dive under tables, waiting for the incredibly violent things that people at Mother's house and people at Daddy's house acted as if Daddy would do if anyone ever did anything Daddy didn't want them to do.

At Mother's house, I waited for Mother to make a face and hold the phone away from her ear and for Daddy's voice to sound in the air, loud and threatening, but that never happened, either. Mother went through the house humming. "Your dad likes your eye," she said. "He just can't admit it. He's doing the fancy footwork in his mind now and just watch: in a little while he'll be acting like *he* had it done."

. . . .

Daddy started getting up earlier than usual and having breakfast in the dining room. Judy said he did that so that he would not have me coming down the corridor to be with him while he had breakfast in his room. He wore the alligator shirt and the gray flannel pants, too, that he had worn when he was married to Rita, instead of the Hawaiian trunks and matching sport shirt he usually wore in the mornings. Judy said he was doing that so that he wouldn't have to go back to his room to change to go to the driving range and have me walking behind him down the corridor. Judy said I was not to go down that corridor, no way. Judy said it made Daddy too sad to see what that doctor had done to my eye, open, staring all black and blue. She shook her head. There was no way I'd ever have a boyfriend now. Judy said she didn't understand why I didn't run like hell from Mother when Mother said she was going to take me to New York and call Daddy. Or once I was in New York, call Daddy from somewhere, I knew how to make long distance calls, and Daddy would have come and gotten me wherever I was. Judy said Daddy couldn't understand why I would want to *leave* him like that.

I peek around the gold doors that lead into the living room to see Daddy sitting there, dressed. Daddy sees me seeing him out of the corner of his eye and starts to smile, but then shrugs his lips back over his teeth and keeps on staring straight ahead.

It was like Mother, telling me detectives were going to go up to me at the hospital, when none ever did. It was like Mother telling me I was going to be beautiful, when that hadn't happened, either. It was, or it seemed like it was, like Mother telling me anything almost anytime, except when it was like Jennifer telling me Busy's voice would get higher and higher, until it broke your eardrums like Caruso's, when all she did was screech. It was like coming out from under your desk after bomb drill, blinking, half thinking that, even though you hadn't heard any noise, you would still somehow find the school in rubble, the teachers wandering dazed in shredded clothing, unable to teach you anymore, or even better, dead, and Grade Five and Cuban invaders (who Kennedy said were mean but were actually very nice) the only people left in the world, with houses full of clothes and Good Humor Bars and cars with keys in them, which the Cubans would let us drive, standing behind us and smiling and saying, "Hasta luego!" as we pulled out, when all there was when we came up from under our desks was Miss Schmidlapp, steely, telling us our homework assignment for that night. And then, when the things didn't happen the way the grownups had said they would happen, the grownups never said, "We're sorry, we're *sorry* things did not work out that way!" when you had had to act as if they were going to happen for so long. It was as if they had *forgotten* what they'd said and expected you to do the same.

"How are you today, Judy Girl?" Daddy says finally, scooping poached eggs off a serving dish while staring straight ahead.

"Fine, Mr. D."

"I like having my Judy Girl sleep well. Don't I like having my Judy Girl sleep well?"

"Yes, Mr. D."

CHAPTER 9

Most of the weekends at Daddy's house now, it was just Sonny and me. Jennifer was in the East and Butch didn't want to go to Daddy's house. He said it was too boring. He went surfing instead. I asked Mother if I couldn't not go, too, but Mother said it was important for me to go to give Daddy and Sonny a sense of family. I asked Mother if Butch couldn't give just as much of a sense of family as I could, but Mother said she didn't want Butch to be influenced by Sonny and besides, he *needed* to surf right then, he needed to have some outlet for the excess energy that his . . . poobitry . . . was causing him to have.

"But I thought he went through whatchamacallit a couple of years ago!"

"His growing up has been difficult."

I then asked Mother if she wasn't afraid I might be influenced by Sonny, but Mother closed her eyes and said, "Just help me, please."

. . . .

Daddy went barefoot and wore Hawaiian trunks and a matching sport shirt all the time now and kept the heat in the house turned to eighty so he wouldn't be cold. Sonny and I opened windows when Daddy wasn't around, but Judy always came running up behind us and shut them. Judy liked the house warm, too, because she was from Guam.

Daddy had gone back to having breakfast in his room, but I had not gone back to going in after Daddy's tray, and Daddy had not called up Busy on the intercom and asked for me.

I could hear Daddy through an open window sometimes, rustling his newspaper and yelling, "Martin Luther King's a communist! Can't those boys in Washington see that? It's as plain as day!"

Daddy had given up going out in the afternoons and had given up seeing Rita. Fewer people had started coming over. Even Dr. Villalobo had stopped flying in from Mexico. Daddy said he'd just get that Judy Girl to give him a little shot. Daddy said Judy Girl was the only person who really understood what was wrong with him.

Judy said the trouble was that not many people had it and so the doctors did not know what to do. They did not even recognize it when they did see it. In Guam many, many people had it. People were stopped up, stopped up everywhere. They called it "urgno," which meant "no come out." Judy got shots to give Daddy from a good Guam doctor. "All doctors in Guam give peoples shots, make peoples feel better," she said.

Daddy pats Judy's knee and says that no one has taken care of little Daddy Boy for a long time.

Judy pats Daddy's cheeks. "Oh, you gorgeous hunk of man, you," she says, her voice faltering. She repeats in a stronger voice: "Oh, you gorgeous, sexy hunk of man!"

. . . .

Sonny lived at Daddy's house all the time now. He had moved into the wing off the kitchen, empty since Midge had left, after graduating from boarding school.

He had been sent to Daddy's house by Mother in the first place spring break of his senior year in high school after Mother had come back early from a weekend and had found scotch and beer bottles strewn over the front lawn, and a bra, and something in an ashtray by Sonny's bed that I never got to see and that Butch only said "oo-la-la" about, that made Mother turn pale and say, "You go on over to your father's house. I'd like to see if he'd put up with that kind of behavior for one minute." Then when Sonny had just stood there grinning, saying, "But, Mom, I didn't think you'd even know what one looked like!" Mother had screamed, "Go on! Go on!" and pushed Sonny out the door, ripping the back of his T-shirt as she did so, so that the two white halves of his T-shirt flapping on his back as he walked on up the driveway looked like angel wings.

Sonny looked different. He wore a different kind of clothes: bell-bottom pants that were too tight for him, leather sandals, and T-shirts with holes in them. He also had a small beard. Sonny looked like the men we yelled "Beaver!" to out the car window on the way to school, like the kind of people who wore love beads and went to sit-ins.

I thought Sonny wouldn't like hearing Daddy yelling that Martin Luther King was a communist but he just grinned and said, "If that's what he thinks, that's groovy."

I thought Daddy wouldn't like Sonny looking like he did but he didn't notice. He just said "Hhrhl" as he looked at Sonny, his voice grinding in the middle: "My little Sonny Boy . . . and some little hhr-girl."

Sonny talked differently. His voice sounded higher and

gentler, as if he weren't opening his throat up all the way, and he said words like "heavy" and "groovy" and "far oooouuuuuuut!," which made me think of paper rockets arching into the distance.

Sonny's friends came to the house. They would knock on the screen door and if Judy was not there, I would answer it, but almost as soon as I was opening the door, Sonny would be standing in the pantry, saying, "Hey, in here." They would go into the wing off the kitchen, then come out a few minutes later, stuffing tinfoil packets into their jeans. They would jerk if they saw me and look around, but Sonny would say, "She's cool."

Sonny would say "she's cool" about me, then after his friends left, he would put his arm around my shoulders and squeeze them and say, "Ooo-ooo!" his voice rising on the last "ooo."

Sonny would say "she's cool" about Judy, too, and put his arm around her. Then they both would look at me and smile.

I would smile back at both of them, stepping from one leg to the other, and then after a while, wander from the overheated house to the terrace and feel the breeze blow over my newly-shaven legs. "I am cool," I would think. "I am *cool*." I would wonder if it meant my eye had finally started to be O.K.-looking and if it meant Sonny was going to be nice to me from then on, and I would smile, thinking it was wonderful and amazing and funny, all at the same time, that Sonny and I knew someone Judy's age, someone thirty-four, who took stock in things we said and knew about things like being cool. I would think of me in the future after having been solidly cool for a year: me in thirty-inch-wide bell bottoms with a giant peace symbol painted on one cheek, me in love beads and Navajo boots, me with my hair down to my knees.

Girls came over. Sonny would go out in one of the limousines and come back with them. Usually there would be one, but sometimes there would be two or three. He would go into the wing with his arms around them and shut the door. They wouldn't come out for hours. Sometimes they wouldn't come out until the next day. Other times the girls would come out, without Sonny, and wander around.

"Where am I?" they would say when they saw me.

I would tell them.

"Far out!" they would say.

They would stand looking at the chandeliers in the living room and say, "Wow, wow," over and over again.

Sometimes they would see Daddy looking at them from the darkness of the hallway.

"Heh, heh, hrrrhll," Daddy would say, coughing, "one of Sonny's little gha-hrrlhhs."

"Who was that?" they would ask me, after he disappeared back into the darkness of the hallway again.

"My dad."

"Far out, oh, *far out.*"

Sonny would go for days without eating but then come out and says, "Judy? How about a big scarf," and Judy would cook an enormous meal.

Judy had started cooking again. She started after Sonny said to Judy that he'd kind of like a little stroganoff sometime. He remembered she used to make it. Judy said, "Well, why didn't you ask?" Then she blew the dust off the stove and made beef stroganoff for us.

Judy made limestone lettuce with green goddess dressing, fried chicken, sweet and sour pork, spare ribs, filet mignon, snow peas, rock cornish game hen, baked Alaska, pigs in blankets, crêpes Suzette, hot turkey sandwiches, quiche Lorraine, mushroom omelets, pizza, banana splits, hot fudge sundaes, ice cream sodas, guacamole, chiles rellenos, flan, and strawberry shortcake. She said that all we'd ever had to do was ask.

I went into the kitchen several times a day to watch all the burners burning, sometimes as many as six. I watched Judy as she cooked. I watched Judy's capable hands. I watched her smooth brown arms. Her skin was a perfect color, I decided, a kind of permanent tan. I watched her eyes, intent on chopping. They were a perfect shape, in between slanted and round. I watched her perfect small nose. I watched her with eyes that were so much easier to watch with now, not having to lift my head up, not having to move my head this way and that to take in the whole scene. Judy was perfect, I decided.

"See, Busy?" we would say as we sat at the table, stuffing ourselves. "All we had to do was ask."

"Ach," Busy said, pushing at the air with her hands.

•   •   •   •

Mother stands by the front door when I come back from Daddy's house on Sunday nights and asks me if it is true that Daddy wears Hawaiian trunks and a matching sport shirt all the time and if it is true that Sonny takes drugs and deals drugs and has girls over to spend the entire night.

"I don't know," I say, and wait for someone to come down the driveway, or for a pot on the stove to start melting or for Na-Na to wander out into the garden with nothing on but a string of pearls, so that I can slip past Mother into my room, but she keeps on looking at me.

Mother says not to play the innocent with her.

"Innocent?" I repeat, and wait for my eye to start stinging, so that I can blink it and rub it and walk past Mother into the bathroom for ointment, but it keeps feeling just the same.

Mother then says in a softer tone that she is sorry to burden me, but I am the only one she has left. . . .

I shrug. "I just don't know," I say, and skirt past her to my room, my round patent-leather overnight case with the poodles and Eiffel Towers on it that I hate banging against my newly-shaven legs.

. . . .

Butch saw my newly shaven legs and sighed, "At last. Finally you're turning into something which is not totally *beneath my contempt.*"

Butch's hair, bleached blond by the sun, hung down over his ears. His face, more tan than ever, caused his yellow-green eyes to glow even brighter. He was wearing baggy surfer trunks, a Hang Ten T-shirt and zorries.

Butch put one foot in front of the other on my bedroom rug, as if he were walking on a surfboard, his arms out. "But you still do homework. That worries me. Walk to the nose. And your pits now, what about your pits?" He reached for my wrist and tried to pull my arm over my head. I twisted my wrist out of his grip. He teetered. "Don't pull me off my board, Robs, don't pull me off my board!" He regained his balance. "Hang five." He pushed one foot very far forward and curled his toes over the end of an imaginary board. "That's pretty good, now . . . hang ten!" He brought the other foot up and curled both toes over. He closed his eyes. "The supreme moment. And all the girls on the beach are yelling, 'Butch, Butch!' And I yell back at them, but very suavely, 'Later, girls.' And all the surfers waiting on their boards are saying, 'He's *so* cool.' And I am thinking to myself, 'You handsome stud, don't you ever die.' Then I back up." Butch opened his eyes and put one foot behind the other. "Then if I see a situation ahead that I don't like, if there are rocks and shit, I just surf around it." He crouched more and leaned on one foot. "There's Mother up ahead! Bank to the left! There's Dad!" He leaned on the other foot. "Bank to the right! You don't want to get involved in those rocks and shit. No no," Butch said, in a way that sounded like "nu nu." "Then, when the wave is no longer big enough to be worth your time and you're close enough to the beach for the girls to be able to check your bod, you pull out!" Butch put one foot behind the other and twisted with a jerking motion. "The board comes up to you and you sit down . . ." Butch opened his legs wide and fell on his hands, "to wait, but for a short time, for another moment of *glory!*" Butch shut his eyes and threw his head back. He lowered himself onto the rug. He stayed with his eyes shut for about a minute, then opened them and said, "So tell me about your girlfriends at school. Tell me about the one that's so ugly."

"Carol?"

"Yeah, Carol. Tell me what bra size she wears."

. . . .

One of the maids has sunglasses on, with black and blue spreading beyond the rims. Another has a bandage over her nose ringed with black and blue marks. Another has her neck in a sling attached to a gauze headband circling her head.

They look at me. "Your daddy sure did a good job on your eye," they say.

"Oh *brother*," Minnie whispers.

We still went to Trader Vic's at least one night every weekend. Daddy would have forgotten but the headwaiter would call up and say, "Are you coming tonight? We have your table reserved for you," and Daddy would say, "Sure, sure!", then call Busy on the intercom and ask her to bring her sister, then call the very newest maids, then call Don and Minnie and Judy. Then Minnie would call Busy, and Minnie and Busy would talk for a long time about how Daddy was too sick to go, then they would sigh and say the company would probably do him good.

"Now, say you've heard of this little old place where there might—" Daddy tilts his hand one way, then the other, over the drink he is making, "be something under the ground. Got to check her out. Got to make inquiries. Got to fight off the other guys and court those farmers for those leases. Got to go every day to those farmers, even though you feel like an asshole, sometimes with a pineapple, other times with a box of chocolates, other times with a Brownie camera and take everybody's picture on the front porch, even the niggers, even the women who look like hell. Got to get 'em to know you, get 'em to like you. You dress neat but not slick. You tell 'em your daddy's a preacher. You even take your daddy to meet 'em. Sometimes, you borrow your daddy's hat and collar and tell them *you're* a preacher, when they're ignorant enough. Then, once they agree to give you a lease, got to negotiate a good lease, one that gives you plenty and that you can get out of. Then, once she's yours, you always have to do a lot of things *to* her before you set up your rig. Got to cut brush. Got to cut fences and build fences. Got to square off that acreage and balance out the number of wells you drill with the amount of draw. Got to make a road. Got to set up trailers for the men to rest in and even eat in and sleep in when it's that far out, with little awnings outside so they don't fry in the heat. Got to set up a Port-A-John and a generator for power and electric lights. Got to do a lot of other things that I'm probably forgetting about now, and then, and only then, can you set up your rig and drill."

Daddy looks down into his glass, swirling the ice inside it. One of the new maids looks at me through her bandages and smiles.

Daddy sighs. "It's so sad to be an ugly woman," Daddy says. He shakes his head. "Men can be ugly and get away with it. There's a certain charm to some ugly men, but an ugly woman, she just has *nothing* going for her. Big calves, a big behind, fat arms, skinny arms, a skinny neck, no neck, curvature of the spine, no chin, no chin coupled with a big nose and buck teeth, so that the chin seems to recede even more, a mustache, meeting eyebrows . . ."

"Chin hairs," Judy prompts.

"Chin hairs," Daddy repeats. He lowers his chin onto his chest and sips his drink. "Ear hairs. I've never heard of ear hairs on a woman, but I'm sure some women have that, too. Ears that stick out. Baldness. Short legs, flat feet, knock-knees, varicose veins, ugly hands, ugly feet, bunions, toes when . . . one toe rides up over the other and then just . . . *sits* there." Daddy shows us with his fingers. "There are so many ways for a woman to be ugly, so many ways." Daddy looks down at his drink and shakes his head. He takes a long sip. Some of the maids shake their heads, too. "Not to mention birth defects and all the crippling diseases, tuberculosis, skin cancer, polio, pelagra, rheumatic fever so that you go bald, multiple sclerosis and all of the other sclerosises. There are so many ways to be ugly. And then you can get a woman with a beautiful face and an ugly figure, or with a beautiful face, a beautiful figure, but with a pair of ankles that just make you want to cry!" Daddy's voice goes up a few notes. He takes another sip. His eyes glisten. "But the saddest thing for an ugly woman is never to know love. Never to be taken in a man's arms. Never to be hugged and kissed and . . . mmh . . ."

Daddy picks up his glass and tilts it as far back as it will go, drinking the rest of the liquid and sucking the ice into his mouth, then spitting it out with a gurgling sound.

"There was this crippled girl. Lived on some land I leased. She loved it when I came. I went there lots of times. She used to look at me with such big eyes. And I mean, you took that blanket away and she was withered from here to here. I mean . . ." Daddy starts to come out slowly from the other side of the bar.

"That's all right, Mr. D., you don't have to show us. . . ." Minnie calls from her corner.

Daddy bends slowly and slices his hand across his hip. "From here—" Daddy bends lower and slices his hand across his ankle, "—to here!"

"Patetic," Busy whispers loudly.

"Gosh, she sounds like she was in really bad shape!" one of the new maids calls.

Daddy clears his throat, then continues in a quiet voice: "I didn't lease it from them, really. They gave it to me. Her father did. Hrmpf!" Daddy coughs. "'Hell, you can have the land for free, son, and besides, we like having you around!' HhhhRRRRRmmmmmmpplha!" Daddy tries to clear his throat, then goes on in a higher, thinner voice. "'Amelia's

—that was his daughter—'s awfully fond of you, y'know.' But she was just a crippled thing. Hrmmm, hrmmm. I tried to give him something for it, but he said, 'Oil, I don't believe it, and besides, we like having you around!' I tried to give him something for it, I tried to get that girl to walk. I'd kneel down by her wheelchair and I'd say, 'Franklin Roosevelt, you know who Franklin Roosevelt is, don't you, honey?' She'd nod her head yes. 'Well, he's actually walking, for an hour every day,' but the father would always be behind me, saying, 'We like having you around.' I'd say, 'You can do it, honey, you can walk,' but the father'd always say, 'We like having you around.' But she was just a crippled thing hhr*rml*rrrrlghggga!" Daddy's voice struggles through choking phlegm.

"She died," he says finally, in the highest voice possible.

"Oh, you're so good, Mr. D., so good," Judy whispers.

Daddy stays silent, his jaw working. Judy runs to the bar for a napkin while Daddy waits with one hand covering his mouth, giving low grunts. Judy puts the napkin into Daddy's outstretched hand. He slaps the napkin over the lower part of his face.

"Let it come up, let it come up," Judy says.

Daddy nods. The napkin bulges in the space between his hands. "Bah!" he says, twisting it off at his mouth. He hands it to Judy. She holds it in her lap, her long fingernails curling over it. "So good," she repeats, whispering.

"It's time to go, Mr. D.," Minnie calls.

"Yes, our reservations are for nine-thirty," Busy says.

"I mean . . ." Daddy croaks, "that's all I wanted to do, just go on, *being nice.*"

"We know, Mr. D., we know you did." Judy nudges the maid next to her. They stand in front of Daddy.

"That's all I wanted to do to my baby girl, just go on, being nice. . . ."

"Oh, you're so good, Mr. D., so good," Judy says, shaking her head.

"But that doctor had to take her . . ."

"And you did it, you gave her a beautiful new eye," one of the new maids says.

"Like hell he did," Minnie says, under her breath.

"I was so worried . . ." Daddy whimpers, his lower lip trembling.

"Poor Mr. D.," Judy says.

Judy and the new maids form a circle around Daddy.

"Come hug Daddy," Judy whispers to me over her shoulder.

I stayed where I was and watched.

Judy and the new maids put their arms around him and kiss him, all at once.

"You're gorgeous, Mr. D.," Judy says.

"Yessir, you are," the new maids say in unison.

"One gorgeous—"

"Sexy—"

"Wonderful man."

"Come on, Mr. D., let's go to Trader Vic's," Minnie says.

Daddy starts reaching for empty glasses.

I just watched.

. . . .

"Tell me you've got a dry hole," Daddy says, looking at me. He sways in his seat.

"*WHAT?*" Judy shrieks. Judy and the new maids laugh.

"Say, 'Daddy, Daddy, I've got a dry hole!'"

"It was Butch who used to say that," I say.

"Come on, precious, don't be so—"

"You should do it, it will make him happy," Judy whispers to me. "Oh, you sexy brute, you," she says out loud. She reaches for Daddy's hand across the table.

I look at Judy. She smiles at me and winks.

I looked down at my plate. I was going to keep looking at my plate, I thought, look and look until it started spinning, like in the movies, and I woke up somewhere else with a whole other family and realized that the family I had been with before had been a strange dream.

"Naw," I say out loud.

"Come on," Daddy says.

"Aw, she's shy, Mr. D. . . ."

"I just don't *want to.* . . ."

"What's this, shy? I want my Baby Girl to say, 'Daddy, Daddy, I've got a dry hole!'" Daddy leans forward. He bangs his fist on the table. "Any Daddy Boy's Baby Girl Daddy Baby Daddy!"

"Go on, say it," everyone—it seems like everyone—says.

"*DADDY, DADDY, I'VE GOT A DRY HOLE!*"

. . . .

Halfway though the teriyaki steaks, Don gets up out of his chair. Minnie stands up, clutching her napkin.

Daddy is staring straight ahead.

"Oh, you gorgeous . . ." Judy is saying to him.

"Would you like to go home, Mr. D.?" Don asks, glaring at Judy.

"Let's go home," Daddy says, still staring straight ahead.

Daddy rises up out of his chair, swaying. Don runs around the table and catches Daddy under one arm. Minnie rises and catches him under the other. He sways against them. Judy and the other maids rise, grabbing purses and rabbit fur stoles. Busy and her sister rise.

"Let's go home," Daddy says.

Waiters come up. Don whispers to them. The headwaiter comes up. "Sure, sure," he says. Waiters walk ahead, pushing chairs out of the way. People stop talking and turn and look at us. Daddy is being supported almost entirely by Don and Minnie. He takes a step only every other step: his toes drag on the ground the rest of the time. Everyone else walks behind.

"That's what the prices at this place will do to you," someone in the restaurant says.

We walk past the giant clam shells and stuffed mahi-mahi, past the shields and spears and under the outrigger canoe, past the three Chinese men sweating behind glass.

"What's with the bandages?" someone else in the restaurant says.

The headwaiter is standing at the door. "O.K.," he says, smiling.

"You're a good boy," Daddy says, pulling a hundred-dollar bill out of his pocket and stuffing it into the headwaiter's pocket.

We go past the shrunken head, through the mouth of the giant tiki that is the door, and into the night air. The limousine is already waiting.

Don and Minnie put Daddy on the front seat between them. He slumps down.

We drive home.

"Where are we?" Daddy mumbles, without opening his eyes.

"Home, Mr. D."

"Good."

Don walks around to the passenger side. He and Minnie heave Daddy up onto their shoulders. "Try to make your legs work a little, Mr. D.," Don says.

"They're working, they're working," Daddy says, his toes bumping over the front steps.

They get to the open door. Daddy raises his head a little. His hand clutches the doorframe. Don and Minnie try to carry him further in but he holds on.

"Just let me be a second," Daddy says.

Minnie looks at Don. Don takes himself halfway out from under Daddy's arm. Minnie does the same. Daddy is still standing.

"I'm all right. Just let me go."

Don and Minnie take their hands away. Daddy sways. They put their hands back again quickly.

"I'm O.K., I said!" Daddy looks ahead through dull, red eyes.

Minnie looks at Don. They let him go.

"You can all go home now," Daddy says.

"But, Mr. D. . . ."

"Judy. I want Judy Girl. Judy Girl'll help me."

Everybody else looks at Judy. She winks at everybody. "That's all right. I'll take care of him," she says, walking up to Daddy. "O.K., Mr. D., let's go," Judy says, touching him lightly on the back.

"Judy *GIRRRRRRRLLLLLLLLLLLL!*" Daddy says. He stretches out an arm.

Judy puts a shoulder underneath his arm, laughing.

"Judy *GIRRRRRRLLLLLLLLLLLLL!*" Daddy repeats.

"Ha, ha, you're pretty funny tonight, Mr. D!"

I watched them move forward.

. . . .

"Andrew," Jennifer said. "Andrew is so brilliant. Andrew definitely has to be one of the most brilliant people I've ever met. He is so much more brilliant than Mark. I don't see how I could have *ever* liked anyone like Mark. Mark. Ew!" Jennifer shuddered, hugging a pillow. "His dumb little cartoons. His family and their smelly dogs. Andrew's family, he actually just has a mother, is so much more, how can I put it, is just so much more refined. Has so much more, well . . . class, if you really want to know. I miss Andrew so much. I hate California."

Mother asked Jennifer if she knew that Daddy wore the same Hawaiian trunks and matching sport shirt every day. Mother was standing in the doorway. She scratched under her curler cap and shut her eyes.

Peter was away. Mother was wearing her pink quilted bathrobe with coffee stains down the front and frayed gray cuffs. Every vacation, Jennifer bought Mother silk and voile bathrobes from Montaldo's and Saks. Mother would shake them out of their boxes and say, "How elegant! How really fine!" She would wear them for a few mornings but then slip back into "quilty," and when Jennifer would confront her, ask her why she wasn't wearing one of "her" bathrobes, Mother would say they were lovely bathrobes, really such good quality, but she wanted to save them for special occasions.

Mother said Daddy was up there at the house under the control of Judy. He wore the same Hawaiian trunks and sport shirt every day, all day long, and drank, and took drugs. Sonny lived in the wing off the kitchen. He didn't do anything all day. It was unnatural for a boy college age to be living there. Mother asked Jennifer if she'd heard of LSD: she thought that was what he might be taking. Mother said Jennifer *had* to say something the next time she went there.

"Oh . . . I   hate . . . California," Jennifer   whispered, sighing.

"What did you say?" Mother asked.

"I said I'll *say* something, I'll *say* something."

.   .   .   .

Mother didn't ask Jennifer right after she got home. She waited until Jennifer was in her room unpacking. Mother asked Jennifer if she'd spoken to Daddy and Sonny. Jennifer said she'd spent the day shopping, looking for a present to send back to Andrew, and then by the time she got home, Daddy was all set to go to Trader Vic's, so the time was never right. Jennifer said she was going to call Alice and find out her recipe for toll house cookies and air-mail Andrew a batch of those, too. . . .

A big noise made me look up. Mother had fallen across the bed towards Jennifer.

Jennifer jumped up.

There was a hairbrush in Mother's hand.

"Mother!" Jennifer said.

"You're selfish, you're all just so damn selfish!" Mother said.

"But Mom, what did I do?"

"I've been trying to explain to you, I've been trying to give you insights!"

"But what did I do?"

Mother pushed herself back off the bed and ran towards Jennifer. Jennifer ran out of her room and down the hall. Mother ran after her. I started to laugh for a minute, then stopped: they were both jiggling so much.

. . . .

"Come here," Jennifer whispered loudly, peeking at me through a crack in the door leading to her room.

"What is it?"

"Just . . . come here."

Jennifer shut the door behind me and locked it, then went back to where she had been sitting cross-legged on her bed, in front of her spectrum of cable-knit sweaters and A-line skirts, photographs of Andrew placed between each overlapping skirt and sweater, so that each photograph was framed by a different color, other photographs of Andrew half pulled out a pink satin stocking bag beside her.

"God, she's so lame when she gets mad. It's like she decides: I'm going to get mad. And you can see it. You can see it in the little trembling way she raises her fist. All those years of not getting mad at things she should have *really* gotten mad at, and now some little thing comes along and she decides to get mad. She's so ridiculous. I mean, I really *like* Andrew! He is the nicest person I have ever known. So what's so selfish about going out and getting a present for him? I'd say that was the opposite of selfish, if you asked me."

"I don't think that's what she's so mad about," I said.

"Well, what does she want *me* to do about Daddy and

Sonny? Go over there and say, 'Daddy, do you drink?' 'Sonny, do you take drugs?' How does she *know* they do, anyway? Does she *spy* on them? I think it's creepy, the idea of her *spying* on them. I mean, she's so *intense*. I don't think Daddy takes drugs, do you? Dr. Villalobo doesn't even go there anymore. And he wasn't wearing his Hawaiian trunks the *whole* time we were there. I mean, he put on gray slacks one day and Judy served us that nice dinner. I don't think Judy's such a bad person. I don't think Daddy's under her *control*, do you? God," Jennifer went on, without waiting for me to answer, "that nice dinner made me feel like we were living like real rich people, like the way . . . Andrew's family lives."

Jennifer's eyes, dark brown like Daddy's, were moving back and forth over my eyes.

"I mean, I want a mother who can get herself *together* in the mornings. Who doesn't come out of her room until she is dressed and until she has made sure that her nails are all right and her hair and her makeup." Jennifer trailed the fingers of one hand over the fingers of the other, as if she were putting on an imaginary pair of gloves. "Or who, if she *has* to come out of her room before, can at least have on an attractive, clean bathrobe. Who, even though she may not *speak* French, at least knows how to *pronounce* French words. Who can say 'mieux' instead of 'mur,' let alone the English words she can't pronounce, like 'puberty' instead of 'poobitry.' *Poobitry!* God, where did she pick that up? All that Virginia shit about being well-born. What well-born person ever said '*poobitry*'?"

· · · ·

Mother parked under the porte cochere. She had called Daddy the day before and had said she wanted to speak to him. She was wearing a hat with a veil stretched over her face and a suit with three-quarter-length sleeves, so that her hands and wrists looked like ostrich heads, coming out.

Daddy opened the door. He was wearing gray flannel pants with an alligator shirt, a red stretch belt with a brass buckle, brown shoes, and glasses.

I was watching them from behind a grill in the wall of the house. As soon as I had seen Mother's car coming up the driveway, I had run to the basement, climbed into the entrance to the air ducts, and crawled on my hands and knees through the air duct that I knew led to the grill that had a view of the entrance and of the porte cochere.

Air ducts led all over the house, I had discovered, not just to Daddy's room and out, to grills that looked outside on different parts of the grounds and inside on different rooms. It was possible, that way, to see almost everything that went on at Daddy's house, though I didn't like to go into the air ducts much, because they were so dirty and creepy inside.

Daddy took Mother's hand and silently raised it to his lips.

"Oh, Cornelius," Mother said impatiently.

"You're looking lovely, my dear."

"Thank you."

"How's your dear mother?"

"Fine, thank you."

Daddy stepped aside for Mother to come in. He led her to the projection room. He stepped aside at the doorway for her to go in first. "Thank you," she said.

I inched back in the air duct to where I knew there was a grill that looked on the projection room.

"My dear?" Daddy said, seating Mother in one of the large Spanish armchairs by the desk. Daddy turned the other

Spanish armchair until it was facing her and sat down. They were face to face.

Mother said the reason she had called was that she wanted to talk to him about Sonny. She said she thought it wasn't right for a boy Sonny's age not to be in college. She said he was missing out on an important stage of life. She said she thought that with nothing to do, he'd probably get into a lot of trouble. She said she was afraid he was already taking drugs. She said she didn't know what to do but that she thought a good counselor might be able to put him on the right track. She wanted to know what Daddy thought.

"Do you know that you still have those same perfect eyebrows?" Daddy said.

"Thank you, Cornelius, but now Sonny—"

"Why don't you come give Daddy Boy a little kiss?"

"What?"

"Why don't you come give Daddy Boy a little kiss."

"Oh, Cornelius, you can't mean that."

"Come give Daddy Boy a little kiss!" Daddy rose out of his chair with his lips puckered.

Mother rose out of her chair and, twisting, stepped to the side. "Cornelius, I can't believe this."

"Kiss Daddy Boy." He moved towards her, his lips still puckered.

Mother backed around the desk, tripping over one of its legs.

"I want to talk about Sonny!" she said. "And Butch! Do you know that he misses an average of two days a week of school to go surfing? And Jennifer! She is so *obsessed* with that boyfriend of hers—"

Daddy rolled the chair aside and stepped forward. "Kiss Daddy Boy."

"Cornelius, how silly, Cornelius, how disgusting!" She ran around the far corner of the desk, then jerkily, on high heels, cut across the room to the door. She slammed the door shut behind her. Groping in her purse for her car keys, she ran through the hall, out the front door, and to her car.

Daddy moved after her as fast as he could. "Mmh, mmh, come kiss Daddy Boy." It echoed in the hall.

Mother stood at the car door looking for her car keys. Daddy was almost on her. "Come kiss Daddy Boy, come kiss Daddy Boy."

Mother slipped out of his way and ran around the front of the car, then, still looking in her purse, walked quickly (even walking, Mother could move faster than Daddy) around the far columns of the porte cochere, around a stand of elephant ears and along a bank of dichondra.

"Mmh, come kiss Daddy Boy, mmh, come kiss Daddy Boy," Daddy said, always behind her.

"Dammit," Mother said, "dammit," her hand churning the contents of her purse, her high heels sinking into the dichondra.

"Kiss, kiss," Daddy said, walking gingerly on the bank.

Mother found the keys as she was rounding the second far column. Her hand dived sharply into her purse and came up with them tinkling in her hand. She ran to the car door with her keys in one hand and her open purse in the other. She opened the car door, got in, slammed the door, turned the key in the ignition, and revved it once. The exhaust blew against Daddy's legs, pushing his pants back against his shins. "Kiss, kiss," Daddy said, shuffling his feet and walking his hands forward along the back fender.

Mother rolled down the window. "Cornelius, you're disgusting and sick and you need help," she called back to him.

"Kiss," Daddy said. He was at her back window now.

Mother pushed the accelerator and moved forward slowly, looking back to make sure that Daddy had stepped back. She pushed it down harder. His hands trailed for a second, then fell off. She drove down the driveway.

"Kiss," Daddy said after her, "mmh, kiss."

CHAPTER 10

The new girl was put next to me. Her last name started with an *A* and there were just enough *B*s, *Cab*s, and *Dal*s to make it around to the next row, where I was. She was pale, with dark blond hair. The side of me that she was on felt clammy. She sat perfectly still, staring straight ahead, while around her, girls sat on desks, talking loudly. They talked about what had happened the year before, referring to an incident with one key word or phrase, calling out "Foss's shoes!" or "Chicken basket!" and then laughing loudly.

Then someone mentioned John and someone else Ringo. Someone else said, "George, George, George." Felicia got up on her desk and shut her eyes. Gradually the noise in the classroom died down, until everyone was quiet and listening to her.

"I can see it all now," Felicia said. She shut her eyes. "This spring, when the Beatles are on tour, Paul is driving down North Ravello Drive in the back of a black limousine. He passes a group of Glenfield girls. They are all wearing bangs. Suddenly, he leans forward and taps the chauffeur on the shoulder. 'Stop, please,' he says, in the politest of voices. 'What is it, Paul, what is it?' Jane Asher asks. 'I don't know,' Paul says, staring out the window. 'I see . . . a vision.' 'Vision?

[219]

What vision!' Jane persists, pulling on Paul's arm, trying to get Paul to turn around and look at her.

"But Paul's back remains turned. He is looking out the window into the group of girls, transfixed. Suddenly, he opens the door and rushes towards the group. Jane is half pulled out of the car from trying to hold him back. 'Erragh!' she groans.

"Paul runs and then slides on his knees (we don't want him to hurt himself now, poor, dear Paul) up to . . ." Felicia looked around the room, "Carlie!" (This week it was going to be Carlie, then.) Carlie beamed in her seat. Felicia went on. "He looks at her with adoring eyes. 'You are the woman I've been waiting for all these years,' he says. 'What?' Carlie says.

"Paul rises. 'Come,' he says, stretching out his hand. Carlie rises and takes it. Hand in hand, they go off, up the iceplant-covered embankment, up Chalon, Bellagio, and Tigertail Roads, all the way up to Mullholland Drive and from there . . . just up . . . and off. 'Paul!' Jane screams at their retreating figures, 'PAUL!!!' "

I glanced at the new girl again. She was taking strands of dark blond hair and pushing them behind her ear, over and over again.

I was glad I was not the new girl anymore. I knew worlds more than she. Things you had to be there for a while to know. Things you couldn't sum up in a word, like what it meant, in our school, if you liked John, what it meant if you liked George, what it meant if you liked Paul, what it meant if you liked Ringo, and then, depending on who you liked, what it meant if you craved him, what it meant if you loved him a whole lot, or a lot, if you just loved him, if you liked him a whole lot or just liked him. You could know, on the surface, what it meant right away, but you had to be there for at least a year to know what it meant right on down through every aspect of your life, what queernesses you assumed, as well as coolnesses, for liking one over the other. You had to be there for at least a year to know why it was so queer to wear pink and green on Friday or fold your socks down only once or why Marcia Sanders, Vicky Jones, and Linda Reilly were so queer. Sure you could tell they were queer right away by the clammy way they looked, but you had to be there for a year to know why they were queer through and through.

I had been the new girl the year before, and constantly absent because of my eye, which was still healing, so that six weeks into the school year, some girls still didn't know my name, or if they did, thought it was a mythical name, under which library books could be checked out and kept overdue, which could be written by monitors on class absentee lists, so that I would be sentenced to Friday afternoon study halls well into the summer.

I wore pink and green on Fridays, they said. I rolled my socks down only once. My bangs were cut *above* my eyebrows and I had bushy eyebrows, too, that met, and sweaty palms, like Marcia Sanders, and deep sweat patches under my arms and I wet my pants, like Vicky Jones, and when my period started, I just sat in it, so that my uniform had a big brown patch on it, and I ate rubber cement, like Linda Reilly.

Then, when I was in school, girls looked at me, then looked at each other and laughed under their hands in disbelief. "I can't believe she's really real!" they said. They rolled their eyes, bit their nails, and wrinkled their noses.

One day halfway into the first semester, Felicia detached

herself from a group and came up to me. She was tall but she still had not lost her baby fat. It puffed out her face, making her eyes two bright blue slits and her mouth a smirk. "Go on, go on," I could hear girls behind her, giving her a little push as she started towards me.

Her baby fat was tinted bright pink on the parts that stuck out the most, so that her chin, cheeks, and forehead were bright pink and shiny.

"Uh . . . hi," she said.

"Hi," I said.

"Uh . . . what's the matter with your eye, I mean . . ." The girls behind her giggled. "Did you get hit by flying glass or something?" She cocked her head to one side and squeezed her eyes shut even tighter.

"No," I said. I told her that I had had an operation. It was still healing.

"Oh, yeah?" Her head went back level. Her eyes opened.

"Yeah." I told her they had hitched my eyelid up because I had been born with no muscle in my eyelid. There was no other way for it to go up.

"Oh, yeah?"

I stretched my eyelid out so that she could see the scar. She brought her head up close. "Eeeeewwww," she said, long and low. It was unlike the abrupt "Ew!" that had always been said by anyone around my age anytime before. It was more like the "Oooooo" that people said at jewels or pretty bugs.

Girls gathered around me. I said the operation had been done the summer before that. It was still healing.

"Wait a minute," Felicia said. "You mean you spent the first ten years of your life with one eye shut?"

"Uh-huh."

"That must have been tough."

I felt my shoulders relax and grow, somehow, wider. Tough: no one had ever said that before, about my eye. Tough: it was as simple as that. I thought of chewing rawhide. I thought of striding into Beverly Hills on huge legs like Paul Bunyan's, sweeping cars and people out of my way. Tough: that's what it had been. Things had been tough, but they were not tough any more.

"Yeah, it was tough," I said.

Girls watched me, but they no longer bit their nails or rolled their eyes. I watched them. I watched them all for about two weeks, picking out the ones I liked the most, then watched the ones I liked the most for a few weeks more. I practiced saying "shit" and "fuck" the way they were said at Glenfield. "Shit" was short and sharp. "Fuck" was long and drawn-out, with a Germanic guttural sound at the end: "f-u-u-u-u-u-ckgh."

Then one day I was near them. I was listening to them. There was room in what they said for a sentence and in that sentence, room for a word. I drew my breath in softly: "Shit."

Girls turned to me.

"F-u-u-u-u-u-u-u-u-ckgh, oh f-u-u-u-u-u-u-u-u-u-u-u-u-u-ckgh."

"Oh f-u-u-u-u-u-u-u-u-u-u-u-uckgh, f-u-u-u-u-u-u-uckgh," they said back, laughing.

Soon after that I cut bangs to look more like Jane Asher and screamed whenever I saw a Beatles' picture, screaming loudest when I saw a picture of the one I'd decided was my favorite, and I learned how to tear it out of whoever's hand it was in without ripping off a corner.

Miss Nicolson entered the room.

"Hi, Nick!" Felicia called.

"Felicia, that's enough!"

I glanced at the new girl. She had stopped putting her hair behind her ears and was watching Felicia out of the corner of her eye.

What really made our school different from anyone else's was that you had to be there for a year to know how Felicia was able to say the things she said to the teachers, how she was able to call Miss Nicolson "Nick," say "Va t'en forniquer" to the French teacher and tell the algebra teacher to stop picking her nose, and how everyone (except Marcia Sanders, Vicky Jones, and Linda Reilly) was able to say the things they said to the teachers in their own little way. You had to be there for at least a year to know who were the teachers you could say things to right away, who were the teachers you could groom, in the course of the year, into teachers you could say things to, how to tell if they were in a good mood, to make them cheerfully receptive to your comments —through sally and retreat, sally and retreat, comment-wise—how to block their retreat from a receptive mood with "My father was in eighty-three movies, Miss Nicolson!" or "My mother had an affair with Anthony Quinn!" causing their glasses to steam, their hands to shake (they were all from Catholic junior colleges in the Midwest, Felicia had found out, and had come to California just to be closer to movie stars), and then to thrust the Ultimate Comment home like a matador so that there were no repercussions, there was nothing more than a shudder.

Sometimes, though, something would go wrong and the teacher would get mad. We could see her expression darkening. It didn't matter what we'd said. It had more to do with timing and rhythm. One comment had followed too closely on another, like waves sloshing. Someone would be about to shout, "Vivien Leigh was at our house for dinner last night! And Laurence Olivier! And Tony Curtis!" But it would already be too late: there would be black rings around her eyes. Her lips would be pressed tightly together.

"You've overstepped the mark," she'd say. "Yes, this time, I'm afraid, you've just overstepped the mark!"

A deathly silence would follow that no one, not even Felicia, would dare to break. We would face straight ahead with our hands clasped together on our desks and think, "Ohwhatadragohwhatadragohwhatadrag," and try to figure out how we'd messed up, after all the time we'd had, and we'd worry that anyone looking in from, we didn't know, Mars, would think that our timing was bad when it wasn't—it was good most of the time—and we'd pray that we would be given one more chance.

Miss Nicolson was making each girl read a paragraph out loud out of the science book.

Olivia, the new girl, started to read. Her voice was so strange that we all stopped what we were doing, recrossed our legs, and leaned onto the other buttock, to cover up the fact that we were listening. I looked at Miss Nicolson. She was staring at her book even harder.

The new girl's voice was hollow. Some of the sounds came out her nose. I leaned forward and, after she had finished reading, turned my head as if I were looking out the window, catching her face for a second in my vision. Lots of other girls were looking out the window, too, or up at the clock.

There was a scar running from the new girl's nose to her upper lip and one side of her upper lip didn't meet the other; it was up higher. Her whole lip was put together crooked, the way you button a sweater when you're in a hurry.

Her voice was shaking.

"All semester," I thought, "all semester!" I wondered if I would ever be her friend. I would never go out of my way to be her friend, the way Mother went out of her way to have Negroes and amputees over for dinner.

. . . .

Olivia made me laugh until the apple I was eating secretly behind the raised top of my desk dribbled out my nose. I opened my mouth and laughed out loud, spraying chewed apple all over the white tips of my saddle shoes and the saddle shoes of my neighbor. Then it was all up anyway, so I let slam the desk top.

"That a way!" Felicia shouted. "That a way!"

I spluttered and choked.

"You two! Stop it! Stop it this instant!"

We looked at Miss Nicolson, grinning. "Victor Borge . . ." I started to say, then stopped. Miss Nicolson's eyes were two hard beans. Her mouth was set. Quietly, she told us to follow her into the courtyard.

Our steps reverberated on the hard stone. The school was Spanish style, built in the twenties. There were bars on all the windows, which the principal assured us was part of the Spanish style. A virgin, her head crusted with bird-do, gazed down on us from a niche.

Miss Nicolson said we had been giggling entirely too much. It was disrupting the class. Even the principal had noticed. She had passed by the teacher's room and had asked Miss Nicolson, "Who *were* those two girls giggling?" It had embarrassed her! Miss Nicolson said she couldn't understand it. I had been such a good girl the year before. Always studying and so attentive in class. And now I was giggling all the time, talking, eating in class, even tearing ivy off the nature trail.

Miss Nicolson's eyes had softened and were moving back and forth, from Olivia's eyes to mine, but now it was our turn to keep our eyes hard, immobile.

Miss Nicolson said our giggling was probably a nervous reaction to growing up. Lots of girls had that. We giggled because we were nervous and we were nervous because, well, girls got crushes on one another. It was perfectly natural.

"Christ, she thinks we're lezzes!" Olivia said, after Miss Nicolson had gone back to class, leaving us in the court-yard for the rest of the period to "think about it," she said.

"*The Group*, page one twenty-seven," I prompted.

"Candy Bergen's flaring nostrils."

. . . .

The Group, page one twenty-seven; *The Good Earth*, page thirty-five, the line "And with a hoarse cry he grabbed her"; *From Russia with Love*, page ninety-three, the line "Their bodies moved like clockwork"; *Quiet Days in Clichy*, all of it; *Fanny Hill*, all of it; also freckles on pale skin, pixie bands, dress shields, the words *nuptial*, *batch*, and *spatula*, Wayne Newton, Edie Gorme, Mel Torme, the Lennon Sisters—all that made us laugh for hours until our stomach muscles hurt and the tears rolled down our faces and saying "Stop, oh stop" only made us laugh more, and the list was constantly growing. All we had to do was mention one thing, at almost any time, in an isolated way or in a slightly different tone of voice, and it would become funny, too. Sometimes it wasn't even a word, sometimes it was just a look, from me to Olivia or from Olivia to me, and the whole situation we were in would become funny. It was exhilarating. It made us feel as if we could do anything: walk to Pizza Hut at milk break, pull ivy off the nature trail, scale the Cyclone fence that surrounded the school when Richard Burton went by walking his dog and land behind him with a sweaty thud so that he jumped, make excursions back into the vestige of boarding school, which housed only retired teachers now, and hidden behind massive pieces of Spanish colonial furniture, gaze upon hawk-nosed, sunken-cheeked old women, who lay open-mouthed under mountains of comforters, dying.

Sometimes, though, Olivia would say things, thoughts really, that wouldn't make me laugh, wouldn't make me say anything right away, except "I know! I know!" It was because they were thoughts that I had thought, too, but had never told anyone about, because I had thought they were *so* strange no one would understand them, and there Olivia was, just *saying* them. It was because I was so amazed that she was saying them that it took my breath away and made the words *I know about that, I know!* roll over and over each other in my mouth, so that I would bounce on my toes and shake my hand, and Olivia would go on explaining, as if she thought I didn't understand.

Olivia was the first one to say that three dots in a triangle (as in the end of a coconut, an overhead light) made a face, though I had thought that all along. "There's one!" she said. "And there's one!"

"I know about that," I said, "I know! There's one and there's one and there's one!"

Olivia was the first one to say that she thought the Beatles were great, but screaming about them was a little too . . . well . . . horny, like twitching your leg in class.

"I know. It embarrasses me when they do that!" I said, even though I had stopped screaming just a few weeks before and Olivia was kindly not remembering.

Olivia was the first one to say that she had thought, sometimes when she was little, that she could see molecules.

"Oh God, yes, I know, I thought that same thing!"

"That . . . graininess in the air . . ."

"What *was* that?"

Olivia was the first one to say that she had even thought sometimes that she was Jesus and that she had thought her thoughts where somehow being *seen*.

"Olivia, it's amazing, I had the exact same thoughts but just never told anyone!"

Olivia was the first one to say that maybe I had never told my thoughts to anyone because I never had anyone I could tell them to.

I didn't say anything. There was a tightness, suddenly, in my throat. You could say everything, I thought, you could talk about everything, except about things like that.

Olivia went on: "God, other children were so mean to me when I was little . . ."

"They called me 'Cyclops,'" I said through the tightness in my throat.

"They—oh, I can't talk about all the things they called me, but it was like they were *mad*, you know?"

"Yeah, it *was* like they were mad!"

"And my parents weren't any help, either."

"No, my parents weren't any help, either, either!" The tightness in my throat disappeared.

"It was because they were always telling me I was 'special.' 'Special, special, special'—God, how tired I got of that! If only they'd said to me once, 'Those are the goddamned breaks . . .'"

"I know! They called me 'interesting'!"

.   .   .   .

I took Olivia quickly through the foyer, projection room, bar, living room and dining room so that she couldn't see how dusty they were.

"Boy, I knew you were rich, but I didn't know you were *this rich*," she said, running after me. She wanted to know if she could stop and look.

"No, let's run!" I said.

We started to climb the back stairs.

"God!" Olivia said, stopping, her eyes fixed on the sill, black with dust, underneath the single window lighting the stairwell. "Don't they ever *clean* this place?"

"Yeah, it's pretty awful," I said, giggling.

I had learned to say things before Olivia said them. Or, if she still managed to say things before I did, I laughed, hoping to get her back into the state in which everything we saw or said was funny.

"And those *cobwebs!*" she said, raising her eyes to the upper corner of the sill.

"Yeah, I know, ha ha!"

"But I mean . . ."

"Ha ha ha ha!"

"It's such a weird environment to grow up in!"

"Ha ha ha ha ha!" I doubled over on the stairs and finished climbing them, panting.

We stopped in the doorway leading to my room and looked across the room and through an open door to the bathroom.

Daddy was in the bathroom with Busy. Daddy was moving towards her and she was moving away from him, taking short little steps. Daddy was making noises and Busy was saying, "No, please sir, no." Daddy couldn't pick his feet off the ground, he could only shuffle them like a choo-choo train. The fact that I couldn't think "train" without thinking "choo-choo" made me feel sick.

"Old lech, horny bastard," I whispered to Olivia and laughed.

"And what was that smell?" Olivia asked after we were back in the hall. "Was that *him*?"

. . . .

Monday morning Olivia caught up to me in the hall. She was out of breath. She said that while she was at my house, my mother—her name was Mrs. Teasdale, wasn't it? We didn't have the same name—anyway, my mother called up her mother and talked about how glad she was that I had a friend. My mother said that I was a solitary, quiet, and lonely child and that she was worried about me! My mother went on to talk about my brother—is his name Sonny?—and my father and how crazy *he* is and her childhood in Virginia "and it was really weird, Robin! She went on for so *long!*"

The tightness in my throat grew into a lump.

"Let's get to class," I said.

"Did I say something wrong?"

"No."

"I *did* say something."

"No, it's just that class is going to start in about half a minute, I swear to God."

．　．　．　．

"Christ, Daddy, you smell!" Jennifer said, entering Daddy's room on her first visit of the spring vacation. "Don't you ever *bathe?* Don't you ever change your *clothes?*"

"Oh, little baby girl, oh, little baby girl," Daddy said to Jennifer, shuffling towards her, reaching out his arms.

"Ugh! Keep away!" Jennifer turned and walked quickly from the bar, still in her Misty Harbor raincoat, carrying her purse. She slowed down when she got to the living room and started weaving from side to side. She flopped down onto the sofa with a sigh, raising a cloud of dust on either side of her. She started looking around the room. "Goddamned dust everywhere!" she said. She got up and walked towards the kitchen.

She found Judy in the kitchen with a cake decorator, squeezing out rosettes of frosting. All the other maids were sitting around the table. Jennifer grabbed Judy by one shoulder and spun her. "You made Daddy smell!" she said. She slapped Judy. Judy's head jerked back. A lock of hair fell out of Judy's French twist and hung down in a beckoning finger. Pink stripes appeared on Judy's brown cheek. "Now get out," Jennifer said. "Get out and don't you ever come back." Judy stood without moving. "Get out!" Jennifer repeated. She grabbed Judy's arms and started pushing her. She pushed her through the kitchen, through the service foyer, and out the door. Judy moved ahead of her, trotting like a small child. Jennifer opened the screen door. She pushed Judy out. "And if you try to get back in touch with Daddy, I'll kill you, I swear!" She turned to the new maids sitting around the table. "I want this place cleaned up. You," she said, looking at one of them. "Clean up the bathrooms.

You. I want you to clean the foyer, projection room, and bar. You. You clean the living room and dining room. You clean Daddy's room and the guest rooms. You two clean the upstairs rooms. You see to the linen. Now let's go."

Jennifer came back into the living room. "I can't believe I did that!" she said.

. . . .

Dr. Fayman came to the house in a business suit, followed by Mr. Fleming, who ran Daddy's office downtown. Daddy was wearing gray flannel trousers, a white alligator shirt with a full sleeved red alpaca cardigan over it and shoes.

Daddy had wanted to wear Hawaiian trunks and a sport shirt but Jennifer had said, "Daddy, Daddy, Daddy . . ." until Daddy had finally put on clothes.

Daddy and Jennifer walked down the hall first, followed by Dr. Fayman and Mr. Fleming. I ran ahead with Daddy's suitcase banging against my legs.

"Daddy, Daddy, Daddy," Jennifer had said, until Daddy had finally agreed to go.

The maids were waiting at the door, and Busy and Don and Minnie. Daddy kissed them one by one. "The doctors are going to find out once and for all what's been keeping old Corny Boy down," he said.

"Take care, Mr. D."

"Yeah, good luck."

"We'll miss you."

Daddy and Jennifer and Dr. Fayman and Mr. Fleming got in the back of the limousine. Don got in the front. The limousine started down the driveway. Daddy turned in the backseat, pressed his fingers against his lips and waved them at us.

"Jeez, I'm gonna miss him," one of the maids said.

"You said it," another one said.

. . . .

Daddy climbed out of a window of the hospital in the middle of the night. He walked to the corner and called Don from a phone booth. Don found him on a bus-stop bench, shivering in his Hawaiian trunks on Main Street. In Santa Monica. In the middle of the night. In the rain.

"*DADDY!*" Jennifer screamed. "*DADDY!*"

"Oh, Baby Girl," Daddy said, "you can't expect Daddy Boy to stay in a hospital full of ugly nurses. Nothing but ugly nurses in that hospital! Hanging necks, close-together eyes. 'You just need to take a little tuck,' I said to a couple of them. 'I know the best plastic surgeon in the country! Let Daddy Boy pay for it!' But all they could say was 'Take this' or 'Turn over' or 'Drink that.' You can't expect Daddy Boy to stay in a place full of ugly women. Why, they just make Daddy Boy's whole spirit sink. Beautiful women, that's all I want. All I want is to be surrounded by beautiful women."

"Da-dee-eeeee," Jennifer sighed.

"A quarter of an inch," Daddy said after a while.

"What?"

Daddy raised his thumb and forefinger and put them alongside his nose. "A quarter of an inch off the end of your nose, Jennifer Girl, that's all you need."

"Da-*DEE-EEEE!*"

CHAPTER 11

Daddy stayed in the presidential suite at the Waldorf; Mother stayed at the Westbury. We went back and forth all day long.

"Just a few more minutes!" Daddy called from the living room when he heard us come in. Daddy had promised to take us to lunch at the Plaza, the Sherry Netherlands, or La Grenouille.

Daddy was sitting in a rush-bottomed rocker, in a gold pyjama top, one foot up on a knee, a stack of unopened envelopes on the floor beside him.

"What's my little girl been up to now?" Daddy asked, picking an envelope up off the top of the stack.

Jennifer was watching Daddy from the hall. Her hair was uncombed and she was holding her beltless black silk kimono closed at the waist with one hand while biting the cuticle on the thumb of the other hand.

"Oh God," Sonny whispered, "if he's opening bills, that means we're not going to eat for another two hours."

Jennifer raised her thumb to her mouth, formed a silent "Sh!" with it, and went back to biting.

Daddy cleared his throat. The sound of rattling phlegm mingled with the sound of paper rustling. "Let's see . . ."

Daddy held the bottom right corner of the page up to his eyes. "Wah!" he shouted breathlessly, as if something had been pulled out of him with a rip cord. He was silent for a few seconds, then his face crinkled. "Ha, ha, Baby Girl, ha, ha, Baby Girl . . ."

Jennifer came out of the darkness of the hall towards him, stepping exaggeratedly pigeon-toed and smiling, though still with her thumb in her mouth.

"Forty-eight hundred dollars! Ha! Ha! Baby Girl! You couldn't have spent more money if you'd tried! Ha! Ha! You little girls just *love* to walk all over old Daddy Boy, yes you do!"

"Oh *Daddy* . . ."

"Go call Busy Girl and Rita Girl and tell them to come look. This is the funniest thing I've ever seen!"

"Let's go back to the Westbury and charge up something there," Sonny said.

"But we were just there!" Butch said.

"There's nothing to do *here*, is there?"

"O.K., let's go."

"See you later!" we called. We started out the door. Busy and Rita ran into the living room in their bathrobes.

"Hey . . ." Jennifer ran after us. We stopped.

"Ah . . . you've got 'out of town' written all over you," Jennifer said, eyeing Sonny's and Butch's Hawaiian shirts and wraparound sunglasses, my short muu-muu and our rubber flip-flops, over which streams of dirty city water washed every time we crossed the street, "so make sure the taxi goes straight up Park (that's the wide avenue) or Madison, with all the shops. The driver might try to take you in a circle, just to make money."

"Oh, Jennifer," Butch said suavely, "you're so urbane."

"That's *urban*, toe-jam," Sonny corrected him.

"No, I mean really," Jennifer said earnestly, tossing her hair.

"Yes, quite the Eastern Miss," Butch said.

"Jennifer, when I get to Mrs. Farnsworth's, I'm gonna take that fingerbowl in two hands, like this, see? And I'm gonna chug it! Glug, glug, glug!"

Jennifer gasped. "Oh, no you're not, Sonny! You're not going to do that!"

"Oh, yes I am!"

"Oh, Sonny, promise me, *promise me* you're not going to do that! You wouldn't be so mean. Oh, Sonny, *please!*"

"I don't know, Jennifer, you're getting to be a pretty big snob. . . ."

"Oh, Sonny, I'm *not* a snob. I promise I won't be anymore, only please, *please* don't drink the fingerbowls at Mrs. Farnsworth's!"

"I don't know. . . ."

"Oh, Sonny, please! I'll do *anything!*"

"I'll think about it." Sonny turned to Butch and me. "Come on, let's go."

We waited for the elevator.

Jennifer came out. "Sonny?"

"Oh, cool it, Jennifer," Sonny said as the elevator door closed.

· · · ·

"Doobie?" Sonny asked, once we were in the cab. He pulled a joint out of the pocket of his Hawaiian shirt. He took matches out of his pocket and lit it, making his lips very thin to be able to hold it and take a drag on it. He handed it to me. I took a drag on it the way I'd seen Sonny do it, holding it between thumb and forefinger (not between forefinger and middle finger, like regular cigarettes) and making my lips thin.

"Robs?" Butch said slyly.

"What?"

"You've let all the smoke out!" Sonny said. "You've got to hold it in your lungs, like this, see?" Sonny breathed in. "And you shouldn't talk, but if you have to say anything, you kind of croak it, like this: 'Whaaat?'"

Butch took a drag and handed it back to Sonny. Sonny took a drag and handed it to me. I took a drag, holding it in my lungs the way Sonny had showed me.

"Hey, Robs's all right, you know it?" Sonny said to Butch over my head.

"Yeah, Robs's all right."

"And she's not too bad looking either, is she, Butch?"

"No, I would say Robs is . . . ah . . ."

They leaned forward. I could feel their eyes moving from my feet to my head.

"Legs, A."

"Ass, A."

"Boobs, C+."

"Face, B−."

"Overall, B."

They fell back against the seat, laughing.

"Hey, Robs," Butch asked, "will you forgive us for all the times we were mean to you?"

"Yeah, we promise not to call you pesky pits anymore."

"Or ugly."

"Or uuuuuuuuuugggggggggghhhhhhhhh-ly!" They laughed.

"Or turdface."

"Or butthead."

"Or dippy."

"Or prissy."

"Or yipicals."

"Yeah, or anything like that. O.K.?"

A silence, broken by one loud "Ha!"

"O.K.? C'mon, yip, I mean, Robs. We've got to stick together when all around us—"

"Everyone's being an asshole," I said.

They laughed.

"So what do you say, huh?"

"O.K.," I said.

"O.K. what?"

"O.K. I'm with you guys."

We sat closer together in the taxi.

．．．．

"Aaouw," Mother groaned as I walked in. Mother had a migraine the whole time she was in New York. The doctor came in every day to give her a shot.

I sat down on the edge of the bed.

"Where are the boys?" she asked.

"They're in the living room eating lunch."

"What are they having?"

"Beef stroganoff."

"That's nice. Aaow. Aaaaaaaoooooowwwwww!" Mother gripped her forehead. "Have you heard how much Jennifer's wedding dress is?"

"No," I said.

"It's forty-eight hundred."

"Hm."

"Forty-eight hundred dollars, I said!"

"Is that a lot?"

"Of *course* it is. Aaow. 'At least do something simple' —that's all I said. That's all I could say, in the end. 'Have it in California, among your friends, or in Virginia,' but no, she's having a wedding on Madison Avenue, in a church to which she has no . . . emotional attachment. Reception at the Cosmopolitan Club. The most expensive caterer. She thinks we don't know how to do things. 'We know how to do things!' I said. Dress too old. Aaow. Aaoooooowwwwww!" Mother rested, panting, then continued: "*No* girl of twenty wears a dress with a stiff bodice like that. It's too matronly. Aaow!"

Mother fell back against the pillows. She was silent for a while, then continued. "I'm well-born. Andrew's well-born. Growing up she repudiated this. But unconsciously, she's been conscious of it all along. So now she responds, but instead of embracing my warm, southern brand of . . . being well-born, she embraces this cold New York version. It's as if she doesn't understand that you can be well-born and *poor.*"

Mother put the back of her hand, a Kleenex clutched tightly in it, against her forehead. "And your father and Rita staying together up there in that hotel: *no* woman goes and lives with her ex-husband in a hotel in front of his children. What could be more confusing for them. . . ."

Mother sighs. A tear trickles out of the far corner of her eye. "My friends said I had to be out of my mind, a man eighteen years older than I was, who'd been married three times, but when they met him, they always said, 'We see what you mean!'

"There was an older woman at the Barbizon named Mildred Smith. She was a kind of counselor to us all. Cornelius was calling me at the Barbizon all the time and I didn't want to go out with him alone, so I said to Mildred, 'Come on out and meet this Texas oilman who's been calling me.' Mildred said that if she were me, she wouldn't touch him with a ten-foot pole, a Texas oilman, eighteen years older than she was, who had been married three times, and I said, 'Mildred, I'm not taking him *seriously*. You *can't* take him seriously, you'll see. Just come on out with us. It will be a fun evening.'

"I didn't take him seriously, but when Mildred saw him, walking towards us at the Stork Club, in an ankle-length camel-hair coat, having just made his second million, Mildred turned to me and whispered, 'Are you out of your *mind*? That's one of the most attractive men I've ever seen!'

"Mildred was very matter-of-fact. She asked him right away: 'But what about this having been married three times?' And he turned his big ingenuous eyes on Mildred and said, 'Mildred *Girl!* Those weren't really *marriages*. I'd come into Houston from two months out in the oil fields, and word was getting out that I was starting to be a little successful and the mothers would get very excited. They'd invite me to their country club dances. And I'd be out on the porch of the country club, holding some little girl's hand, and it would be a beautiful May night and the magnolias would be shining in the moonlight, and I'd have been out on the oil fields for two months, with nothing but old roughnecks to look at, sleeping on the ground with rattlesnakes crawling up my pantlegs when the next thing I'd know, I'd be step-pin'—' Daddy walked one finger after the other on the Stork Club tablecloth, 'down the garden path at the country club towards a preacher with some little girl I hardly knew!' And Mildred, who had always been the voice of reason until then, patted his hand and nodded and said, 'I *understand!*'

"I didn't take him seriously, but when Mildred said that, that 'I *understand*,' that's when I started to lose perspective." Mother shuts one eye and, palms upright, pushes one hand forward and pulls the other back, as if she were trying to figure out how things changed, up close and far away. "That's when I started trying to convince myself that, with effort on my part and my innate sense of . . . knowing how to do things and my buoyant personality, it would work."

Mother put her hands down and pushed herself up on the pillows. "Peter's been wanting me to settle East with him, in a little town in Maryland that he's discovered. I don't think it's a good time to go, but Peter's stomach just can't take California anymore. It would mean taking you with us but leaving Butch in California for his last year of high school. It would also mean putting you in boarding school in Washington as the schools in the little town have just gotten integration, and you know I like colored people as much as anyone, but I'm just afraid there might be violence. You'd be going next September after we got back from Maine. It's April now so that means you'd only have two months left of weekends at your father's house . . . with all those . . . influences.

"There's a school I've been looking into: it's a good school, full of nice, ladylike southern girls who would teach you how to squeal. . . ."

I rolled my eyes.

"Sh. It's nice to squeal. Every little girl should squeal."

"Mom?" Sonny put his head in the door.

"Take off those sunglasses!" Mother said.

Sonny sighed, drew his head back and shut the door.

. . . .

A chauffeur had driven us in a limousine to Andrew's mother's house in the country, where we were to have lunch: Mother, Daddy, Jennifer, Sonny, Butch, and me. Andrew had stayed in town.

It was a black limousine.

Daddy was wearing a gray double-breasted suit that reduced his paunch (though he could have actually *been* thinner, and we unable to see it, for Daddy had spent every weekend up until the time for Jennifer's wedding in his room—then at the Waldorf, he had always been sitting down in his pyjama top), a white shirt, a maroon necktie with small white dots on it, a matching handkerchief in his pocket, polished black shoes, and fine black socks, through which his ankle shone, thin and delicate, in flashes.

"Why, Daddy, you look *wonderful*," Jennifer had said, that morning, as Daddy emerged from his dressing room at the Waldorf.

Mrs. Farnsworth was wearing a sleeveless flowered blouse, moccasins and Bermuda shorts, the fly of which arched over her large stomach. She had skinny legs knotted with veins, large brown spots on her skin, a puffy face, and a helmet of curled, sprayed bluish hair.

"Just because Mrs. Farnsworth will be wearing shorts doesn't mean the lunch won't be formal," Jennifer had said.

Sonny, Butch, and I looked at her.

"Well, that's the way people *are* in the East. They have a kind of studied casualness."

"What?"

"That doesn't mean Daddy or any of *you* should try that, for heaven's sakes!"

A month before, Jennifer had called us in California to say that Mrs. Farnsworth wanted us to come to lunch at her house on the day before the wedding while Andrew was busy in town. Jennifer said Mrs. Farnsworth thought that would be a good way to get to know us. There was panic in Jennifer's voice: "She wants you and *Daddy* to come."

"That's appropriate," Mother said.

"But *Daddy* . . ."

"Peter will understand."

"But what I mean is . . . Mrs. Farnsworth's not the kind of woman Daddy likes. He won't even be nice to her!"

"Jennifer," Mother laughed gently, "haven't you realized by now that your father likes *all* women?"

"He won't like Mrs. Farnsworth, though. She's one of those . . . low-voiced-type women."

"Jennifer, I'm sure your father will understand the situation. He can be a very charming man when he wants to be."

"But what I really mean, Mother, is . . . he won't get drunk and fall down, will he? He'll wear nice clothes? He won't order a *white* limousine to take us out there? He won't goose Mrs. Farnsworth, will he? Because really she wouldn't be amused."

"Jennifer, please . . ."

"Mrs. Farnsworth likes horses and genealogy, and Limoges and Sevres and Duncan Phyfe—"

"Jennifer . . ."

Jennifer went on as if in a dream: "And Hepplewhite and Sheraton and marine oil paintings and crewelwork and oriental rugs—"

"Jennifer, stop it."

Jennifer called Daddy and asked him if he was going to get drunk and fall down, then called Mother back to say she had asked him that. Mother said she shouldn't have said that to Daddy like that and Jennifer said, "I know, but I just get so nervous!" Jennifer said Daddy hadn't laughed or said anything on the phone, he had just hung up. Jennifer had tried calling back but no one answered.

The next two of the three weekends at Daddy's house before going east for the wedding, Daddy didn't come out of his room at all. Busy said Daddy had said to her that his Baby Girl had hurt him "worse than if she had stuck him with a knife," but Jennifer said she wasn't worried: it was like after my eye operation, he'd get out of it in time. The third weekend, Daddy came out of his room once, looked at me with eyes that didn't see me, then walked out onto the terrace and yelled, "You've got to work on that backhand, Dolores Girl!" at people playing tennis below.

Jennifer called us every day, sometimes two and three times a day. She asked Mother what kind of dress she was going to wear; she asked Mother if she had gotten her dress yet. She sent me a scrap of material, then called me and asked me if I'd received the material, then when I had, told me to have my shoes dyed the color of that material, because that was the color my dress was going to be. She called me and asked me if I was sure I could walk on high heels. She called me and told me to be sure I went to a good shoe dyer, one who would dye my shoes with a color that wouldn't run in case it rained. She called Mother and asked her how she was going to *be* at the wedding. Mother said she was going to be just fine. Jennifer said she didn't mean that, she meant, how was she going to *act?* Mother said she was going to act like a suitable mother-of-the-bride. Jennifer asked Mother how she was going to *be* with Mrs. Farnsworth.

"I'm going to say, 'How do you *do*, Mrs. Farnsworth?'"

"Not like that! Now pretend I'm Mrs. Farnsworth."

"How do you do—"

"No! You've got to say it more . . . clipped."

"HowdoyoudoMrs.Farnsworth," Mother said, all in one tone, with an English accent like Henrietta's in "Topper."

"That's fine." Jennifer turned to me. "Now, tell me how you're going to be with Mrs. Farnsworth."

"I'm going to say, 'HowdoyoudoMrs.Farnsworth.'"

"And you're going to shake hands."

"Uh-huh."

"And there are going to be fingerbowls. And what are you going to do with the fingerbowls?"

"Dip my fingers in them."

"And then what are you going to do?"

"Flick my wet fingers in Mrs. Farnsworth's face!"

"Oh, no you're not, Robin! Don't be mean! Say you're not going to do that!"

"Ha, ha! Yes I am!"

"Oh, Robin, please don't do that! Please!"

"Ha, ha!"

"Robin! Mother!" Her voice started to tremble.

"Oh, Jennifer, I'm not going to do that."

"You promise?"

"I promise."

We shook Mrs. Farnsworth's hand one by one. "HowdoyoudoMrs.Farnsworth," Mother said, her voice even more subdued than it had been when she was practicing. Daddy took Mrs. Farnsworth's hand and held it, looking down at it (it was wrinkled, with swollen joints and brown splotches) with a slight smile on his face. Daddy then raised his head and looked directly at her.

I expected Daddy's face to fall and his eyes to become dull the way they did when Daddy was introduced to a woman who wasn't pretty, but Daddy's eyes kept shining and his mouth kept smiling its special small smile, scrunched up to half its normal size and turned up at the corners.

"Mrs. Farnsworth?" Daddy's mouth now somehow managed to ask.

"Call me Denise."

"Denise."

I held my breath, waiting for "Girl" to come after "Denise," but instead Daddy said: "That's a beautiful name. French, isn't it?"

"Well, you see," Mrs. Farnsworth laughed shyly, "Mama [she pronounced it 'ma-*ma*'] was *mad* about French."

. . . .

We passed slowly through the house on the way to the dining room. The rooms were small, with sloping, creaking floors. The wallpaper, curtains, and stuffed furniture were all of different prints. The wooden furniture was scarred and gashed.

Mother stopped to look at each room. "Charming! Charming!" Mother said. "See, Robin? This is what a house *should* be like!"

"But it looks all beat up," I whispered, "and the furniture doesn't match."

"That gives it charm," she said.

The dining room was small, with a low ceiling. Sonny's

head almost touched the ceiling; Daddy's shoulders seemed almost to touch the walls on either side. The dining room table was covered with gleaming silverware, sparkling glasses, three for each place, and shining plates. Plates that were in front of us when we sat down were removed by the maid and came back with tiny white asparagus on them, covered with cream.

Jennifer picked up the smaller fork. She looked at Mrs. Farnsworth to make sure she wasn't looking, then raised the fork in the air for a second, eyeing Sonny, Butch, and me significantly. Sonny and I picked up the smaller fork. Butch made as if he were about to pick up the larger fork. The color rose in Jennifer's face. Butch made a face and picked up the smaller fork.

The asparagus was cold. I looked at Sonny and Butch to see whether they were surprised. Sonny left his on the plate after dipping a tine of his fork in the sauce and licking it with the tip of his tongue. Butch's lips were pressed together and bulging, as if he were swishing Listerine around in his mouth. I could see him keeping the bite in a bulge in the front of his mouth, between his front teeth and his lips, until it was soft enough, then sliding the bulge around, on the outside of his teeth, to the back of his mouth, and pressing it with his cheek through where I knew there was a gap in his back teeth down his throat.

"Five dollars left in the whole wide world!" Daddy was saying. He leaned forward in his chair. "Do you know what that means? Do you, Denise? Five dollars . . . in the Depression?"

"Daddy . . ." Jennifer said.

Mrs. Farnsworth shifted in her seat. "No, Mr. Drayton—"

"Call me Cornelius."

"No, Cornelius, I assure you, I—"

"So what did you do with the five dollars?" Sonny asked, as if he hadn't heard the story five hundred times before.

Jennifer frowned at him.

Daddy went on as if he hadn't heard the question: "You may ask why I didn't go out and buy a few things for myself. Five dollars went a lot longer in those days, didn't it, Denise? Tell the children how much longer five dollars went in those days."

Jennifer laughed, embarrassed.

"What are you laughing at?" Daddy asked, looking at Jennifer. "Come on now, Denise, tell them how much longer five dollars went in those days."

"Well, yes, five dollars really did go a lot longer—"

"No, Denise, I mean . . . tell them a story!"

"Well," Mrs. Farnsworth said, rolling her eyes up for a second, "I remember once when I was seventeen or so. I had borrowed Papa's car and driver for the day so I could do a little shopping. Papa had given me some money, I don't know, a graduation present or something. Anyway, Papa and I had gotten our signals crossed, about the chauffeur, so that at the end of the day, I came out of a shop carrying a lot of packages, and there was no chauffeur. No chauffeur and all these packages and five dollars, yes, I remember, five dollars left in my pocketbook. Five dollars was probably enough in those days for taxi fare to Grand Central and a train ticket to Greenwich, where we lived. But what did I do? Nothing sensible like that, of course. I went back into the store and bought a hat I'd seen in the window on my way out. I remember it so well: it was green felt, about so big—" Mrs. Farnsworth formed a circle in front of her with thumbs and index fingers, "and it cost five dollars exactly.

Why, it was the sort of thing that would cost probably a hundred dollars today."

"Heh, heh," Daddy said. "See what I mean, children? That was a good story, Denise."

Children, I thought. Daddy had never said *children* before. *Daddy had never listened to other people's stories. Daddy had never said a name without "Girl" or "Boy" after it.*

"So how did you get home?" Sonny asked Mrs. Farnsworth.

Mrs. Farnsworth thought for a minute. "I can't remember. Let me think. Oh, yes: the manager of the store . . . the manager of the store let me make a call to Greenwich as I had spent so much money there. I simply told Mama that Papa's chauffeur had abandoned me and that I had no money to get home with. She sent her car and driver down to pick me up. When I got home, Papa gave me a stern lecture about always keeping a little money on me. He said—yes, I remember it now—that I should always have at least five dollars on me! Ha, ha, ha! Yes, hm." Mrs. Farnsworth took a drink of water.

"Denise Girl, that's a marvelous story."

Girl: he'd said it now, but slipped in in a way that Mrs. Farnsworth didn't really notice, in a way that made her just settle down more in her seat. And *marvelous:* Daddy had never said *marvelous* before.

I wondered if Daddy was being the way he was before we were born, the way he was when he met Mother, when he wore ankle-length camel-hair coats and people said, "We see what you mean!"

"Do you think so? Oh yes, well, *I* rather like it."

"Yes, yes." Daddy breathed in deeply. "So you see, children, Elizabeth," he nodded to each of us, "now that Denise has illustrated, through her marvelous story," Daddy nodded to Mrs. Farnsworth on the word *marvelous*, "that five dollars *could* go a lot longer in the Depression, it is not so ludicrous for me to tell you . . ."

Ludicrous.

The way he was when he flew ahead of Mother's train in giant leaps, his ankle-length camel-hair coat flapping out behind, and stood at the steps leading down from Mother's sleeping car, roses in hand, the train station gleaming, and yelled, "More roses! Candy! Water! A wheelchair! Blankets! Pillows!" and all that had floated to him, in the arms of running, white-coated porters, just like in old movies.

" . . . that I was keeping those five dollars intact," Daddy held his hands out, palms up, "because I was planning on making an investment. My investment was going to be in land. Land for oil. But I didn't know when and I didn't know where. I was just keeping my eyes, keeping my ears open.

"Every morning I went into the same coffee shop. The owner would let me have a cup of coffee free because I had worked there when I had first come to town and he knew I was hard up. Sometimes he would let me have a doughnut, too.

"Every couple of days, this guy, Ted Simpson, would come in. He'd been with me on the deal I'd lost so much money on. He was a good guy, though. He had asthma. Was in Texas for his asthma.

"He'd come in huffing and puffing. 'Hup! Hup! Hi, Cornelius! I've got one for you. Hup! Hup! This one can't miss. Three miles outside of Ruckles.'

" 'North, south, east or west?' Always important to know the direction.

"He'd say which direction. Then I'd ask about four things: I'd ask about salinity. I'd ask about topsoil, the depth, the composition. I'd ask about moisture. I'd ask what its proximity was to the nearest strike. He'd answer something. 'No good,' I'd say. 'But Cornelius, you look like hell! How much longer can you go on?' 'I can go on, Ted Boy, as long as I don't hear of a deal that looks good.' 'Hup, hup, well, it's your funeral!' He came in a couple of days later. He was wheezing extra hard. 'Well, did that one work out?' 'No, but Cornelius hup! Hup! Hup! Hup! I—' 'Take your time, Ted Boy, sit down.' I pulled out a chair for him. He sat down. We were sitting at one of those little old bitty tables they had in drugstores. 'Stevensville,' he panted, 'eight miles west . . .' 'Salinity . . .' Etcetera.

"Everything sounded good. 'Sounds good,' I said. 'Let's take a ride out there.' 'But Cornelius, we don't have any time! Hup! Everett Libby has an option on that lease. He got it just this morning. I don't know how in . . . blazes . . . fellow—' Actually, Denise, he used some very ugly terms to describe Libby, but, then, Libby was a very unsavory character."

"I understand, Cornelius."

"'—got it but he did. He's looking for shareholders. He hasn't sent out the general word yet, but when he does, there's gonna be a stampede!' 'I don't know . . .' 'Cornelius Boy, you're gonna invest in that well if I have to throw you down and *drag* the money out of your pocket.'

"Suddenly, something snapped in me. Ted had used this tactic on me many times before. He was such an excitable fellow. Sure, the conditions were favorable for a strike and Libby had gotten the deal together and he *was* pretty knowledgeable. But there was something else.

"You know what they say about first impressions? Well, it was as if my first impression, you know, the one that goes by so fast you can't recognize what it is so that you have to replay it three or four times in your head before you can recognize it and all the time secondary impressions are trying to pass themselves off as first impressions and you don't have time to examine them but you know they're not the ones so you say to them, 'Get out of there!'" Daddy took a deep breath.

Mrs. Farnsworth let her fork hang limply in her hand and looked at Daddy. Jennifer, Sonny, and Mother looked at Daddy. Butch stopped sliding a lump of food behind his cheek and looked at Daddy.

Daddy had never talked about how a *mind* worked before. Daddy had never talked about how things *seemed*.

The way he was when he sat at tables in nightclubs with soldiers and sailors fanning out on either side of him while Mother was out on the dance floor dancing and he heard their war stories and said, "That must have been terrible, son, terrible . . ."

Daddy continued: "Well, it was as if my first impression, it was as if my first impression—"

"Was what?" Jennifer broke in.

"Was that it would come in!"

A silence followed, in which I thought I heard something that sounded like a bicycle tire deflating. Then Daddy reared back his head and started to laugh. "Hee, hee, hee," he laughed, wrinkling his eyes so much they finally shut, his shoulders bouncing. He leaned forward and coughed one rattling cough into his handkerchief, then reared back his head again and laughed some more. "You were rich and I was poor but I'll be damned if we don't both have it now!" Daddy shouted, laughing.

Mrs. Farnsworth started to laugh at the other end of the table: "Eaugh haw, haw, haw!"

[253]

"Damn!" Daddy said, laughing.

"Eaugh, haw, haw, haw!"

Or the way he was before he met Mother, when he had black hair and did the box step at Arthur Murray's and people, women mostly, stood around the half-open door, craning their necks . . .

"I don't get it," Jennifer said to Butch through her teeth, but just as she was saying it, Butch reared back his head and started to laugh, too.

Mother was smiling.

I laughed, too.

just having to see that, just having to see what the others meant, just having to see our Daddy.

Jennifer, looking at us, giggled nervously.

"So did the well come in?" Sonny, the only one who hadn't laughed or smiled, asked after the laughter had died down and Daddy, Mother, and Mrs. Farnsworth were reaching for handkerchiefs and water glasses.

"Why, yes," Daddy answered.

"And how much money did you make?"

"I can't remember now," Daddy said, scratching his head. "About a thousand?"

"Good gracious," Mrs. Farnsworth said.

"What happened to Ted?"

"Ted who?" Daddy asked.

"Ted, the guy who helped you."

"You mean Ted Simpson?"

"Yeah. Did he invest in the well?"

"No."

"Why not?"

Jennifer looked pleadingly at Sonny. Sonny looked at her quizzically, then as if remembering something, moved his two hands towards the fingerbowl and puckered his lips faintly. Jennifer frowned.

"I don't know," Daddy said.

Daddy had never said *I don't know.*

They were standing on tiptoes, craning and craning, but never were quite sure what the others meant, they only knew that they were laughing, laughing with surprise at something ticklish drawn out of them, and at the tenderness they felt.

"Why was he so nice to you?" Sonny asked.

Jennifer wrinkled her eyebrows, stretched out her mouth, and shook her head once.

"Is something wrong, Jennifer?" Mrs. Farnsworth asked.

"Oh! Nothing," Jennifer said, giggling nervously.

Daddy looked at Sonny. "Ted liked young fellows, I guess, liked to see them do well . . . so I had this thousand dollars," Daddy continued to the group, "enough to buy a lease, rent a rig, and start drilling on my own. There was a farm I was interested in. The farmer and his wife had a daughter. She was crippled." Daddy leaned forward and looked at Mrs. Farnsworth. His eyes were wrenching now.

"The human dramas I would become involved with, Denise Girl, just looking for a lease! Visiting those farmers, scratching a living out of the soil, seeing their daughters, their sons with so many dreams, one a beautiful artist, another with the potential to become a concert pianist. And you come to them from Atlanta, Richmond, St. Louis, all the places they'd ever dreamed of. Denise, I would like to show you my holdings. Not to demonstrate my wealth, well, heh, perhaps a little. I *am* proud of what I have done, but more to show you that your Andrew Boy will be well taken care of. Not that he is not well taken care of already—" Daddy made a sweeping gesture with his arms, "but I believe a marriage should be, well, a marriage, if you know what I mean. Can we make a tour of your property, Denise? Now? I don't get around so much anymore, Denise, and when I come to a new place, I just like to walk around. Is there some hill we could go to from which we could have a good view of your property? There must be."

In a flash, Daddy was up out of his chair and behind Mrs. Farnsworth's. "Wha, whu," Mrs. Farnsworth said, automatically rising to her feet as Daddy pulled out the chair for her, then tottering to one side.

Daddy stepped to the side and caught her. "Oh, Denise, how could I have been so—but do you think, if you took my arm?" Daddy stretched out his arm. Mrs. Farnsworth put her hand through it. "Ah, that's better," Daddy said, patting Mrs. Farnsworth's hand with his other hand. He led her out of the room. She smiled an embarrassed smile at us as they were leaving. "Um, see you," she said shyly.

You could hear her laughing down the hall.

. . . .

Daddy and Mrs. Farnsworth were standing outside, on the rise of a hill, against a fence of gray, weather-beaten logs. Daddy had one arm across the small of Mrs. Farnsworth's back and was making wide, sweeping gestures with his other arm. The back vent of Daddy's jacket widened and closed with each gesture. Mrs. Farnsworth's back looked small with Daddy's arm across it.

They turned. Daddy came walking towards us with Mrs. Farnsworth holding his arm. They were talking. Daddy smiled at Mrs. Farnsworth, putting a hand over the hand that was on his arm occasionally, for emphasis.

The dryness had gone out of Mrs. Farnsworth's face. It

was possible to see what she must have looked like when she was younger: rosy-cheeked, beautiful in sweaters, a great skier, hair that was too curly throwing off barrettes that tried to hold it down.

"Fast foods," Daddy was saying, "they're the wave of the future. If I was going to do it all over again, *that's* what I would involve myself in. I *know* your little town was built before the Revolution, but let me tell you something, Denise: every little town in America is going to have one of those avenues with fast food places on them, where a poor fellow, a poor fellow like I was, is going to be able to go get something to eat, cheaply and quickly."

"Oh no!" Jennifer whispered beside me.

"Now, Denise, I know you like your privacy out here, the big trees and all, and I know you're not hurting financially, but if I were you and if the day ever came when, well, I might need a little extra something, that piece of property closest to town, first I'd build a nice golf-ball driving range on it. That would get people coming out here. You might even meet some nice fellow that way. Corporate executive. Mayflower stock. You're still just as pretty as a Broadway showgirl."

Mrs. Farnsworth laughed. "Oh, Cornelius, you're not serious, you are *not serious!*"

Daddy stopped, turned and looked at her. "Denise *Girl!*" he said.

Mrs. Farnsworth looked at him. You could see her expression change five times in three minutes. She put her lips together and spluttered. "This is so amusing!" she finally said.

"Can I see something here, Denise?" Daddy asked, still looking at her. He put his hands on either side of her head.

She stood still obediently in front of him. He tilted her head back until he was looking directly at her face. He pushed the skin of her face up slightly.

"*Oh no!*" Jennifer whispered beside me again.

"Beautiful," he said, as he let her face go.

. . . .

Mrs. Farnsworth transferred to Jennifer's arm and said softly and quickly to Jennifer as we walked to the limousine, "Why, Jennifer, I don't see why you were so terrified of our meeting. He's charming, really, quite charming! Such an *original* sense of humor! I don't know *when* I've had a more amusing afternoon. And so handsome! I really can see how he could—" Mrs. Farnsworth paused.

"Could what?"

"Charm people. Bye now, Jennifer dear," Mrs. Farnsworth said, in a louder voice, to Jennifer, who had turned to her with an opened mouth. She kissed Jennifer on the cheek, then turned to us. "See you at the wedding. Bye, bye."

CHAPTER 12

Mother drove the seventy miles from her and Peter's house in Maryland to my boarding school in Washington several times a term. She wore a raincoat and sunglasses and took me out to restaurants, each one a different nationality, in the time we were allowed out from school, between four and six.

Mother would call me after she got to the city. She would ask me what kind of restaurant I wanted to go to. I would say what kind and look it up in the phone book, then call them and find out whether they were open but I wouldn't make reservations because I knew what they would say, with our going at a time like that.

. . . .

We arrive at the restaurants as the waiters are setting up tables. They come towards us with long white cloths dangling from their hands and say, "Sorry, no," and Mother says, "We have family problems," and the waiters, looking at her raincoat and sunglasses, say, "Ah, I see, yes, please!" and gesture towards a table.

It is in a French restaurant that Mother tells me that Daddy has completely broken down after Jennifer's wedding. Four or five double bourbons every night and nose drops and uppers and downers and injections that are supposed to be live sheep cells but that are in reality nothing but dirty water. Daddy has complained about being stopped up for years but no one knows for sure because he still refuses to go to a serious doctor, one who will tell him what to do instead of being told by him. Jennifer can commit him, she is over twenty-one, but you just don't commit a man like that; that would kill him sooner than being sick would.

It is in a Chinese restaurant that Mother tells me about Sonny saying drugs were the greatest thing since Jesus Christ.

It is in a Lebanese restaurant that Mother tells me about Jennifer and Andrew, Jennifer especially, acting like they aren't married, Jennifer going off on long tennis dates with some fellow.

It is in a Russian restaurant that Mother tells me about being in California because of Sonny's problems and, while she was there, being said "fuck you" to, by Butch. Butch had said this to her many times before, but this time, because of Sonny, she thought she would just tell Daddy. "I'm going to tell your father!" she said to Butch. "Yes, this time, I'm going to tell your father!"

Daddy was waiting for Butch at the front door, barefoot in Hawaiian trunks and a matching sport shirt. He was carrying a golf club.

"What do you mean, 'fuck you,'" he bellowed. "I'll teach you not to say 'fuck you'; I'll fuck you over, boy! If I'd ever hit my little mother, if I'd ever cursed her . . ." He was crying. He swung the golf club at Butch's head.

"Dad, control yourself!" Butch said, wresting the golf club from him.

Mother's lip is trembling. Mother says she wanted Butch to go east to boarding school, too, like me, so that he would not have to . . . witness, and Daddy was not against it, just as Daddy was not against my going east, but she thought that that was just because Daddy was already so far gone, but then when Butch kicked a hole in the door with his bare feet when Mother spoke of it as a possibility after Jennifer's wedding, Mother realized that it was too much of an uprooting for him with only one year left of high school, and so, even though it made her sick to do it, Mother put Butch in Daddy's house, in that wing off the kitchen with Sonny, thinking that, well, at least that way, for better or worse, Butch would get to know his father.

Butch spent the night in Don and Minnie's apartment. Don drove Butch to school in the morning. One of Butch's friends came up to Butch in class and said there were men waiting outside for him. Butch climbed onto the roof of the gym and spread-eagled on the hot, spongy tarpaper. Other detectives spotted him from a helicopter. The helicopter dived at Butch a few times. Butch ran, cowering, and hid under the metal arch of the ladder. Then the men who had been waiting outside the classroom climbed the roof with cans of what Butch told a friend, and that friend told Mother, was mace jiggling in their back pockets.

The detectives put Butch on a plane to Arizona. More detectives met Butch at the airport and drove him to a boarding school—I'd probably heard of it—it was advertised in the backs of magazines.

Mother searches in her purse for a Kleenex. Mother says she never thought she'd have a son of hers in the kind of school that was advertised in the backs of magazines.

It is in a Greek restaurant that Mother tells me about

Daddy's heart, lungs, liver, and bladder being all stopped up. They are stopped up from the years of Daddy having fantasies of them being stopped up until they became stopped up for real. That was a classic psychological phenomenon: fearing imagined things until the things became real and really *did* hurt you. Then, when you thought about Daddy's main activity, drilling holes in the ground, the oil coming up, it all fit together with the kind of— Mother laces her fingers together—"kindergarten logic" psychological things had. It was as if he thought he didn't *deserve* all that oil flowing and so took it out on himself. The way Daddy was about his . . ."department," for example —Mother points with her ice cream spoon to a place somewhere underneath the table. Even in her day, Daddy thought the tract was blocked and had doctors go up it with probes. Of course, it didn't have to do with going wee-wee as much as it had to do with . . . other things boys worried about. Daddy wouldn't believe the doctors when they said there was nothing wrong. That was when the doctors went to Mother. "'We think you should know that your husband insisted we do this very painful test. We think you should know, he has nothing wrong with him physically; the problem is up here—'" Mother taps her head. That was when Mother felt so much tenderness for him. That was when Mother felt that, even though he had dragged her along the rug, she had to stay.

It is in a Czech restaurant that Mother tells me about Butch being sent back from the school in Arizona advertised in the backs of magazines because he first walked into the principal's office and said he hated the school, then when that didn't work, sat on the floor of his room and refused to go to class or the dining hall or sports or anyplace and said over and over again, "I want to go home, I want to go home," for days.

It is in a Turkish restaurant that Mother tells me about finding out that, the whole time she and Peter were in Philadelphia to lend Jennifer moral support during her divorce trial, Jennifer had her tennis-playing boyfriend stashed in her hotel room.

It is in a Peruvian restaurant that Mother tells me about Sonny going to Daddy's house one day and finding Daddy waiting for him at the front door with a raised golf club.

It is in a Japanese restaurant that Mother tells me about going to California again and finding Sonny, under the name Art Arbanzo, living in the Hollywood Hills with a group of people, one of whom was colored. Mother says he is trying to repudiate his class. Mother says she doesn't understand why he would want to repudiate his class.

It is in an Indonesian restaurant that Mother tells me about Butch paying someone to write the ten papers he still had due so that he could graduate from public high school.

It is in a Mexican restaurant that Mother tells me about Daddy finally finding out about the condition of Don and Minnie's apartment.

Daddy walked up the rickety staircase with his back to the wall, saying, "Man, man!" as each step shook. He stood at the entrance to the kitchen and told Don and Minnie to pack their bags and told them he was putting them up at the Hilton until he got their little place fixed up because their place was fit for neither man nor beast. Minnie said they'd stay with her sister but Daddy said, "No, the Hilton, the Hilton." Then, Minnie told Mother she didn't know why she did it, they should have just gone to the Hilton and let Daddy find out about it later, or maybe she thought he would forget about the Hilton after they had packed and just let them get away to her sister's, but she just had to show him the place where the bugs were, she had lived with them so long. She picked up a corner of the linoleum and showed him the white things, scrambling, and Daddy, looking at them, said, "No, a suite, a goddamned suite at the Beverly Hills Hotel, with three goddamned meals a day, and I don't want you to come and work for me, either. I just want you to lie in bed and get a little rest and watch TV." Then Daddy called his friend who had a steel company and when the friend said he only did high rises, only couple-of-million-dollar jobs, Daddy said he didn't care what the thing cost, he just wanted to make Minnie Girl and Don Boy's place solid.

They tore the whole garage down and put up a steel frame and made a garage and apartment exactly like the garage and apartment that had been torn down, with steps on the outside made of steel and supported by I-beams.

Don and Minnie watched TV until they were sick of it, then told Daddy they wanted to go back to work, but Daddy said, "Relax." Then Don and Minnie told Daddy they were sick of watching TV, they wanted to go back to work, and Daddy sent them tickets to Hawaii.

After they were finished building, Daddy took a decorator through the big house and said, "This, this, this, and this," and had all the things he liked at his house reproduced on a smaller scale for Don and Minnie's apartment.

There was a white, thick-pile carpet running throughout, Minnie told Mother, and a white tufted sofa running the length of the wall in the living room, with an extra large color TV in front of it and two Louis the Sixteenth side tables. On one was a small Laocoön clock and on the other, a dish full of fake grapes, and scattered among them, little wooden hairy people with signs on them, which Daddy had gotten from Rita or one of his girlfriends, and which Daddy had given them because he already had plenty of them, scattered all over his dressing table. There were antiqued mirrors in the bedroom and a bed with a canopy over it, hung from the fist of a flying cupid. There was a slidey silk bedspread on the bed and in one corner, halves of a ping-pong table that couldn't fit anywhere but that Daddy wanted them to have because he had one at his house and it couldn't be reproduced in smaller scale because it had to be regulation size.

It is in a Thai restaurant that Mother tells me about Jennifer marrying her tennis-playing boyfriend and then moving out one month later. Mother says she doesn't understand why Jennifer always has to *marry* them. Mother says she wants to know why Jennifer can't just have affairs.

It is in an Italian restaurant that Mother tells me about Sonny riding up to Daddy's house on a motorcycle, bleached blond hair down past his shoulders.

He knocked at the front door, but one of the new maids, looking out the peep hole, didn't recognize him and wouldn't let him in. Sonny walked around to the service entrance and through the kitchen, brushing people aside. He walked through the dining room and down the hall to Daddy's bedroom. Daddy was lying propped up in bed. Sonny kneeled down beside him. "You don't have to die, Dad," Sonny said. "No one has to die. I know the way. I *am* the way!" There were tears streaming down his face.

Daddy reached over his head and started pressing buttons. Male nurses came running. "Get this damn fool out of here," he said.

There is a silence. Mother's chin is trembling. "Do you

know what Butch said, that time your daddy tried to wrap a golf club around his neck?"

"Yeah, it was, 'Dad, control yourself,'" I say.

Mother is balling and unballing a piece of Kleenex up near her eyes. Mother says she wants so much to be in California right then, where she can get Sonny and Butch to good counselors, talk to Cornelius, get their allowances cut off, so that they won't keep on just . . . helling around, get Butch finally tested for the dyslexia she always suspected he had, get their brain waves taken and other kinds of tests, because it can be *chemical*, not just psychological, but she has so much on her in the East, what with Peter's health being so delicate and Na-Na, whom she has brought East with her, in the nursing home. Mother says she's asked some men in California she knows who have it pretty "'together,' as they say now," with solid jobs, fathers of children who are all turning out all right, to talk to Sonny and Butch, because that was what they needed right now, strong men they could look up to. . . .

Mother says the psychiatrists said, about Daddy, "If only we'd gotten to him in time!" They said he was in a box, psychologically speaking, that was getting smaller and smaller, limiting more and more the reactions he could have to any given situation. Mother makes a square with her hands in front of her face and shrinks it down.

It is in a Persian restaurant that Mother says that about a month after she threw the candelabra, a technician came to wire the house for a stereo system the technician said Daddy had ordered. "Stereo," Mother thought, "how nice." Mother thought it was a sign of something normal. Mother thought it meant that perhaps they were going to have some kind of permanence in the house.

The technician was there for several days. He got to know Mother and Mother guessed he understood the situation and felt sorry for her, because on the third day, he took Mother aside and said, "I think you ought to know that this is no stereo system I'm putting in. I'm wiring the house for listening devices. That's what your husband wants." He lowered his voice. "You'd better get out of here," he said.

It is in an Indian restaurant that Mother tells me about Butch, sometime before he moved in with a surfer friend in Malibu and after the Sonny incident, walking into Daddy's room and saying, "You're a goddamned fool, Dad."

It is in a Spanish restaurant that Mother tells me about Daddy at the Mayo Clinic.

He had decided on his own and to go right away, and the secretary, by some miracle, had managed to get a room from someone who'd canceled. Daddy took Samantha with him. Samantha was Daddy's new girlfriend but Mother believed that they didn't, they couldn't have any kind of . . . sexual relationship.

When they got there, Daddy said he wanted to put Samantha across the hall. The nurses said the Mayo Clinic was *not* a hotel.

"What do you mean, it's not a hotel?" Daddy roared. Daddy was about to check out right then but Samantha calmed him down. She said she didn't mind; she would find a room in a real hotel downtown. Then Daddy said he wanted a double bed in his room. He told Samantha to call a furniture store and order a double bed to be delivered. The delivery men arrived with the bed. They started to bring the double bed in through the doors of the room. They were about halfway in when the nurses came running. They stood in the doorway, blocking the bed's entrance, while Daddy stood behind them, yelling, "Let me have my goddamned bed!" Daddy "escaped" in the middle of the night. He could have simply checked out and left, no one was forcing him to stay, but he climbed out a window instead and called Samantha from the corner. He waited for her on a park bench. In his hospital gown. In Rochester, Minnesota. In March.

Mother's chin is trembling again. "Did I tell you what Butch said, that time . . . ?"

" 'Dad, control yourself.' "

. . . .

I found out the time from the waiter and told Mother I had to get back to school. Mother went to get the car, leaving me enough money to pay the bill. I paid the bill, got change, and counted out a tip. I sat at the table, looking out the window, and waited for the car to arrive. Minutes passed, five minutes, eight minutes. I sipped water. The headwaiter looked at me. Ten minutes passed. Our waiter, brushing crumbs from the tablecloth and finally removing everything from the table but my waterglass, said, "Mommy, Mommy, where's Mommy?"

Outside, a black boy loped by with a pink Afro comb in his hair.

The headwaiter came up to me. "Please, miss," he said. "Dinner guests coming soon."

I got up from the table, put on my coat, and waited by the door, peering through the iron grillwork over the glass in the door's upper half.

I imagined Mother lying on the pavement, her head broken, blood trickling along the sidewalk and collecting in a pool in the gutter, her purse open, the contents of her purse dumped onto the sidewalk beside her.

A black boy comes up to her. "Give me some money," he says. "No, honey," she says, "you're supposed to say, 'Would you *please* give me some money.' That's much more gracious—" Crash. Then, a white light with purple shell-less snails unrolling and rolling on their own. She tries to talk to them, to invite them over to her house to meet other purple shell-less snails. They are not paying any attention to her. "Flat," she says about them. "Yankee." She sees a pool of blackness growing around her. I chuckle at her confusion. God is about to come in any minute and tell her she is dead.

Twenty minutes passed.

"Just let her come back," I prayed. "Just let her come back."

Mother opened the door to the restaurant, jabbing me in the stomach with the doorknob. "Oh, there you are, I didn't see you!"

"Where were you?"

"I got lost."

"But the car was only two blocks away!"

"Sh," Mother said.

"Miss Kreps'll make me stay an extra two hours in study hall!"

"Sh."

"But you don't know her!"

"Sh. Just leave it to me."

We drove back to school.

"It's my fault!" Mother chirruped, approaching Miss

Kreps's desk in its glassed-in room just inside the entrance to the residence hall. Miss Kreps laughed. Mother held out her hand to Miss Kreps. Miss Kreps half rose out of her chair and took it, smiling.

"How are you, Miss Kreps?" Mother asked.

"So nice to see you again, Mrs. Teasdale!"

"Miss Kreps?" Mother continued in a subdued tone of voice, lowering her eyes. "I got lost driving back from the restaurant. I'm a very bad mother!"

"Oh yes, you're a very bad mother!" Miss Kreps said, mock seriously, shaking her head.

"That's why we're so late. Will you forgive us?"

Miss Kreps lowered her head and tapped on the desk. "Well, you *are* seven minutes late, and the rules are that if a girl is even *five* minutes late, she will have to spend another two hours in study hall."

"But surely, Miss Kreps, if the mother is the *cause* of her being late . . ."

"I'm sorry, Mrs. Teasdale, but if we were to make one exception, we'd have all the girls coming in late. There would be absolute bedlam here!"

"Miss Kreps—"

"I'm sorry, Mrs. Teasdale. Have you got your books?" Miss Kreps asked me, looking at me over Mother's shoulder.

"Yes," I said after a pause.

"You won't be coming out of study hall until . . ." Miss Kreps looked at her watch, "ten-thirty. Now go along."

I swung out of Miss Kreps's office and waited by the door.

"Good-bye, Miss Kreps," I heard Mother say.

"Hope to see you again, soon, Mrs. Teasdale!"

"I hope so, too!" Mother said. She came out of Miss Kreps's office smiling.

"See?" I hissed at her once she was out in the hall. "I *told* you she would make me stay another two hours in study hall! I hate this place! You promised me that if I didn't like it here you would let me go back to California! I want to go!"

"Sh."

"But I hate this place!"

"Sh, sh. They have to keep the rules . . ."

"But it's not fair! And it's all your fault! If you weren't such a—"

Mother started to walk towards the door.

"Oh, I-don't-know-what, about directions, I wouldn't have to spend another two hours in study hall!"

"Sh, sh," Mother said. "This is a very good school. You'll be glad someday you went here."

"But that's not the point! I, you—"

"Sh, sh," Mother said. She closed the door behind her.

"I *hate* you," I said to the door, kicking it.

CHAPTER 13

Two steel tanks, with long rubber tubes coming out of them, glinted in a shaft of sunlight shining through cracks between and underneath the curtains in Daddy's dark green bedroom.

There was a mound on Daddy's bed. It was wider than it was long. At first I thought that Daddy had gotten so fat that he was actually wider than he was long, but then I realized that Daddy was lying sideways across his bed with pillows on one edge, underneath his head. He had no covers on. His stomach rose, tight and huge, through the crack below the one buttoned button on his gold pyjama top. He held the end of one of the rubber tubes in his hand and sucked on it from time to time.

I had just come to California for semester break. Mother thought it would be a good idea if I went and saw Daddy, but over semester break so that I would not have to stay long.

After a while, Daddy stopped wheezing, removed the rubber tube from his mouth, coughed up loosened phlegm from the bottom of his throat, and turning his head to the side and up as far as it would go, spat a ball of spit over the edge of the bed.

The rug was squishy under my feet.

"I've tried everything," Daddy said, "even Mazola Oil."

Busy came in. She walked gingerly in her cha-cha heels on the sodden rug, trying not to grimace. "Mr. Kurtzman to speak to you on one nine."

"Who?"

"The television producer. Does Bozo."

"Oh."

Daddy pressed the button. "How you doin', Kurt Boy? . . . Oh, I'm doin' fine now . . . Just a frog in my throat . . . What? . . . You wrote a cookbook? . . . What's borscht? . . . Oh, some kind of Russian soup . . . I love soup . . . What? . . . *'Course* you can have a promotion party here! . . . I'm feelin' fine now! . . . My lungs are fine! . . . I've just come in from driving a few golf balls . . . Had to run to the phone, that's all . . . What? . . . *Pay* for the party? Kurt Boy, I wouldn't *dream* of taking any money from you . . ." Daddy motioned to Busy to hand him the nozzle of the oxygen tank. He took one long drag on it while Mr. Kurtzman's voice sounded in the air. Daddy put the phone back to his mouth. "It's my pleasure, Kurt Boy . . . Fine, fine . . . Two hundred people? . . . In one week? . . . No problem! . . ."

"Oh no," Busy whispered.

"What? . . . I feel fine! . . . And besides, nothin'll make me feel better'n havin' a party! . . . I haven't seen any of my friends in so long . . . Bye, Kurt Boy . . . Bye . . . Yeah . . . Bye . . ."

Daddy stayed breathing on the tank for about a minute, then took the tube away and said, "Busy Girl? Go call Susan Girl . . . and tell her we're . . . havin' a party . . ."

"But Susan doesn't work here anymore. You haven't had a social secretary for almost a year."

"Oh yeah. Well, hire some little girl."

"But Mr. D—"

"We'll put an oxygen tank in a party favor . . . if we have to, but that's what I need right now . . . a little old . . . big party."

．．．．

I stood in front of the bathroom mirror and practiced making up my eyes like the eyes of the models I'd seen in *Vogue*, the ones who stood alone in desert landscapes, in padded, op-art minidresses, net stockings, white Courrèges boots, and large Lucite earrings. First I put heavy fish-shaped eyeliner around my eyes, then I extended the lines beyond my eyes on either side Egyptian-style, then I put above my eyes first white-out, then red eye shadow, then pink, then green, then blue, then glitter from Paraphernalia. A little bit of makeup made my eye look just like the other and a lot of makeup on its slightly stranger shape made it somehow look even *better* than the other, so that I then had to make the other look like it.

I thought of Mother closing her eyes and saying, "Sh."

Just two more years, I thought, just two more years. Then I would be in college and I wouldn't have to see any of them anymore. I wouldn't even go home for vacations. I would figure out something else to do. I would take my junior year abroad in Paris and sit in cafés with the kind of people that if people at Mother's house or people at Daddy's house saw them, they would call the Bel Air Patrol—black people, communists, really skinny people, people with their hair down past their knees. We would talk in perfect French about philosophers whose names I had seen flipping through the Philosophy section of Campbell's in Westwood while Butch sneered, "Aren't *we* the little intellectual miss?" They would not know where I was from or what my parents had done. Finally, one of them (a man) would start to like me. He would take me back to his garret. It would be very messy. It would be a clutter, though, more than a dusty mess, of musical scores, African statues, Egyptian mirror symbols. He would say we'd spent too much time talking about philosophers: now he wanted to know about me. He would say all the people at the café had been wondering—Fernande, Che, Omar. I would say it wasn't important. He would say he couldn't believe that. He would ask me every night, putting his arm around me on the one piece of furniture he had in his garret (it was a sofa) and squeezing me gently, he would say, "Tell me, come on, tell me, please."

I would tell him finally. I wouldn't know what would make me do it. I would tell him about how my father discovered oil and how my mother was discovered and was in the movies and how I was born with no muscle in my eyelid and my father had everyone in the world's face fixed but mine, so that my mother had had to kidnap me, sort of, to have it done and how my brothers and sister were, well, pretty screwed up, I was serious, but how could you blame them with what they'd had to go through, and so was I, probably, though it was harder when it was yourself to see exactly how.

He would laugh, embarrassed, not knowing whether to believe me, and so to prove it, I would take off my eye makeup with a little jar of Noxema I carried in my purse at all times, and, holding up a candle (his electricity having just been cut off a few days before), show him the scar and its slightly irregular shape.

It would be like those stories of travelers or old men who

told seemingly fantastic tales, then displayed a monkey's paw or a dead albatross (whatever that was) to prove them. It would be the one thing I had. Or like the sailor who swirled alone in his boat as Moby Dick with Ahab on him went down, down.

. . . .

The party was on Valentine's Day. For decorations, Don and the gardeners had hung up all over the house big, foldable fluffy hearts made of red tissue paper honeycombing out from red satin ribbons. The morning after the party, the caterers had cleaned up the house but Don and the gardeners still had not taken down the hearts. They were still up on the second day. On the third day, I asked Daddy when they were going to be taken down.

"But they look nice, don't they?"

"I think they look weird."

"Weerrrrrd . . . weerrrrrrrd," Daddy repeated, imitating me.

They stayed up for almost a year.

. . . .

Mother cried on the phone, said it was "the end of an era."

Miss Kreps's eyes were on me as I stepped out of the phone booth. I stood with my back to her, staring down the hall. The hall stretched, long and silent, from her office to the reception room, where we'd had teas every Wednesday afternoon until they were canceled, after a maid had been nearly trampled in a rush for cookies.

It had always been the most depressing hallway I'd ever seen. Dim overhead lights canceled out whatever natural light came through transom windows over classroom doors on either side.

I heard Miss Kreps rise. I knew what she was going to do. Maybelle Dixon's father had died two weeks before. I heard Miss Kreps's arms rise in her nylon blouse to hug me.

The hall stretched in front of me, the hall in which we had been forbidden, ever, to make any noise.

I opened my mouth. A sound came out. I couldn't tell what kind of sound it was, but it was loud.

"Sh!" Miss Kreps said, "sh!" I heard her arms drop. Maybelle Dixon had not made any noise.

I made the sound again. I could hear it this time. It was like a cow mooing, only more gravelly.

Lamps swayed. The dreary hall seemed to brighten. You could imagine parties happening in it, almost.

I made the sound again, pitching it higher at the end.

I thought of sunshine, the radio blaring, and me in a convertible in a gorgeous landscape with no school. No school forever.

I felt something warm and smooth on my elbow. It was the nurse's hand. She guided me into the old-fashioned elevator girls were allowed to use when they twisted their ankles or broke their legs. The cage door opened. The black maid at the controls looked at us inquiringly.

"Her father passed away," the nurse said.

"M-mh," the maid said gently.

I felt a lump in my throat suddenly, a small lump. It was because of the way the maid said, "M-mh," the way black mammies in old movies on TV said it about something sad, movies at the ends of which you saw rays shining through clouds and heard a thousand voices humming "Swing Low, Sweet Chariot." Even though I knew it was dumb to cry at the ends of movies like that, I still did sometimes.

The nurse led me into the infirmary. There was no one else in it. I sat down on one of the beds. The nurse gave me two red pills in a paper cup and another paper cup full of water. I wondered if they were the same pills the nurse had given Carter Beaufort the day she had started eating Doritos and just couldn't stop. I swallowed the pills and drank the water, then lay face down on the bed.

The cage door opened again. I heard footsteps, then felt a hand on my back.

"There, there," Miss Kreps's voice said. "I know how you feel. Vacation is coming up soon and you wanted to see your daddy again."

"Go away," I said. I was busy, my forehead propped on my fists, staring up close at the patch of the bedspread I was lying on. It was a white cotton bedspread, like the kind they had throughout the school, with loops sticking up all over it in patches that made patterns you either couldn't make sense of or could make into anything you wanted them to be.

This time I saw a big hand going down to all the people at Daddy's house to move them. "Busy will go here now," I thought, "and Don and Minnie will go there and those people," I thought, looking at a group I couldn't identify, "they will be thrown across the board, like jacks."

I shivered. All it took was just one thing. It was like going through a door or a cave entrance and then finding yourself, hurtling.

The air duct roared like the sea in my ears. Long strings of dust swayed like seaweed. I crawled through the air vent on my hands and knees, my hands and knees filthy, my white dress brown. I broke through swaying cobwebs. They disintegrated, covering me with brown powder.

The roar in the duct died down. I heard a door open some-
where above me. I heard voices at the mouth of the air vent.

"She's in the air duct."

"She couldn't have crawled in there!"

"It's too dirty."

"She'll suffocate."

"No, she won't. Air ducts are for air."

"She'll choke on the dust."

"Roooooobbbbiiiiiinnnnnn!" It boomed through the air
duct, hurting my ears.

I heard a voice above me, from the top of the stairs. "She's
in the air duct, Mr. D.!"

I crawled further in. I was in the very middle of the house,
in the passage I had once thought Daddy's girlfriends had gone
through, on the way from his room, the girlfriends Jennifer
had said we would never be able to see.

I heard footsteps going up the stairs. I heard a door slam.

Ahead of me, I could see light, shining like a ghost on the
side of the duct. I crawled forward cautiously, wondering how
fast I would be able to crawl backwards if I had to. I saw dark
lines in the light: it was a grill, opening onto the outside. I
crawled to the grill and looked out.

I could see the porte cochere, coming off one side of the
house, and the limousine underneath it, with the strange chauf-
feur who had driven Daddy and me from the airport with the
four strange doctors waiting beside it. I could see also the drive-
way, the lawn, and all the trees and bushes around it. I sat
down in a ball, tucking my knees under my chin. I knew this
grill. I had seen it from the outside, when Jennifer and I had
sat in the bushes, whispering about what Daddy did with his
girlfriends, but I had never thought that I would be able to see
so much through it.

Then I remembered, as I had to every once in a while, that my eye had been operated on and that I would be able to see more of everything now, just by staring straight ahead.

I heard another door slam. Outside, I saw the four doctors climb into the limousine and drive off. I waited, expecting to hear other noises, but there were none. A gardener passed, hauling a coil of hose.

A beige Thunderbird drove up. Colette stepped out, her three toy poodles scrambling out after her. They started trotting rapidly back and forth across the lawn, their noses on the ground.

"Ho cho cho cho cho cho cho cho cho," Colette said to them after they had done their business. They jumped back into the Thunderbird. She shut the door and drove away.

Another limousine backed up under the porte cochere from the garage beyond. Don was driving.

A woman appeared under the porte cochere from the front door of the house. She walked tiredly, carrying a sweater.

"Come on!" Don said to her, half whispering, out the car window. She speeded up, her backless high heels clacking on the asphalt.

It was Judy. She was wearing an evening dress. It was red with a low back and had gold threads in it that glinted in the sunlight. Seeing that dress was like seeing a little piece of night in the middle of the day, so that seeing it if my eye had not been operated on, I would have had to get as close to the grill as possible and look up, just to make sure the sun was shining. I could now see everything just by looking straight ahead. Seeing Judy like that was like seeing what went on at Daddy's house, on vacations and on weekends when we were not there, happening right in front of me; it was like seeing all the things that happened in all the times and in all the places I couldn't see into, in little islands, happening now.

The words plunked dully in my mind like the dull ache in my eye: Judy's been with Daddy: she's spent the night. *I knew, then, why we would never be able to see Daddy's girlfriends leaving: it was because they were right there.*

My eyes started to sting, harder than before, harder than it ever had in the hospital, so that I had to blink and turn away.

I had known that I would be able to see more, but I did not think that I would be able to see so much *more, so* soon.

The cage door opened again. I could hear girls' and the nurse's voices whispering.

"Is she crying?" one voice whispered.

The nurse mumbled something.

"I can't imagine her crying," the voice said.

The cage door opened again. The voice of Peter's daughter Sophie. Sophie lived in Washington and took me out of school on weekends.

I sat up and dangled my feet over the side of the bed.

"I never really loved him, you know," I said to Sophie, pushing the hair out of my face.

Part Three

CHAPTER 14

Jennifer says it is like one of Daddy's parties, without Daddy there.

Dolores comes, and Tamara and Pepita and Ingrid and Shanti. Midge comes, her face shiny with moisture cream, a smudge of mascara under each eye. Carmen comes and other former maids who have to remind us of their names. Daddy's lawyer friends come and their wives and actors and actresses, the tacky and the less tacky ones, and Dr. Fayman and Dr. Grass and Dr. Villalobo.

They come into the living room sneaking looks up at the Valentine's Day decorations hanging from the ceiling, all covered with dust.

I waited for the surge of embarrassment that I expected I would feel, thinking about how people were thinking about how Daddy died, died in a house full of Valentine's Day decorations, Valentine's Day decorations that had been up for almost a year, and we were his children—but that didn't happen.

It was because it was all out there, I thought; *it was because there was nothing you could do.*

"Just look at the bridgework he had done on me," one of the lawyers' wives says, pulling her lips back and tapping an incisor so near my face I have to lean back to see it.

"He treated me to a bunionectomy," a former maid says. "The man was a saint."

"He took care of my adenoids," another former maid says.

"I didn't think about my overbite until Cornelius suggested it might be something that was keeping me from getting more parts in movies. And it was, because Cornelius had it done for me and I'm doing so well now. . . ." Pepita says, her voice breaking.

"Oh . . . God . . . " Dolores says, sighing.

Jennifer gets a coffee urn and silver trays, newly polished by Minnie, off a high shelf and orders sandwiches and cookies from a caterer. She says even though she knows it is all for . . . well, what it is for, it still makes her feel good to serve things the right way.

Mother comes. She sighs and says, "Oh dear, oh dear," about twenty times when she sees the Valentine's Day decorations, then brushes a tear out of the corner of her eye and takes a deep breath and says, "It's almost like a play, isn't it?"

She greets people as they come in the door. She kisses them and smiles at them and puts her arms around the ones who look like they are going to cry. "He was a dear man, wasn't he, in so many ways," she says, then if they keep on talking, says in a softer voice, "What could *anyone* have done, really, what *could* anyone have done?"

I thought Mother wouldn't know most of the people there. Then I reminded myself, as I still had to sometimes, that

Mother *did* know Daddy, she had been *married* to him and had lived there, and a lot of the people, the less tacky ones, but the tacky ones as well, had been her friends, too.

It was all the people from Mother's house and all the people from Daddy's house being together in front of me with my two eyes open.

Alice comes walking into the living room with six dozen chocolate chip cookies in a Tupperware box while Melvyn waits for her in the car. "He's surely in heaven now," she says.

Some of the people who come by during the day call back that night, after they have had a few drinks, and say that Daddy was so nice, he always said he would do something for them and they just want to know if anything has been mentioned.

Rita stands under the hearts in a short white fur coat and asks straight out about the will.

Butch tells her to shut up and go away.

Colette comes, hobbling into the living room on a walker, her face riddled with facelift scars, her dogs scrambling ahead. She takes Mother and Jennifer into a corner and says she wants it to be known, just for the record, that even though everyone else in the world may have had an affair with Daddy, *she* never did.

"'I really never did,'" Jennifer tells us later Colette said to her and Mother. "'Incredible, isn't it? He came after me many times. He really was like an old billy goat, that Cornelius, but I always said to him, "Cornelius, I saw you learning to do the box step through an open door at Arthur Murray's. Leslie Howard's more my type."'"

Jennifer sits on the sofa in the projection room, shaking her nails dry as the first limousine pulls up under the porte cochere. She goes on: "Fifteen years older than Daddy, looking like a dried prune. God, I was thinking, if Daddy had ever even *contemplated* going to bed with her, he would have been even sicker than I thought he was."

"I think that was kind of sweet," Sonny says, "Colette telling you."

"*Sweet!*" Jennifer repeats. "You *are* sick."

There is silence, then Jennifer says in a softer voice, pulling herself forward on the sofa, "At least let me do something about the hair on the back of your neck."

Sonny had long fingernails and long straggling hairs growing down the back of his neck for he'd cut off his long bleached-blond ponytail with a pair of lawn shears when he'd heard Daddy'd died, and had missed a few places.

"No, that's O.K., Jennifer."
"But it'll just take a second."
"It's O.K., I said."

Jennifer had made all the funeral arrangements. She called all over Los Angeles looking for a white hearse, until someone suggested she call a place that specialized in children's funerals, and she said, "Children's funerals, of course!" She picked out a pair of Hawaiian shorts and a matching sport shirt. She never liked them, "but, well, he did." She reserved the church and the minister, saw to it that only family and "help" were to attend the service, and arranged for Daddy to be buried at Forest Lawn. She hated Forest Lawn just as much as we did, but Grandaddy Drayton was there and she had looked into cemeteries and there *weren't* any others in Los Angeles.

Busy comes in.

"Hi, Busido," Butch says.

"Hi, Busy," Jennifer says.

"Hi, Busido," I say.

"Biz," Sonny says.

"Hi," Busy says. She has a large wastebasket in her hands and is going around the room emptying smaller wastebaskets into it.

Busy empties two wastebaskets, then picks up a third, holds it in her arms and stares down into it with a kind of smile on her face.

"Busy," I say, giggling at her expression, "*what* are you doing?"

Butch shoots me an angry look and stands up. He walks over to Busy and puts his arms around her. Busy puts the wastebasket on a counter, then stands on tiptoes in her backless plastic shoes and puts her arms around him. Her shoulders shake silently.

"It's all right, Busido, there, there," Butch says.

It was still very big, what had happened, I thought, *not only Daddy dying but Daddy living. Daddy living and making you be so many different ways and then dying with you all built up in those ways. Ways that were not needed now.*

"It'll just take a second," Jennifer says again to Sonny.

"Oh, O.K.," Sonny says.

Jennifer goes into the bathroom and comes back with a razor. "Turn around," she says.

Sonny turns around, kneels on the sofa cushions, puts his elbows on the back of the sofa and looks out the window at the white limousines lining up down the driveway.

Jennifer starts scraping at the back of Sonny's neck, making a rasping, embarrassed sound.

"God, Jennifer, can't you use a little water?"

"It's not worth bothering about water for."

The rasping sound fills the room.

I watch them through eyes that have suddenly become blurry.

It is still very big, what happened, and it is hard to see it all the time. It takes practice to keep it all out there in front of your eyes without one end falling off or the other while you call the others to come look. Calling the others to come look takes the teeth out of Daddy somehow. But as you call the others to come look, just as free as you please now, driving cars, getting into bed with men, getting married finally and having babies, you have the sensation that you are out there, calling, but back there at the same time, a crazy, built-up jigsaw monument to Daddy.

"I think they're ready now," Sonny says.

We walk out under the porte cochere and climb into the front limousine.